APOLOGY FOR THE

WOMAN WRITING

Also by Jenny Diski

APOLOGY FOR THE
WOMAN WRITING

JENNY DISKI

virago

Virago Press
An imprint of
Little, Brown Book Group
100 Victoria Embankment
London EC4Y 0DY

An Hachette Livre UK Company
www.hachettelivre.co.uk

www.virago.co.uk

For Ian

1

1645

There her mistress lies in the bed, gasping like a fish. Sucking at the air of the world with those dried-up lips, dragging it in, trying to fill her rusty lungs. It never gets down deep enough to satisfy before she has to release it, the air escaping through her open mouth in a crackled wheeze, so that she can try again. She sounds like a pair of ancient bellows making a final desperate effort to be serviceable. Nothing to be done to help her. Only she can breathe or not breathe.

Nicole Jamyn sits, hands in her lap, on a stool beside the bed, not looking, because she doesn't have to, but also because it hurts to twist her neck. Her head is heavy. It pains her to let it drop. It pains her to hold it up. For the most part she sits looking straight ahead towards the small window opposite, above the desk, trying to keep her head painlessly balanced on her neck, waiting, and listening because she can't help but listen. Nevertheless from time to time, Jamyn turns – she feels and hears the bones in her neck crunch unwillingly at the disturbance – and sees the loose skin around her mistress's closed eyes tense up with discomfort when she breathes in. The cold air scours her desiccated lips as though she were inhaling sand. It must be an automatic response from the unconscious old woman, but even so Jamyn leans over painfully, takes up the cloth in the bowl of water, squeezes it out a little, and dabs at her mistress's parched mouth in the hope it will bring some relief. She has no idea whether it helps or not.

It is not as hard sitting at this deathbed as she had imagined. The few who come to pay their respects call her loyal. A paid servant is not required to hold a death-watch over the final earthly struggles of her mistress.

'She is fortunate to have you, Jamyn,' they whisper as they leave.

They call her loyal, but she can see they pity her, supposing her here because she has nowhere else she could be. A sad creature sitting with a sad creature. It seems they think that if she had a choice, another place to go, a family, she would certainly do no more than what is necessary for her mistress. Only the pathetically lonely would sit day and night, waiting, keeping vigil with the depleting soul and skeletal body expiring on the old woollen mattress beside her stool. They are wrong. Not about her having nowhere else to be. It is true she has nowhere else, no one else, but she is here, sleepless and useless, for the same reason that Piaillon lies curled at the foot of the bed. They both belong with her. She is their home. They will wait until the end, and after that they will wait some more. Then Jamyn and Piaillon will remain together until one or other dies, and at last the last of them will be alone as neither of them has ever been. The chances are it will be Jamyn. Piaillon is already blind and her teeth no longer serve. All she does now is sleep, hardly more quietly than her mistress. She licks at her food when Jamyn puts a platter with a few soft scraps beside her on the coverlet. When she needs to relieve herself she yowls, and Jamyn raises herself slowly from the stool and takes the cat from the bed and carries her all the way down the four precipitous flights of stairs to the street. After she has finished, Piaillon comes back into the house and Jamyn closes the door behind her, letting the cat follow her back up the stairs while she hauls herself up to the topmost floor, hand over hand on the rope that does for a banister. Piaillon climbs as stiff and painfully after her.

'Come on, come on, you,' Jamyn calls in an uninflected trailing voice to the trailing cat. 'We'll get there. Or we won't.'

She hears occasional creaks behind her. Either a stair suffering from age as they all are, or the cat feebly complaining at not being carried. But Jamyn tires on the upward climb, and they arrive at the door of their dying mistress together. It's a little exercise for both of them.

Jamyn also does a bit of shopping. They have to have food, she and the cat. Although she could now afford to pay a sou to the lad downstairs to get it for her, she risks the journey away from her mistress's side every other morning, perhaps to feel a sour gratification that the world really is going about its business without any concern for the predicament of her mistress and herself. Otherwise she sits next to her failing mistress, her lady, with her stiff hands in her lap, slowly and slightly raising or lowering her head occasionally as if it might relieve the pain.

The attic room, with its sloping roof, is sparsely furnished. Her mistress's small iron bed with the slight hump of her tiny, diminishing body under a rough blanket and a grubby but pretty embroidered coverlet; across the room her work table, once quite a good piece of furniture but now untouched by polish for years and scratched and stained with ink. Jamyn is not allowed to disturb the chaotic jumble of papers and books to keep it looking nice; plain floorboards, the planks knotted and uneven, what could be seen of them under the labyrinthine piles of books and papers that seem to have spilled over and spread from the over-burdened table. It is only possible to cross the room by walking sideways and around the unorganised stacks of printed and inked words. The walls are bare except for a crucifix over the bed. In any case, they don't offer enough space to get half the stuff off the floor, even if they had been shelved. Jamyn's stool is next to the bed, and in one corner there is a small chest. Opposite the bed and stool, above the table, set into the sloping roof, there is the small window through which, when it is open and the uneven glass does not distort the world, Jamyn can watch clouds move across a rectangle of sky, or the rain slant across the driving winter wind. She lets the light come and go as it will unless, rarely, she has some task to do at night for her mistress that requires her to light a candle. Her eyes are no good now for sewing or reading – not that she ever reads in the presence of her lady. But she does not find the waiting tedious. There is, after all, a life to consider, the life coming to its end beside her. A difficult life. Difficult enough to live, but just as difficult for Jamyn to grasp properly the reason for so much going so wrong. What was it that made her lady's impossible necessity so necessary? What made it impossible? Jamyn was not trained to think by scholars and professors as *he* was, but she knows the dying woman's life through and through, better even than her mistress, better even than her own. At least she sees it more clearly than her lady ever did, and Jamyn, the faithful servant, works very hard to under-stand how it was for her mistress. It is the only way she can hope to understand her own disappointments. So boredom is not a problem, she has enough to do with the time while she waits.

1592

Michel de Montaigne lies in bed, dying. This time there is no doubt. Nothing is left to do but comfort those who weep, and make his formal peace with God. Soon enough. In the meantime, he considers whether God will wish to make peace with him.

In 1588, when the letter from the young woman arrived, he was fifty-five years old. The excellent classical education with which his father had provided him ensured that he was aware of Pliny's opinion that 'there are three kinds of diseases people have been accustomed to escape from by killing themselves: the fiercest of all is the stone in the kidney when the urine is held back by it.' He had the misfortune not to need Pliny to point this fact out to him, though the confirmation was oddly comforting. For ten years a stone in the kidney had been bestowing on his body an intermittent but regular ordeal of excruciating pain, and filling his mind with the inevitability of more and probably worse to come, to say nothing of the inescapable prospect of the same agonising death his father suffered.

Added to which, it had been a long time since a woman looked at him with hungry eyes, and a few years since he'd dared rely on his once-virile member to rise to the occasion if by some marvel it should happen. There were, alongside the exquisite pain from the colic paroxysms and a faltering penis, rotting teeth, fading eyesight, unseemly stomach disturbances and occasional bouts of the quinsy which vied gaily with the stone for the honour of carrying him off.

None of this was surprising. All of it was to be expected. He was fifty-five years old; an age that many would be grateful to attain, an age when the end of life is so close that every morning he woke slightly surprised to be doing so. Everything that ailed him would only get worse until the day came when all pain and discomfort ceased.

He was fifty-five years old with a mother who still regarded him as a wastrel for failing to maintain the family estate, let alone increase its fortune. She and he argued constantly over how the household ought to be run. It was undignified for both of them. The worst of it was that he had not the slightest desire to run a household; he did his duty by it, but could give it no more of his attention. It would have been far more to his taste to have his mother run the estate (if only it didn't mean that she would believe she had the right to run him too), but duty required that he, the oldest son and heir, take responsibility for it. It had been his father's wish, which he could not set aside, and therefore duty also required that his mother complain to him at every turn. She nursed a grievance against him for his father's will that cut her out of any decisions that needed making and made her virtually a ward of the son she was so unimpressed by. He would meet her on the staircases muttering and crossing herself. When she saw her son, she'd shriek her contempt at his hurriedly bowed head.

'Here is the son in charge of his mother. Such a son! Spoiled by that foolish father of his. A child woken in the morning by paid musicians playing outside his window, if you please. Such a special boy. Only Latin, the finest Latin, was allowed to be spoken to *him* because Latin, if you please, must be his first language. So even the servants, even his mother had to learn it. With what result? With the result that I have an ingrate for a son. A lazy ne'er-do-well who lets the place go to rack and ruin. A son with no respect and no love for his mother.'

He was fifty-five with a wife, Françoise, to whom he was also well mannered, who complained almost as much as his mother, in her case of neglect and at being left with the burden of running the estate (and coping with her testy mother-in-law) whenever he had to conduct his political duties in Bordeaux, or decided he wanted to travel through Europe for a few months, visit friends, or spend most of his days (and sometimes nights) in his tower, scribbling. He listened to her complaints, as he did to those of his mother, with a lowered head and in silence. He never argued, or said anything at all in reply. He waited patiently and politely until they had finished and then he continued on his way. His mother was a burden. But he did not blame his wife for her nagging dissatisfaction with him. Who could, all her children having died except one? Five of them. They lived minutes or days, sometimes a month or more, but they all died. Apart from the one girl. It affected his wife badly; she did not grow so inured as he had to their loss, being naturally not so distant from those particular losses as he must be. He grieved for the children, but he didn't brood excessively over their deaths. They were, after all, infants. He and they had no chance to make each other's acquaintance.

He made a bad mistake, however, after the death of the first child, Thoinette, when, in an attempt at comfort, he dedicated his translation of Plutarch's 'Letter of Consolation to His Wife' to

Françoise and expressed his regret to her that she had to lose her babe in only the second year of its life. In fact, Thoinette had died in her second *month* of life. A slip of the pen, but slipshod. (Later, he carefully recorded all five of the deaths with complete accuracy for the official family records.) Relations between Françoise and himself became cooler. He attended the marriage bed at appropriate, regular intervals after the death of Thoinette and respectfully made more children to die before they were weaned. Except when Françoise lost her patience with his distant ways, they were remote but always polite to each other in bed as well as out. Which is just as a marriage should be, he believed. How else could it survive? It was, compared to many he'd known, a good, orderly marriage. And, once, when he had been quite certain he was about to die after a terrible fall from a horse, when death gently whispered in his ear and he didn't mind at all, his first words to the servants carrying him back to the house, when he briefly regained consciousness, were to express concern that his wife be given a horse as she came stumbling down the road to reach the scene of the accident. Was not her comfort the main thing on his mind even at the hour of his death? Or so they said; he had no recollection of it.

In the year 1588, he was fifty-five. He had been Mayor of Bordeaux, and done the job well enough, though of course he always kept something back, retained that back room behind the public shop where no one was permitted to enter. Duty must be fulfilled, but not at the cost of your soul.

He had gained a literary reputation after retirement. His book of essays – a form he invented himself, he knew with modest vanity – was selling all over France and receiving praise from the most serious thinkers of the times. They wrote to him to say so. But his wife and only daughter were not much impressed and neither had read his work. His neighbours were amused and contemptuous. They were, for the most part, men of his own noble rank but they conformed better to the requirements, being men of action who found the idea of sitting in a room writing laughable to say the very least. He had shown by public and military service that he too could be a man of action (up to a point – everything up to a point), but they were baffled by the fact that he chose to retire from a public life *to become a book writer*. They suspected that the mere three generations of nobility on his father's side, and the fact that his mother was said to have come from a family of Spanish *converso* Jews might account for it.

And so too, initially, was he baffled by his choice of occupation at retirement. It did not, at any rate, go as he had expected when he readied the tower in the west corner of the château for his new meditative writing plans. Far from fine thoughts clothed in grand rhetoric coming at elegant intervals to him when he settled to his study in the tower, his mind, presented with the endless possibilities of everything and anything, with limitless words, limitless but disorderly thoughts, with the rest of its time alone with itself, was attacked by a blank, black nightmare, a shapeless nothing that was in itself a monstrous form and threatened him with madness. He wrote doggedly through this fearful agony, hanging on as best he could to the mane of the ferocious unbroken stallion thrashing in his mind: the hopelessness of his life, the total lack of a point to his existence, the cavernous loneliness. He wrote neat little arguments about grand subjects, pro and con, well scattered with classical references, while his head pounded with the dreadful emptiness, the deadly vacuity that was no longer being kept at bay by a busy life.

Gradually, through the nothing, he edged towards something. Small, seemingly ridiculous forays beyond the proper rhetoric led him there. He allowed himself to follow thoughts that he should have excluded but didn't from his impeccably balanced debates. Personal thoughts, reflections about himself. And niggling questions that arose from the conventionally uncontroversial subjects he took up demanded a reply not from books read or quotations learned, but from furthest inward, deep inside his troubled mind. A soul-search, call it. Thinking, is how he came to think of it. He made a decision, borne of desperation, to be led by those thoughts, to demand answers to the questions his mind put to him about himself and write them down, to make, if they might, the shape of a human being. And what he made, some say, and he knew, was something entirely new in the world. A unique form, like his own self, somewhat and not at all like everyone's own self, that might stand for its particular singularity and yet also address the questions all men ask about their being in the world. Others, of course, did not think so highly of him for this innovation. And a part of him, the part that wished only to be what he was supposed to be, and to simply get on without any *trouble*, agreed with those who termed him vulgar and self-regarding.

He was fifty-five years old in 1588, and all these things were his present existence. Only once had he known complete companionship, a camaraderie of the spirit, the love of and the experience of fully loving another human being, and it was long ago, brief as a single sunrise and sunset in the eternity of the world. Often he moaned his agony in the silence of his library. *Oh, my friend.*

Since then he'd lived in loneliness – the special kind of loneliness that came from having once known what it was to have another *you* with you on the earth. With the passage of time, it had become a treasured solitude, painful, certainly, always, but special, because it recalled constantly the unique communion that had been lost. He would not have given it up, now that his beloved friend was beyond reach. It was all he had left of him, that loneliness. Perhaps it was more even than having him alive and with him. But to have no one with whom you can sit in comfortable silence, to whom you can talk and be certain of their understanding, whom you can trust with your deepest thoughts and fears without hesitation, whose advice is as wise as any good father and who forgives, like any good father, your hesitation in taking it – to have had and lost such a friend, that is hard. No father, no friend. Not even a son, though a son could hardly play the part of a lost friend, but a son would have been something. His daughter, Léonor, was no son. She was her mother's child. A nice enough girl. Perhaps he once had unfeasible hopes in spite of her sex, but at sixteen her intellect was no more than ordinary and her soul was already moulded and content with itself. He smiled to see her frowning over her lessons and sitting like a lady at the dinner table, but there was nothing more than a distant affection in his heart for her. She would, of course, be his heir, but in spite of the careful instructions in his will, he feared for the fate of his library and his work after his fast-approaching end. He had friends, of course. But they were elsewhere, and though he enjoyed their occasional visits and the chance to get away and see them, they never came close to filling the empty place in him that Estienne de La Boétie left behind.

He was fifty-five in the early months of 1588 and he had just spent weeks travelling from Bordeaux to Paris on an urgent and secret mission, getting robbed and almost murdered on the way. He was a Catholic who had been entrusted by the Protestant Prince Henri of Navarre with the task of making an alliance with the Catholic King Henri III against the Catholic League of the Duc de Guise, who was even then marching on Paris, with the unsurprising result that both Catholics and Huguenots distrusted him. Perhaps rightly so, because, without denying his Catholic faith in any way, he was more concerned with bringing peace to France than supporting one side or the other. He arrived for his mission in Paris two weeks late, exhausted to the point of death by the journey, and its vicissitudes, and in shocking pain. His life could easily have ended in the forest of Villebois, a victim of the robbers or members of the Catholic League or whoever they were. His life did not end then. He charmed and reasoned his way out of death that time. He had a job to do, a duty to fulfil. He recalled, however, a very slight twinge of disappointment when the gentlemen in the forest sheathed their knives and left him to get on with his journey and what remained of his life.

He was fifty-five and coming to the conclusion that what was most important in life was to take what pleasure it offers you. To notice it and enjoy it, even momentarily, for what it is. No pleasure was to be disregarded. Only fools despise the pleasures of the God-given body more than less tangible joys. Once the worst fear you have – in his case the terror of the stone – has fallen on you, you discover that pleasure still lives in and around your body, beside, beneath and beyond the pain. Once the end of life is clearly visible, you find that pleasure in its moment is all the sweeter. He knew this, but it was no easy thought to hold in his mind all the time while he lay in bed in his fine Parisian accommodations, depleted with travel, tormented by pain, trying to rest and gather his strength. Other thoughts kept coming, his past life laid itself out before him, his future trickled away barely ahead of him, and he was not sure how he would manage to rise the following morning looking like a man with a purpose. It was 1588. He was fifty-five. There was a knock at his bedroom door and a servant entered with a letter for him.

Marie de Gournay is alone. She is thirty years old and for the
seven terrible long years since 1588, her life has been a desert.
Now, here she stands in the centre of the circular room, barely
breathing for fear of exploding with excitement. She has always
been liable to be overwhelmed by her uncontainable feelings, but
here alone in this place for the first time, she wants to be clear and
calm. She has found her own way to the tower and up the wind-
ing staircase to the library on the top floor. The widow and the
daughter will be awake and up by now, and in all likelihood looking for her. She hopes they will assume she has gone for a walk.
She is here at last, in the place that she has spent so much time –
eleven years – picturing. She remembers how she used to visualise
this room when she was far away from it, from him, but she
can't be sure whether *he* was ever in that study in her mind's
eye. It was as if he were there, but not as an actual person in a
particular spot. The room contained him, but in her picturing
of it her view had been from behind his eyes, so she never saw
him. She couldn't: her view was his. She became him in the carefully imagined study.

Now she is here, actually and alone, seeing what there is to be
seen, and no other presence disturbs the air. The study is vacated.
Except for her. Flesh-and-blood *here*, inhaling the woody scent of
the timber beams above her head and seeing the light that streams

in through the three windows, cutting swathes through the shadowed turret room; feeling the coolness of the curved stone walls behind the bookcases surrounding her, and the dawn air against her cheeks. No phantom, both she and it solid, present, real. Here she is. At last.

It looked no different, however, from her imagined room. His table and chair were placed exactly as she knew them to be against the only flat wall, and all around the other curved walls, from floor to ceiling, there were the five rows of shelves overflowing with manuscripts and books, some bound in tooled leather, others in bright white vellum, some lying flat on top of each other, others upright, side by side, the front edges facing out, in the modern way. The three windows across the room, to the left, right and almost directly ahead of the table, let in the glare of the early-morning southern sunlight to intersect the circular space with three brilliant golden beams, vertical lozenges crowded and glinting with motes performing a frantic dance. Outside, under the windows, three floors below, hens clucked and scraped at the dry earth in their enclosure, a gardener examined the shrubs for unruly shoots, another tended the herb beds. Tradesmen and servants were already coming and going about their business, clattering through the gateway at the base of the tower. When she stood squarely in front of the window to the left of the table she could see the sweeping, patched green valley over which this tower watched, and beyond it the neighbouring hills, dark velvet-coated, rolling away in the distance towards the rest of the world. She turned and paced deliberately across the flags, towards the window diagonally opposite, counting off aloud.

Fourteen . . . fifteen . . . yes, sixteen – if she adjusted her stride to one not hampered by skirts and delicacy, or shortness of leg. Not that his legs were long. He was not a tall man. And her strides were hardly delicate. So, sixteen paces. Correct. She was pleased that it was all exactly as he had described, and she had imagined, having put so much effort into imagining it accurately from his description. Word perfect. Picture perfect.

But, quite separately from her careful re-creation of this place, there had been another sort of imagining during all those years before she got here. It was still of this library, but it was animated, not the careful static picture, more of a reverie in which both of them were there together, as they never had been. She did not see from his eyes in this less considered mode of imagining, but from behind her own. And he was showing her, in her vivid daydream, around his special place. His *solitarium* he had called it, laughing, when they were together at Gournay. She didn't know why he laughed. He pulled out this or that book for her to take to the table and examine. He stood behind her at a window, his arm hovering over her shoulder, almost brushing her cheek, his forefinger extending from a closed fist in front of her, pointing out a feature of the distant view. She could smell the stuff of his sleeve, fine clean linen, the must of heavy silk. He took her into the small side room where a fire blazed and warmed the stone around it, creating a circle of heat and warm yellow light that contrasted with the chill radiating from the other walls. Then he led her down the narrow spiral stairway to the room below, the one with the bed in which he slept when he wanted to be alone even at night.

That dream (sometimes actually a dream from which she

would wake) was of a different quality to her immaculately constructed conjuring of the tower which she (and, it had to be said, his other readers) knew so well without ever having, until this day, visited. The dream that contained the two of them could never now become a reality.

She had got up early, dressed in a careless assortment of warm clothes, underskirt, chemise, plain wool dress, thick stockings, all pulled, without more than a glance, from her travelling chest. She pinned her back hair roughly into a bun and stuck a woollen cap over the short curls in the front; tied a shawl around her shoulders, wrapped an enveloping woollen cloak over everything, keeping the resulting disarray from view as well as the cool morning air at bay, and left the main house as quietly as her clumpy shoes would allow, to be on her own in the tower, at least this first time, fearing more than anything that her dream of him introducing her to his study would be usurped by the two women finding her in time to show her around. It was essential to be alone with the room. If her vision of being in the tower with him had definitively failed, her picturing of it at least had become a reality, and here she was (as his other readers were not) fully in the picture: the eyes that looked about her were her own, she was no longer obliged to look through his. The presence in the study was that of the Demoiselle de Gournay, Marie le Jars, herself.

She pulled the high-backed chair out a little from the table, taking care not to scrape it on the floor, and sat down, resting her forearms flat along the gnarled oak arms. A disbound copy of the edition he had published in 1588, the left edge loosely laced with cord, lay unopened, set to one side, aligned with the right-angled corner of the table. The unlaced side of the book bulged unevenly, showing the edges of the loose leaves he had attached to many of the pages, which she knew were covered in his amendments and additions to the text. There had been no new work after this edition, but he had been revising since then in this disbound copy, scribbling his inked embellishments to the printed words in every bit of marginal space on the thick, creamy woven paper, and gluing in loose sheets of extra thoughts where they were to be added, making ready for the next edition. He hardly ever crossed out, but only supplemented what he had already written. In Picardy she had seen how he revised; he showed her.

She was sitting now in front of the very copy he had worked on while he stayed with her and which he had brought back here to Guyenne with him. Then he had worked on it for four more years. The only other copy of these amendments and changes had been sent to her in Paris the previous year by his widow, Françoise. After his death, his friend, Pierre de Brach, had worked here in the tower, collecting and collating the handwritten alterations in this original, and duplicated them in his own hand into a second copy which she received. The printer to whom she sent it with her own newly written Preface, to produce the new posthumous edition, had destroyed the Brach copy in the process of typesetting. This disbound volume in front of her, filled with minute scrawl and pasted-in scraps, was now the only evidence that remained of his intentions.

She did not pull his book towards her, nor touch it. Time enough. She sat upright in the chair, her hands flat against the deeply furrowed grain of the old tabletop, and looked around her at the circular library. She breathed in the stillness carefully,

inhabiting the entire panorama, overseeing it, seeing over everything, the whole wide world beyond. After a few moments she
leaned back, resting her head on the polished wood of the chair
and looked upwards.

'*Homo sum humani a me nihil alienum puto*,' she read, burned
on to a transverse beam ahead of her. '*I am human; nothing human
is strange to me*', she translated. She turned her head to the left a
little. '*I know nothing*' on one of the two great longitudinal beams.
To the right, on the other beam stretching along the room:
'*Iudicio alternante. Judgement comes and goes*', she interpreted, and
then reinterpreted: '*Opinion changes.*' She let her eyes roam the
beams furthest from the table: '*I define nothing . . . I do not comprehend . . . I hold back . . . I examine . . .*'

Her father's library.

Her *other* father's library was the greatest treasure he could have
left her. Not that he did leave it to her, not particularly. Who
would leave a library to a twelve-year-old girl? It was, of course,
part of her mother's legal property, held in trust until Charles
came of age. But Marie took it for her own and no one, except for
her mother, cared one way or the other. It wasn't the grand library
of a thousand volumes her adopted father had collected, but it
was substantial enough. There were two hundred or so books,
along with a chair, a table and a lectern, in a small, previously
unused first-floor room of the château in Picardy. Guillaume le
Jars – *that* father – wasn't a great reader. The library was a con-
ceit. Something a well-born gentleman as he was should have,
and when at last, through his efforts as a treasurer at the Court,
he became a gentleman with the means and land he previously

lacked, he had, when Marie was just three or four years old, instructed an agent to purchase the basis of a gentleman's library and have it sent to the château on his newly acquired gentleman's estate at Gournay-sur-Aronde.

Marie doubted that he had found much time to read before his death eight years later. His life in Paris was filled morning to night with maintaining and bettering his position in Court and with keeping up in society. The books were bought and sent to the room he had shelved for them in Gournay. Perhaps he intended to retire there and read his books when the time was right. As her other father had done. He more likely imagined himself hunting and dining with neighbours and disputing with the peasants who so aggravatingly had somehow acquired the rights to graze their cattle on his land. He might have travelled occasionally. He surely planned to lead the comfortable, easy life of a landed gentleman (assuming that the never-ending, or always-beginning wars continued to remain remote from Picardy), but sometimes he might have retired to his book room and leafed through one of his volumes, or just sat there at the table staring at the pages of an open book while actually looking back over the life that was the only one he had. But before that could happen, he died, quite unexpectedly, falling down lifeless for no reason that anyone could understand on the rue Royale, en route to or from some mission in the service of the King.

Marie had already discovered her father's library on her occasional visits to Picardy as a small child. She found the room that no one used, with its dusty, unread volumes waiting like silent sleeping princes for their reader to creak open their leather bindings and release the laboriously printed words inside into the world and a ready mind. It was the one place in which the tightly nerved child could be calm and at ease. She took the room for her own, and on every visit to Gournay until she was twelve years old, she lost herself in it, ignoring the calls from her mother and the servants for her to come and make herself useful around the place. Instead of being useful, Marie inhabited her father's library and began to learn to want the impossible.

Marie sat now in the far grander library of her adopted father. After he died, it belonged to his widow. When the widow died, the library would become the property of the blood daughter. Like her real father, he had not left her anything. It was said that he had written her a letter on his deathbed, but it had never arrived. What finally came to her was that copy of the amended 1588 edition, worked on by Pierre de Brach, with a request from the widow, from Françoise, that Mademoiselle de Gournay find a publisher for it in Paris. Also included in the parcel, which unlike his deathbed letter *had* reached her, was the manuscript of her own and only work of fiction, the romance she had sent him after his visit: *The Promenade of Monsieur de Montaigne*. The one he had never returned. The one about which he had never written her a word. That manuscript was included in the package with the great man's final amendments to his work. It was found among his papers, wrote the widow in an accompanying letter, and she believed that Marie would want it back, and if she would be so kind as to find a publisher for a posthumous edition of her late husband's work, since she knew how much Marie admired it, and being in Paris would be in a position to find the most reliable printing establishments, she would count it a great service to herself and her late husband. Signed Françoise de la Chassaigne – Madame de Montaigne.

Marie de Gournay knew that this was as it should be. The adopted daughter, not the widow or the natural child, had to be the keeper of the work, maintaining it and his memory as only she could. Marie le Jars de Gournay sat at her father's desk, in his library, and took in the fact that the impossible thing she had wanted for so long had, after all, become her life's work.

2

Guillaume le Jars left his family well enough off when he died in 1577, but their fortune suffered catastrophically in the continuing and perpetual wars between the Catholics and Huguenots as taxes spiralled and rents remained unpaid, tearing their security, as well as the order of things, apart. Three years after Guillaume's death, Marie's family left Paris for the estate in Gournay, where life for a widow and her six children would be less demanding and considerably less expensive.

Marie missed her father and those occasional times when she was in his presence in their Paris house. He seemed a kind enough, careful man, and to a small child, wonderfully clever and filled with understanding about the world. At twelve she was sorry to lose the opportunity of knowing him for longer, but at the age of fifteen losing him was nothing compared to her loss of Paris. It was the brilliant centre of the world, where everything was available and life's possibilities appeared to her endless when she watched men and a few women moving with such delibera-tion through the streets as if they all knew exactly where they were going and what there was to be done. She always tried to imagine herself, free of the constraints of childhood, joining them, and debating fiercely in the fashionable salons, which were surely the destination of the bright-eyed purposeful ones, where knowledge and wit – she had no doubt – soared back and forth like sweetly hit tennis balls. It was clear to Marie from the way they carried themselves in their fine clothes, with their cloaks jauntily flung about them, tip-tilted hats and polished buckled shoes, that they knew all there was that was important to know about being alive. Their understanding shone in their confident, focused eyes. Not the mothers and the children and servants, of course, with whom she spent all her childish time, but others, unencumbered, glowed with their possession of a world of knowledge that seemed so immense and mysterious and yet quite possibly *achievable* to the little girl. And just as she seemed almost ready to discover how to join them, how to apprentice herself to them, her mother's decision to leave Paris meant Marie's exile from all that promise. She was dismayed, as she would have been dismayed in the final moment of consciousness, by the sudden end of her actual life, at having to move permanently to the château in Gournay-sur-Aronde, surrounded by its moat, which was surrounded in turn by an endless wilderness of smallholdings, woods, fields and dirt tracks. The countryside. When her mother told her of the decision to make their home in Picardy instead of Paris, her bright future ploughed into darkness. She screamed her refusal to move, and lay on the floor wailing and kicking out at anyone who came near. It was hours before she stopped sobbing, and days before she spoke to anyone. It was the worst fit of passion her mother had seen from her easily enraged oldest daughter. Nevertheless, the decision was for the best.

Gournay was a full day's ride north by coach from Paris, and as they went clattering along after their wagons of household goods, Marie, pale as linen, eyes swollen with a last night of mourning for her beloved Paris, watched the vivid world disappear with the spire of Sainte Chapelle and the towers of

Notre-Dame, until finally civilisation's last outpost, the cathedral of Senlis, vanished behind her, and they plunged into the shadows of the vast forest of Saint-Christophe for what felt like hour after hour of deep green gloom. When eventually they emerged into the daylight there was nothing: the great green and brown nothing of the countryside. They continued along the coach road with no more to see on either side of it than gatherings of a few cottages that barely deserved the title of villages, and *Nature* – overgrown land, cultivated fields, rivers, bushes, trees, small animals fleeing in front of them, birds screeching warnings in the branches, a blazing sun in a senseless blue sky, earth, stones, dust – until they arrived at their final destination, Gournay, where not a palace or a cathedral was to be seen. No shops or fashionable streets, no famous salons in fine houses where courtiers and intellectuals congregated to talk about philosophy and poetry and who was doing and saying what. Busyness in this vacuous place was visible only as hard work on the purpled, weather-scoured faces and thick, bent bodies of the peasants, their voices harsh as squabbling crows, carrying through the unobstructed air. People were seen in numbers only when they were harvesting their crops in the autumn or shrieking at each other on market days. This place, this provincial world was bereft of anything that mattered to Marie's vision of her future. Hope expired.

Marie was a sullen, angry girl when they moved to Gournay from Paris. But it wasn't only the sudden anger triggered by her change of circumstances; there was also a slow-built rage, beginning she would never remember when, living inside her, an expanding bubble filling slowly with fury, and visible to the world in her pinched, downturned little mouth and protuberant glaring eyes with pupils like tight black knots. Marie went sourly about her life at home before Gournay when she wasn't gazing through a window to watch the Parisian world go by. Her daily existence was dedicated by her mother, Jeanne, to preparation for her future. Daughters married. They were born to marry. Very occasionally a sublime beauty might blind a potential suitor to her lack of a great fortune or an important name, but Marie, her mother would remind her from a very early age, did not possess such a quality. The le Jars name was old enough and respectable, but not so impressive that it would compensate for the very modest portion that would be her dowry, even before the death of her father left them in difficult circumstances. There were loans to the Crown that never would be repaid as long as the wars continued to suck the life out of the nation's coffers. There were the careers of her two brothers to fund, and her three younger sisters to marry off. Girls in her position, Jeanne insisted when Marie failed to excel in her domestic duties, had better become skilled housekeepers if they were not to end up in the only other place they could be: the convent. A mother had a duty to face the facts about her children. It looked very much as though the youngest girl, Léonore, was going to wear the habit. She was at least as plain as her older sister, but a quiet girl who dreamed of nothing so much as being wedded to Christ. Which under the circumstances was a blessing. It was respectable, and Jeanne could not hope for anything more for the child. Her ambition rested with her other daughters. Madeleine and Marthe would marry. They were useful, practical girls a mother could do something with when they were old enough to be presented. They weren't great beauties, but they had aspirations and were efficient at their household tasks. Perhaps they would make quite decent alliances that would boost the family name.

But, long before the time of Guillaume's death, Jeanne was close to despairing of her eldest daughter. The child had no talent for anything that was to be expected of a woman. No domestic skill came naturally to her. Her hands were large and maladroit, not made for the delicate and intricate tasks that women could excel at. She moved with a jerky awkwardness, her eyes flicking away when in danger of making contact with others. Her embroidery and sewing always had to be unpicked, and no matter how patiently she was shown the stitch and the desired result, she produced the same clumsy, uneven work that was nowhere near the lines she was supposed to follow and out of all proportion to the original stitches of anything she was mending. She found food planning and preparation tedious and cared nothing for combining delicate flavours or spicy aromas. She ate whatever was in front of her with complete lack of interest. She would not dance in spite of her forced attendance at the lessons of the dance master her mother provided for her children. She would not sing, and anyway had a thin, tuneless voice that no one would ever enjoy listening to. Nevertheless, Jeanne persisted in trying to teach her oldest daughter how to run a household, to budget, to plan so as not to run out of supplies of food and fuel, to instruct servants and monitor their work. She showed her daughter how to dress to best advantage without extravagance of either money or taste. She told her what she needed to know about the getting, bearing and rearing of children. Because what else could she do with a plain female child who showed not the slightest interest in devoting her life to God?

Marie found these lessons from her mother intolerable. There were terrible arguments, with Marie running out of rooms and shouting.

'I won't! I don't care. I don't want to marry! Leave me alone!' Often her voice would reach a peak and disappear, cracked by a scream.

Her father's library in Gournay was the place of escape from her present and from her preordained future. She slipped through the dark panelled door at every possible moment of the day and night, whenever she could avoid being tutored on how to be someone's wife, some house's keeper, some child's mother. Jeanne or one of the servants only had to take their eyes off her for a second, and she was gone. And strangely, although they called out her name in mounting aggravation, and climbed the stairs breathing heavily in search of her, they only ever opened the library door, called out her name once again, paused for the briefest moment before crashing the door closed behind them, and giving up the search. Marie was invariably there. She sat half-curled or flat out on the floor behind the table under the dusty window, with a book or manuscript in front of her, unsighted from the door. They entered, called out her name, and then left.

'Mademoiselle Marie? Where are you? You are wanted in the kitchen.'

'Marie, come here immediately. You've got work to do. Don't you dare hide.'

And then silence, waiting for a reply. 'I'm here, I'm coming . . .' But she never answered, the silence extended and finished in an impatient sigh, the slamming door and footsteps fading up or down a staircase. And yet they surely knew she was there; that the library was her home in the world, her particular place, where she always wanted to be. Certainly they knew: 'What is in that roomful of words that you like so much?' her mother often demanded angrily, without ever waiting for her daughter to formulate an answer.

It was her mother's question, to which she required no reply, that first made Marie wonder what actually it was that she liked so much. For the first few years, she could barely read, but she manhandled what volumes she could reach down to the floor and turned their pages, heard the creak and crackle, inhaled the papery, cottony scent, almost like her newly laundered chemise but more acrid, and the warm, spiced smell of leather, like a wild horse tamed. She ran her fingertips over the calf bindings and the embossing, catching the ridges and smoothness. Turned the pages, stiff woven paper heavy with inked markings that gradually became separated and recognisable as words, then sentences, until eventually, so gradually that she never knew when, the full existence and meaning of a book came clear to her. So at first it wasn't a roomful of words as her mother had delightfully suggested, it was a roomful of objects that had no other place in the world. Two hundred, once she could count that far. The bindings were pored over, the pictures gazed at, the pages turned. First they were objects that gave pleasure to all her senses. Toys. And then more. Objects with a function. A room full of words, a room full of sentences, a room full of meaning if she could only interpret it.

The library became the only world she chose to explore. She began to associate the books with more than sensual pleasure. She pulled down volume after volume and when she found one written in the French she had by now been taught, she started to read, at first in a scattered way, here and there, book after book, as a bee dances over a flowering bush, and then beginning at the beginning, reading on in a single book, getting the idea of each being a discrete entity devoted to an interest of its own. And finally, coming to understand that behind each individual book was a mind. That a book was an object filled with the thinking of a mind which belonged to a single person, alive or once alive. Thoughts bound between leather boards and kept for ever ready for another mind to explore. *Her* thoughts came and passed and went she could never know where. But a book held a person's thoughts so that someone else could entertain them, borrow them, roll them around and look at them, enjoy them, wonder about them, and then come back another day, month, year and consider them all over again. Marie learned that books were boxes of thoughts, held fast by writing, made by a special breed of beings called writers. Eventually, the answer to her mother's question was so detailed that it was impossible to articulate. Simplified, she would have said: Words, no . . . writing . . . no, writers was what she liked so much about that room full of words. But by the time she got the answer Marie also knew that her mother did not want to know it and would have been profoundly unimpressed with the one her daughter had devised.

Some of the books were incomprehensible, even once she had learned to read. Opening volume after volume, she found the letters danced as meaninglessly as they had when she was an illiterate baby. Her shock was physical, and her anger at discovering that there were still secrets the library withheld from her was sharp. She did not know Latin. No one thought it a necessary skill for a female child. She spelled out a title: *A. . .e. . .n. . .e. . .i. . .d.* One day, on another shelf she discovered a second copy with the title *Aeneid* and wondered why there were two. When she got it down, she saw that only the title was in Latin and that the text was in French. She read it, and instead of leaving it at that and allowing the Latin version to rest on its shelf, she had another thought. Translation was an unknown idea to her, but if it was possible to take a book and turn its words into another language then each word must have its counterpart in that language, in every language. She imagined Latin as a code, like the codes her siblings sometimes devised for keeping things from the adults and from her. Latin was a secret writing to which she believed she might have found the key. If the two books were the same, apart from their language, then if she read them side by side, word by word, sentence by sentence, she might learn Latin all by herself. She scoured the shelves and discovered several books in both languages. The child may not have had domestic skills or God-given good looks, but she possessed tenacity, and a dogged desire to understand everything that was written or printed between covers. She had no idea of the difficulty of the solitary task she set herself so she simply got on with it, and on and on until very slowly and after years of work she was quite fluent in reading and even writing Latin. It was a game, an assignment, a marvellous never-ending puzzle to be solved, as producing succulent meals, intricate embroidery, and a perfectly run household might be to another girl. Marie lived in her father's library in every possible way. It was her breath, her heartbeat, and, when she moved permanently to Gournay, it became her Paris, with all its hopes and dreams.

The stolen library hours of Marie's youth in Gournay were a preparation, though it was fifteen years before she knew for what. Apart from her bookish explorations in her father's study, nothing of any moment had happened to her by the time she was eighteen. It looked very much as though nothing was going to happen to her – so her mother feared. Neither marriage nor piety appeared to hold any interest for her and she remained practically and determinedly useless at the only possibility left for a useful life: to be domestically competent enough to take over the household duties from Jeanne as she got older. So far as Jeanne was concerned, at eighteen her eldest child might as well still have been eleven for all the progress she had made towards a functioning worldly existence. She had become a woman in the sense that her body was ready for its duties: she bled regularly each month and her awkward, angular childish limbs and torso had rounded somewhat. The narrow, pointed chin and fleshier cheeks gave her a heart-shaped face which almost softened the sharpness of her childhood severity, and she looked in some lights if not pretty, then striking at least. But her beady raven's eyes were too prominent, her nose too emphatic without being classical and her mouth too small and her thin lips too tightly pressed together for most lights. She was far from beautiful, even though her plainness was a little alleviated by the momentary succulence of her passage through youth. She looked tense, always. Even when she smiled there was a mistrust at the corner of her eyes, and an ambiguity in the curve of her lips that could easily be read as disdain. When she wasn't smiling, which was most often, her features contracted into a clouded concern in the centre of her face, which hovered on the verge of crossness. Preparations were already in hand for Madeleine's betrothal to the Lord of Bouvray, a more than satisfactory alliance, though it was a test to find the dowry, and Marthe, two years younger than Marie, but far more personable and accomplished, would not be looking for a husband for long. So for her oldest daughter, as for her youngest, Léonore, it would have to be the convent.

Few of her father's books were left unread now, not even those in Latin. Marie's progress with Greek was slower (her Uncle Louis had helped her understand the unfathomable characters when he visited), but there was very little hurry. The more she read and the more Latin she learned, the more it seemed to Marie that an entire and good life might be spent in the company of books. Any other of the few possibilities open to her else would be an interruption to her reading. To become a nun would be a continual interruption. Nuns were, she knew, less free than children to secrete themselves in a corner and read whatever took their fancy. Marriage, too, would be an interruption. What moment did her mother have to read, even when her father was alive, even if she had thought it a decent use of time? A widow's life, taking care of a household and children took up all the hours in a day, though Marie could not understand why, and a living husband might interrupt a wife even more. She resolved to be neither a nun nor a wife. She could see nothing wrong with just reading books. But could a grown woman have a life that was devoted to reading? That is, did such a life exist in the world to be lived? According to her mother, even reading in one's spare moments was a waste, and she had never heard of anyone who could live only by reading books. If such a one existed – she could barely imagine it – it was certain it would not be a woman. Yet, the more she thought, the less reason there seemed to be why she shouldn't. Except for the matter of money. Once a husband, a household and religious vocation were renounced, only a too limited income might prevent such a life. Money was very short these days, with the preparations for her sister's marriage and the dowry. Marthe would need one also. Charles was already costing a good deal in his military career in Italy, and Augustin was still a baby whose future would have to be paid for. After the cost of upkeep for the chateau, there would be very little left over from their ever-dwindling resources to keep a single woman in a life of reading. But what would she require? Food, clothes, a roof over her head. She had no interest in elaborate garments or fine suppers; she could forgo any unnecessary travel if she was in the right place to start with. Why should she not live a frugal life, reading books, translating them, thinking about them? Of course, she was not, and if she remained in Gournay without marrying she never would be, grand enough to have a literary salon of her own, nor even to attend one like those in Paris she had heard tell of, where the thinkers of the day came to discuss and share their thoughts.

As Uncle Louis learned of her interest in books, he began to tell her about the learning of Catherine de' Medici and Marguerite de Valois, and the salons they kept where *everybody* went. Mary Stuart, he said, had composed a Latin prayer and recited it to the entire Court when she was just fourteen. So women *could* be learned and spend time talking about books and writing, if not quietly live their life in libraries. Certainly, she had heard only of great queens and princesses, with retinues and vast wealth doing so, but surely, if she determined to want very little and was prepared to be content to read and think quietly in her own company, rather than discuss ideas with the elite of Paris, there would be enough money left over from her sisters' dowries and the cost of supporting her brothers for her to lead a modest, quiet life, her only expenditure books, in some small accommodation in an unfashionable quarter of Paris, uninterrupted by domestic or religious duties. Who could mind if she did that? Why shouldn't she?

Because it was just a dream of a life. There was no precedent that she could think of in any corner of the social world into which she had been born. Though she could imagine it, the fact that she had no knowledge of anyone actually living it made it seem very unlikely that she could actually have such an existence. Why, apart from the fact that she wanted to, would she achieve what she wanted? Could simply wanting make the impossible occur? She thought not. There was no evidence in any part of her life, not even in her reading, that dreaming of something was enough to make it come true. And yet the dream was so compelling. Why did she have it, and so strongly, if she was not destined by the desire to live it in reality? Surely just coming up with such an unheard-of thought must indicate her capacity and the necessity for such a life. The thought remained with her although she knew not to mention the idea to her mother, who would have reiterated – horrified – Marie's fears that such a life was not available to be lived, and doubtless made immediate arrangements with the local convent.

There were few visitors to Gournay, but from time to time her father's brother, Louis le Jars, visited from Paris and brought with him the scent of the sophisticated literary world Marie so ached for. He was a secretary at the Court of Henri III, but she discovered also a playwright, almost one of those, it gradually dawned on Marie, who was recognised and even justified in the world for the words he put down on paper. His plays were performed. People paid for tickets to watch them. There were those, she had come to understand, who not only lived a life reading, but who also wrote what others read, *for a living*. It had dawned on her surprisingly slowly that some of the books she read were written by actual, living, breathing persons, and that these persons were what might be called writers, as others were called wives or nuns, some of whom, she now supposed (the writers, not the wives or nuns), might actually be paid for their efforts. Books cost money to buy – she knew that only too well – so were those who wrote them in receipt of payment? Aristotle and Ronsard, Plutarch and Erasmus wrote, were writers, just like Uncle Louis. Writers by profession. They had spent, and did spend, their time poring over manuscripts and writing down their thoughts and ideas. What they wrote was printed. People bought their books and discussed what they read in them, waited even, from the living ones, for the next volume to come out. Behind the words between the covers of the books she read, people actually existed. They were all men, of course, as far as Marie knew, but one of them, Uncle Louis told her, though there was no copy of her work in the library at

Gournay, Christine de Pisan, writing over a hundred years ago, was neither a man, a nun or a princess.

Louis liked his niece and her oddness. After he discovered her secret passion, he always brought her a book of poetry or the newest romance when he came to visit, to Jeanne's disgust. 'A household manual would be more useful,' she would snap at him. Uncle Louis took some pleasure in telling Marie stories of his life in Paris; she responded to them with a rare excitement. He had actually been a friend of Ronsard and was acquainted with other members of the Pléiades and brought her the latest volumes of their poetry. Quietly, when his sister-in-law wasn't nearby to scold them both, he would tell her who was saying what, in which salons they were saying it, and, though this was of little interest to Marie, what they were wearing when they said it. Marie listened and took in every nuance she could grasp, like a young animal learning the scents on the air, but there was also an anguish in knowing that she could not be there among them, in the streets and salons of Paris, nodding to d'Aubigné, and passing the visiting Giordano Bruno on the street, attending Garnier's latest play, or buying the new collection of de Baïf's verse. Aged eighteen, and as removed from nodding, passing, attending and buying as it was possible to be, she hated Gournay, in spite of the life-enhancing library. It was her prison, her tower, where no prince would ever come to her rescue. Often at night she lay in bed and imagined returning to Paris with Uncle Louis, but for all her uselessness at home, it was out of the question that she would be allowed to leave, or that, in truth, he would want to take responsibility for an unmarriageable niece who was not even able to make his life more comfortable.

In that spring of 1584 Louis came to stay for a few weeks and brought Marie two volumes of a work which he told her had been gathering momentum among the most discerning sections of society for the past two years. Louis explained that the books contained what were called by their author 'essays' – attempts, try-outs, testings – it was hard to define this word in its new literary coining. The writings that made up the two volumes were not poetry, not polemic, nor rhetoric, but whatever they might be, they were really remarkably interesting.

'They're not quite like anything else – not to say in parts,' Louis whispered with a collusive smile, 'quite unsuitable for the delicate mind of a young unmarried girl. But don't tell your mother, eh?'

Marie thanked him with her awkward smile which, though genuine, she knew failed to convey her pleasure and gratitude. Except when she was angry, there seemed to be an unbridgeable gap between her feelings and what her face managed to express. In the presence of another human being, even Uncle Louis, her body tightened, her shoulders rose and her eyes glared and slid away from contact when she meant them to express warmth and gratitude. She could feel the inaccuracy of her body as it took instruction from her intentions and then continued on its own unfluent, impeded way. Yet behind her clumsily polite acceptance of the gift, the fact that Uncle Louis, the playwright from Paris, the bosom companion of the great Ronsard, considered her someone who would want to read what everyone with discernment was reading made her heart thunder with pride.

Marie, her head thrust forward purposefully on her thin neck, the books clasped to her chest with both hands making a safe cage for them, rushed the two small volumes to the library to await her, before her mother could take them and tell her that she might read them only once she had unpicked the mess of her last embroidery effort and satisfactorily completed another attempt. She would save up Uncle Louis's gift for when he had left and there were no more stories of Parisian life to divert her. Who knew when he would come again with another book and more tales?

Once or twice lately, Marie had imagined, though she tried not to, a moment arriving when all the books in her father's library had been read, twice, three times. Could a time come when, after who knows how many readings, the idea of beginning all over again would fill her not with that warm wash of so much pleasure to come, but with the same deadly tedium as her mother's instruction to organise the following evening's dinner? At present it seemed impossible that she would ever have enough of her books, but it seemed a little less impossible with every volume she finished and returned to the shelf for a second, and then a third time. A new book extended the possibility of her reading life so that she could avoid the alarming idea of using up her library. Of course, new books could be ordered from Paris, but the cost was immense and her mother would never permit it, though Marie would have been happy to spend her wedding or convent dowry on books rather than a husband or that other secure place in the world. She worked hard at suppressing panicky thoughts about a time when she would no longer want to re-read the books she had, and persuaded herself that she could not help but be content so long as she had her place in the library (she still curled up on the floor behind the table, for all her eighteen years) and there were pages to turn. A new book was the greatest of treasures.

In the world beyond the salons of Paris and the château in Gournay, the wars between the believers in the old and new religions had reignited after a lull. Towns were laid siege to, battles devastated the countryside, impoverishing and killing citizens of both, but miraculously, at least for now, Picardy was calm in the midst of the troubles. It was unlikely to be immune, however, from a season of plague which was beginning to sweep through southern France and work its way north. All the more reason for staying where one was, living inside the protective, provincial walls of the château and keeping oneself to oneself.

Marie had started to make translations of Virgil. Jeanne, harried and getting older, fretted about Madeleine's forthcoming marriage arrangements, encouraged Marthe to refine her domestic and social skills before her presentation in Paris once the danger of plague had died away, and permitted Léonore to spend all the time she wanted with the nuns of the local convent even if it did mean a certain risk in breathing the air of the outside world. There was little she could do about Marie. Louis returned to Paris, the Court, the salons, the theatres, the writers, rested but enthused to be back in the real world in spite of its dangers. It was time now for Marie to attend to the books on the library table and discover what all the years of her reading and devotion to the library had been preparing her for.

The two small volumes waited for Marie on the library table, side by side. Louis had had them nicely bound. Nothing elaborate, no

44

tooling, just plain tanned calfskin, quite smooth to the eye, soft to the touch, though with the lightest of strokes her fingertips could discern the natural irregularities of the leather. Marie picked up one of the books and held it in her hand. It was thick and quite weighty, but no more than the height and width of her prayer book, and lay comfortably, barely overlapping her palms. Closing her hands, as if making ready for prayer, she trapped the bulky volume solidly in her grasp, brought it up close to her face, and with both thumbs parting the pages she opened it and snapped it closed several times, causing puffs of air, the life's breath inside the covers, to blow on to her skin. She opened the book again and lifted it right up against her nostrils to inhale the smell of new leather and freshly produced rag. The sharp scent of paper hit the back of her throat, then deepened and darkened into the complex smell of treated hide, chemical and animal, and finally she caught the special high note of newness. None of the books in the library smelled quite like this any more. The perfume of a new book was like nothing else. After she had read these volumes and they had lived on the shelves beside or beneath the other books, they would take on their smell. Old library. A much more intricate scent than newness, which included the indefinable odour of having been read. These days, being herself an integral part of the library, a hint of Marie mingled with leather and rag, wood, dust and time. She hoped too that the aroma of books had merged permanently with her own personal smell so that she carried it with her everywhere. She never opened the windows of the library, fearing that its perfume would escape, or that the scent of bright spring or autumn, icy winter or torrid summer would enter and be incorporated into the library air, detracting from the precious aroma of stale bookishness. The library had become a living, developing entity to Marie. It had a creatureness into which she hoped to become inextricably merged. It breathed and brooded, waited, and once when she was younger, had expressed itself to her directly. One stiflingly hot, dry day, as she crouched on the floor behind the table leafing through a hefty book of maps, a sudden commotion on the other side of the room made her jump up in fright. There was a loud snap like a whip being cracked and then the thud of an object landing heavily. When she got the courage to go across the room and investigate, she saw an octavo, vellum-bound edition of Plutarch's *Lives* in French lying open, face down, on the wooden floorboards, several feet away from where it had been shelved. Unless there were ghostly others in the room (an idea she considered and set aside to think about later), it had leapt out and away from its place on the shelf of its own accord. Had it made a bid for freedom? Had it wanted to be read? Had the book jumped from its shelf, a wilful book that desired to make itself known to her? An army of ghostly others could not have excited her imagination more. She let the ghosts out of her mind to go their way, and picked up the book. Acceding to its wishes, she took it back with her to her place on the floor behind the table, mar-velling at the life it contained, even before she discovered the life of the words she read between the yellow vellum binding.

Marie opened one of her new books and looked at the title page:

ESSAIS

DE MESSIRE

MICHEL, SEIGNEVR
DE MONTAIGNE,
CHEVALIER DE L'ORDRE
du Roy, & Gentil-homme ordinaire de sa Chambre,
Maire & Gouuerneur
de Bourdeaus.

*

EDITION SECONDE,
reueuë et augmentée.

A BOVRDEAVS.

Par S. Millanges Imprimeur ordinaire du Roy.

M. D. LXXXII.

Auec Priuilege du Roy.

No one saw Marie for the rest of the day. Eventually her mother forgot she wanted her, or at least had been determined to have her practise the art of being a woman. There was always an element of relief, in spite of the overt annoyance, when Marie took herself off. The sullenness was very wearing; the raging arguments were worse. When Marie finally appeared in the doorway of the family drawing room it was already well into the evening, long after supper, and her name had been echoing around the corridors and staircases for a good half-hour to tell her to join her mother and sister before they retired for the night. The cries of the servants searching for Marie had reignited Jeanne's fury, and she was in the middle of a tirade about her oldest daughter refusing to take the slightest responsibility for the household, caring nothing for her sisters, her brothers, her mother – they could starve for all she cared, for all the effort she put into helping about the place, or learning anything useful, or interest she took in the dwindling finances, or the career and marriage prospects of her siblings, let alone her own. She was in full flight, voicing even ancient resentments.

'And where was she when the peasants rioted and tore down our trees after they'd been forbidden to graze their filthy beasts on our land? Do you remember how they filled in the moat and threatened us with their sticks and axes? No, you were probably too young. We were trembling in fear of our lives, and where was she? In the library, her nose in a book, as if all the trouble in the world had nothing to do with her. A little madam who thinks reading will fill her belly and wrap her in warm clothes and stop the peasants from murdering her.'

'But, Maman, that was years ago,' said Léonore, who saw it as part of her training for a holy life to make peace between the irreconcilable. 'She was very young.'

'Yes, it was years ago, and I stood there with my young children, even younger than her, quivering behind my skirts, you and Augustine just babes in arms, and I had to confront the villains. I had to pacify those murderous animals. I had to make terms with them as if they were our equals. I had to let them off their fines and give them grazing rights to stop us being murdered in our beds. With no husband, no man to deal with them. Who was there to support me?'

'You dealt with it in a truly Christian way, Maman. You were wonderful. But Marie was a child, too, like the rest of us.'

'She was never like the rest of you. *She stayed in the library.* She wasn't frightened like the rest of you, clutching at me for safety. She refused to look up from her book. If I'd been screaming, flayed alive, assaulted and murdered, all of us stripped and gutted, that unnatural child would still have sat in her wretched book room and turned pages. And she isn't a child any longer. Where is she? She's still in the library. If she can't marry, at least she should be able to look after me in my old age. Can she cook, can she sew, can she instruct the servants, does she know what remedies are needed when I get sick? When you take the veil, what comfort will I have in life?'

'She just isn't like others. And she's very sensitive. I'm sure she will help more when I'm gone, but you will have God, Maman, always, whenever you are in need . . .'

Jeanne's hiss of fury at her youngest daughter's unhelpful piety was abruptly halted by a shriek from Léonore that made her mother swivel round in the direction of her stare. Marie was there, leaning heavily against the frame of the open doorway, clutching it with white knuckles, as if having her body held up by the structure of the house would not be enough for very long to keep her from falling to the ground. Her face was white as plaster and gleaming with sweat, her short curls stuck damply to her forehead, and her alarming eyes were wide and fixed, apparently seeing something no person had ever witnessed before. Her breath came so fast and heavy that she appeared to be rather drowning than inhaling and exhaling. Léonore's face became a mirror of her sister's amazement. Evidently, her oldest sister was having a vision, the sort of vision that a devoted girl like Léonore might eventually expect to receive after decades of prayer and self-sacrifice. Léonore fell to her knees, as Marie would have, had the doorway not been holding her up.

'Marie,' Léonore cried, pressing her hands together and raising her arms in praise towards her sister. 'The Lord has called you, after all.'

Generous Léonore's eyes filled with tears of happiness. Jeanne having had a paralysed moment of intense staring at the sight of Marie was shaken out of her astonishment by her younger daughter's words, and turned around to see her on her knees, her head dropped and muttering in grateful prayer.

'Get up, you stupid girl,' she shouted, running to Marie and prising her away from the supporting door frame. She half carried her daughter to the couch and let her collapse on to it full length. 'Léonore, *get up this minute* and go to the scullery. Tell Louise to bring some tincture of hellebore in hot water. Immediately. Hurry up!'

'But Maman, you don't understand,' Léonore remained on her knees. 'You mustn't interfere in a vision. The good Lord has singled out our Marie for something special. I'm sure of it. Sister Frances told me it often happens that the least religiously inclined are suddenly called on . . .'

'For heaven's sake, Léonore,' Jeanne barked, flapping air into Marie's face with her hand. 'Stop talking nonsense and do as I tell you. Now! Your sister is having a seizure. Either that or she has become mad. Go, girl!'

Marie in the meantime tossed her head distractedly from side to side on the couch and was gasping out incoherent sounds that might have become words if she'd had the control to articulate them, until, moments after Léonore finally got up and ran out of the room to get Louise, she fell into a dead faint, one arm flopping to the floor, her face bright pink, her bodice drenched with sweat. Jeanne loosened Marie's clothes and flapped harder. It was quite clear to Jeanne that those wretched, godless books had finally worked their evil on Marie, and that her solitary life in the library with nothing but words as companions had driven her to melancholy madness. If only she had ignored the tantrums and been more forceful, insisting on her daughter taking regular walks and leading the proper, ordinary, healthy life of a young woman. Now she had an invalid as well as an unmarriageable daughter. She considered for a moment whether she would rather Marie was having a seizure or had gone mad. She hoped the former, but feared the latter.

Marie came round a little as the foul-smelling, steaming cup of soporific was held to her mouth and Jeanne dabbed the pale liquid on to her lips.

'Drink this. It will help you.'

Louise and Léonore stood behind Jeanne with worried expressions. Marie pushed the cup away and struggled to sit up a little.

'I'm not ill, Maman,' she whispered, still breathing fast, her face changed from dead white and vivid pink to the yellowish pale of parchment. 'It's Monsieur de Montaigne. He has ravished me.'

There was a gasp from the three other women, each of whom instantly reassessed their usual picture of Marie in the library.

'His books . . . the ones Uncle Louis gave me . . . they are . . . extraordinary . . . I've never imagined . . . they are . . . remarkable. No, remarkable is too small a word. Nothing, nothing, in all my life I've read nothing like these *essays*.'

Three images of nothing much happening in the library but Marie reading books returned to their owners' imaginations, and they breathed more easily. But Marie was panting harder, overcome once more.

'Be calm, be calm,' Jeanne said, gently pushing her back down on to the couch. 'Are you talking about a book you have read? What is an *essay*? How can a *book* have caused this commotion, this distress?'

'Maman, this is completely new. No one has *ever* done such a thing before. Monsieur de Montaigne has invented a new way to write. He writes about himself as if he were describing the world, and the world as if he were describing himself. He calls them *essays*. Attempts, efforts, trials, oh, I don't know. But they aren't attempts, they are complete, a complete new method of writing. A new way of thinking. It's . . . overwhelming. Dazzling. Everything is changed. Everything is possible. Everything has become so clear. It is as if I had written them myself and yet in a million lifetimes I could never have imagined them. Both. Completely strange and like the inside of my own mind . . . my soul . . .'

The words came out in a mad babble. Occasionally, Marie drew in a great breath in order to run on with the words that were backing up, insistent on being said so that new ones, better ones could come along after. She looked wildly at her mother and up at Léonore and Louise, imploring them to comprehend the importance of her discovery, though had she been in her right mind she would not have spoken of such things to them. Relieved as they were that Monsieur de Montaigne's ravishing of Marie had only occurred through the pages of his books, the women grew increasingly convinced – and in Léonore's case disappointed, too – that Marie had indeed taken leave of her senses. If a *book* had caused this distracted passion in Marie, whose usual response to the world impinging on her was a furious tantrum, or sullen resentment, then only madness could account for it. Books did not *do* things unless a person had dropped the real thread of life and plummeted into some unimaginable dark chasm. It was already clear that by nature Marie was of a predominantly melancholy humour, otherwise she would not have spent so much time alone, refused to join in with regular life, and have read so much. But now the melancholic humour had overrun her entirely and tipped her into madness, as it eventually must if great care is not taken to keep it in check. All imbalances of the humours were to be avoided, but melancholy was by far the most dangerous.

Jeanne pushed the glass of hellebore forward and insisted that Marie drink it.

'No, no, it will make me sleepy. I need to be awake, completely alert. I must read the *Essays* again. I've barely begun to grasp their meaning. Oh, Maman, that such a being walks among us. That he is actually alive, in a real place that can be reached in a matter of weeks. That he exists and breathes now, and is perhaps at this very moment writing. Now I know what it was to be living in the time of Aristotle, of Plato, of Christ.'

This brought horrified exclamations from the three women, and a firm slap with an open hand on the face from her mother.

'Marie le Jars de Gournay, don't you dare talk like that, not even if you're mad,' her mother said.

If the hellebore did not calm Marie's extreme excitement, it at least enabled her to control it somewhat, and consider the folly of speaking as she had spoken to her mother about Monsieur de Montaigne's work. Her admiration, so much more than mere admiration, had caused a passion in her that she should not have revealed to others. It was impossible that her mother or sister could understand what had happened to her over the past day as she consumed the *Essays*. For them it was just another book, and her enthusiasm just another sign of her unbalanced nature. Well, she *was* unbalanced. That is exactly what the

Essays had done to her. She had read so many books by now, some of which she considered miraculous achievements by mere human beings, but her reading of these experiments by Montaigne took her far beyond admiration. With each word she read, with each essay she finished, she drew closer to its creator, until eventually she felt that she had actually entered that most extraordinary mind, that it had invited her in, because she alone was capable of fully understanding the enormity of what he had done, and had allowed her to experience what it must be like to be possessed of such a soul. Of course, she had read other books by men who were still living, but none of them, not one, not one sentence of one of them had offered such a channel into the very being of the man who wrote. Such intimacy – some of which, Uncle Louis was right, she could hardly bring herself to approve of, yet it made no difference. The intimacy of his confessions, no, not confessions, simply his unapologetic descriptions of himself, his thoughts, his person, his foundering, his conviction, came to her as if he were whispering directly into her ear about what it was like to be a human being. What it was like to be her. She recognised herself in his descriptions, wonderfully transformed into something to think about as well as vaguely and wordlessly *to feel*. He was describing her as if he had known her all her life, and she, as she read him, felt as familiar with this man from the far south of France as she did with her own mother. Oh, much, much more. She knew no one as she knew Monsieur de Montaigne, the complete stranger and intimate friend. And the knowledge of him had become part of her – physically. His thoughts flew straight to her viscera, to fill her body with a thrill she had never experienced, until she shook and trembled with the new ways of knowing her feelings. Eventually, her whole being had erupted, mind and body, with the words of this great thinker, as if they were dancing inside her, filling her and bursting to get out into the world through her.

She had to keep this knowledge from her mother who would surely march her straight to the convent if she understood even a fraction of what Marie felt, or she would think her mad, as just now, with much the same result. In any case, her feelings, her understanding of Montaigne was private. Her extreme excitement had caused the error of revealing her state of mind. Now she must force herself to become outwardly calm. Ask her mother for forgiveness. Say that perhaps she was coming down with a fever.

Michel Yquem, Seigneur de Montaigne, and the Demoiselle Marie le Jars de Gournay had to have a private relationship, one that no one else could participate in. To talk about it would be to betray it. She had made an understandable but serious mistake by exposing her profound and passionate response to the *Essays*. She would read and re-read the work of the man she already knew as if he were herself, until no corner of his life and thought and being was unfamiliar to her. Then she would meet him. No one must know this was her plan. Somehow she would meet him, even if she had to walk all the way to Bordeaux to do so, and she couldn't doubt that he would immediately recognise her capacity for knowing how he was to be read; how much, how well, how perfectly and uniquely she understood his work. He could not possibly have imagined such a reader. She was young and not properly educated, but that did not matter. Her understanding of the *Essays* was like an arrow; it flew directly to the heart of the work. At last, her father's library had fulfilled its promise. It had made her ready for this moment. She had learned to love books. Books had become her life. Now she had found the *Essays* and their author. What everything had been leading up to. There was no doubt in her heart and her intellect that she had discovered her destiny.

For a while, the household at Gournay suspected that Marie had permanently lost her mind. Once she had recovered from her fainting fit and the ensuing bedrest, she quite forgot that she had decided the wisest course was to keep secret her real feelings on the sublime work of Michel de Montaigne. She could not help herself. No more than the Christian martyrs could help spreading the Word of the Lord. She was a convert, an evangelist, and in her determination to enlighten the world about the incomparable thoughts and wisdom of the *Essays* she spared nobody who crossed her path. She still spent much of her time in the library – for which people, even the book-averse Jeanne, learned to be grateful – but when she was about the house or walking the grounds, she always had one of the volumes in a pocket or open in her hand, and if she noticed anyone in her vicinity, she would insist on stopping them to read out marked passages and then command them to wait while she found something she had read yesterday that was even more remarkable, quite astonishing, beyond all human thought.

'. . . just listen, listen to this . . .'

The gardeners leaned on their implements, their faces stiff with patience while she quoted Latin poetry to them and Monsieur de Montaigne's comments on it:

'No one dies before his time. The time you leave behind was no more yours

than that which passed before your birth, and it concerns you no more.
"Look back and see how past eternities of time are nothing to us."'

'What do you think of that?'

It was not enough that they had to listen, she demanded a response.

'Yes, very good, Mademoiselle. He's a one. Quite a fellow.'

Cornered in the kitchen, Louise continued to stir the soup, nodding to indicate her attention to the argument being made:

'We should have wife, children, goods, and above all, health, if we can; but we must not bind ourselves to them so strongly that our happiness depends on them. We must reserve a back shop all our own, entirely free, in which to establish our real liberty and our principal retreat and solitude.'

'It's something to think about, Mademoiselle Marie. If only I had the learning, I'd be reading him every day.'

At which, Marie would offer, excitedly, to teach Louise to read there and then.

'It's very good of you, Mademoiselle, but I've to see to the soup and then bake some bread ... No, Mademoiselle, on Sunday I go home and do the washing for my father. Yes, next month, perhaps, if I've got a moment.'

Léonore and Jeanne were less polite when confronted by the words of the master:

'... men's opinions are accepted in the train of ancient beliefs, by authority and on credit, as if they were religion and law. They accept

*as by rote what is commonly held about it. They accept this truth, with
all its structure and apparatus of arguments and proofs, as a firm and
solid body, no longer shakeable, no longer to be judged. On the contrary everyone competes in plastering up and confirming this accepted
belief, with all the power of their reason, which is a supple tool, pli-
able, and adaptable to any form. Thus the world is filled and soaked
with twaddle and lies.'*

'For pity's sake, be quiet about that wretched book,' her
mother would snap. 'If I hear another word about Monsieur de
Montaigne I'll take his *essays* or whatever you call them and feed
them to the pigs. If you want to dedicate your life to someone,
why not dedicate it to Christ? They eagerly await you at the convent.'

And Léonore, who truly and enthusiastically looked forward
to the time when she would be old enough to enter the convent,
put her carefully nurtured immortal soul at some risk and actually silenced her sister with an unheard-of show of temper:

*'Wonderful brilliance may be gained for human judgement by getting
to know men. We are all huddled and concentrated in ourselves, and
our vision is reduced to the length of our nose. Socrates was asked
where he was from. He replied not "Athens", but "The world".'*

'Shut up! Shut up about that wretched man and his stupid
book! I don't care what he thinks or how original he is. He isn't
Christ and if he was you'd make me stop believing in Him!'

But nothing, not even the sound of Léonore blaspheming,
dampened Marie's devotion to the *Essays* of Montaigne or made

60

the look in her eyes when she spoke of him less fevered. Nobody paid attention to what Marie read out, but they worried a good deal, as she continued to do so, that her mind was not right. Jeanne had Louise drop a little tincture of hellebore into Marie's night-time cup of hot milk, but even after weeks of being dosed there was no obvious lessening of her obsession with the book and the man who wrote it. He was her passion.

There had been times in the past during her youthful battles with her mother when Marie wondered why she shouldn't simply give in and live the life expected of her; why not be married, a nun, or anything at all for the time she was on earth? For a moment, every now and then, it flashed through her mind, unbidden and unwelcome, that an individual life was no more than a puff of air in eternity: that her individual life was no more significant than any other, and that none were significant in the sweep of time from the distant past to the far-off future, in the march of birth and death and generation after generation. It was only because it was *she* who inhabited her life, who lived and looked out from behind her eyes, that it seemed so particular and urgent to her; as it must, it crossed her mind, for everyone. But it was a false, a minutely partial view. This came with stark clarity to her only very occasionally, for no more than a passing instant, like a shudder, not from any act of thought, but as if a mist had cleared and made evident the truth, the obvious reality that was there all along. With that initial realisation, her thoughts would of their own accord slide from considerations of her own insignificance to Christ himself, who in that terrifying, brash light looked like no more than another individual life that had flickered and died, leaving nothing but a memory, to be nurtured and spread with who knew what accuracy by bystanders who had had such hopes for being in the midst of something more than the great, impersonal sweep of time. Was even that life just another example of humanity clinging to an illusion, a pathetic hope of immortality and substance beyond their allotted time? Perhaps none of it mattered? Indeed, how could it when you came to think of it in that . . . Then almost immediately, before she could become fully convinced of the implication of the thoughts she was having, the mist began to return, and the bald insight started to fade. They passed, those rare, shocked moments and left nothing behind them, not even the memory of themselves. Like wounds, the unasked-for thoughts healed over and whatever scarring occurred remained hidden beneath the surface. In this, at least, she was no different from the rest of the world.

But now that Marie had found her home, the centre point of her soul, the reason for her purposeful rejection of what was expected of her, she never again wondered, even without knowing it, whether it mattered what she was in the world. She would not marry a suitable husband, would not be a nun, but would devote her life wholly to books and literature. She would translate great works, write poetry, and attempt the new form of the essay. Perhaps Monsieur de Montaigne might read her work. She *would* meet him somehow. Perhaps one day she would be published. Nothing would distract her from such a life, not now that she had an overwhelming focus for the direction of her thoughts and her very existence. She must meet Michel de Montaigne and tell him how perfectly she understood his work, how in spite of their differences in age and gender she was nonetheless his ideal reader. At least she must correspond with him. She read and re-read the

Essays, and the conviction grew that there was a vital, an extraordinary connection between their author and herself. Though what he had written was like nothing else she had ever read, or imagined might be written, her immediate understanding of it was, she knew, as remarkable as the work itself. If that was not modest, it was true. It made her special. A soul did not have an age or a gender, and it was as a soul that she understood the soul of Michel de Montaigne and his works.

When she pored over Montaigne's words, they came to be also hers: it seemed to her that she actually *invented* them as her eyes took them in. Her mind appropriated them, absorbing their meaning – making their meaning her own, understanding them as she did, so uncannily. It was as if she rewrote them verbatim as she read, so that she, the words, their meaning and their original author existed all together as one, taking up exactly the same space inside her head. He had marked them down on paper, but they were exactly the words, describing exactly the thoughts which she would have thought and written herself. The *Essays* were the ghost of her future as a writer. But she did not for one moment resent the fact that Montaigne had written them first. Not that she could think of herself as possessing more than a minute fragment of his talent, originality and quality, but his words came to her as if they had been conceived in her own mind. And, to put it bluntly, could she be so remote from his talent if she understood them so well? The *Essays* possessed her, but she also possessed them, absorbed them, and after the first time she read them they belonged to her heart and mind and became a joint work by Michel Yquem, Seigneur de Montaigne, and La Demoiselle Marie de Gournay.

When in the past she had thought of being a writer, she could not exactly imagine what she would write. She read Aristotle and thought she might write philosophy. She read Ronsard and thought she might be a poet. She read Uncle Louis and wondered if she might not be a dramatist. But when she read Montaigne, she knew she had found the crucible in which her own work would be developed, and that whatever form she might write in, its source would always be the *Essays*, and Montaigne always her master.

His style was startling, however, for a self-educated girl who had tutored herself by reading classical authors. Certainly it was learned and elegant for the most part, yet in places it was bluff, regional, and coarse enough to make her painfully embarrassed. Her mother would indeed have thrown parts of it to the pigs. The truth was that so would Marie, had she not read what those strange lapses were embedded in. Some of it was vile, and Marie squirmed to see it on the page; some of it was actually incomprehensible to a well-brought-up young woman, though it was clear enough to what bodily and private processes it referred. But nothing the author of the *Essays* wrote could loosen the bonds that tied the two of them together heart to heart, soul to soul, for all that she was just an ignorant girl and he was a nobleman, a former Mayor of Bordeaux, and a genius, and everyone thought her mad for repeatedly saying so. Shocking though the language of the essays might be, it became hers, and acceptable because it was of him. The living being of Michel de Montaigne behind the words was as compelling and persistent to Marie as the calling of a dove.

The news came with Uncle Louis from Paris, who, three years later, arrived in mid-February late one evening at snowlit Gournay-sur-Aronde in order, after a recuperating visit, to escort his sister-in-law and his nieces to Paris, where Jeanne hoped without too great an expectation to present Marie at Court and find a man with suitable status and some fortune to make her his wife. And the expedition would also, she hoped, take her now twenty-two-year-old daughter's mind off the wretched book of essays that she had never been without and whose praises she had not stopped singing in all this time. Really, she was prepared to find a husband with a very modest fortune and of no more than acceptable status, if it meant getting her impossible, and frankly unstable daughter set up in life. Marie was delighted to be going to her beloved Paris, but had no intention of co-operating more than minimally in the search for a husband.

Uncle Louis clapped the snow and frost off his cloak in the doorway after his frozen twelve-hour journey, begged for a warming pan and a hot toddy to be taken to his room, and disappeared wheezing and coughing up the stairs to bed. Marie did not see him until long after breakfast the next morning. She sat in a most unladylike fashion with her legs stuck out in front of her, bony ankles poking out from under her dress, on the rug beside his chair in front of the great fire, where he reclined swathed in shawls and woollen bonnet, recovering slowly from his arduous winter journey.

'The icicles grew as fast as I could break them off the window and the carriage found every single pothole from Paris to Gournay. Then the wheel had to be repaired, so I sat shivering on my box in the snow for an hour while the coachmen huffed and puffed at it. My bones have been shaken and rattled like dice in a cup. Oh, my dear, my poor, poor back.'

Marie attempted a sympathetic smile. He would have a week or two to get better before they returned to the city, but Marie would have been happy to leave the following day.

'Will you take me to meet some of the literary people you know in Paris and to a printer's shop where I can order a book of poetry? I've got quite a lot of money saved up.'

'Yes, we can manage that, I think. No shortage of printers in Paris. We might drop into a salon or two and introduce you to some of the writers. It's a shame Ronsard is no longer with us, but perhaps you wouldn't mind meeting Monsieur de Spond, or Monsieur de Papillion?'

He was fond of awkward, ungainly Marie, and couldn't help but warm to the way she looked up to him as the oracle of all things literary. He liked his niece's curious taste for serious and classical literature, odd creature that she was. It was unexpected in a girl, and truly impressive that she had managed to teach herself Latin. She had sent him some of her translations of Virgil and they were very good indeed. Even her Greek, in which he had given her some tuition when he was in Gournay and her mother was not around, was not at all bad. But what use was that to such a plain, nervy little thing and quite impecunious with it? The girl had a poor carriage, rounded shoulders and an indelicate stride. Her worried, pinched face and solemn mind was far too serious

66

for an unmarried young woman with a meagre dowry to offer. He admired Jeanne's determination, but wondered how she would manage to find this daughter a husband. Perhaps it would be no bad thing if she remained single and took care of her mother as she grew older. Jeanne said she was hopeless at household management, but she would learn when she had to, and if she was happy reading in the library, so much the better for ensuring she wouldn't become skittish about her responsibilities. A confirmed spinster could keep Gournay in order and manage it for her brother. And she wouldn't be a great charge on the estate; a book every now and again was cheaper than fine clothes and fancy coaches.

'Tell me what's been happening in Paris, Uncle. Who has published a new volume of poetry? Are you going to have another play performed?'

'Your mother tells me that you've been quite unwell. Rather . . . preoccupied.'

'Oh, Mother wishes I would stop talking about Monsieur Montaigne's essays. She thinks that one should just read a masterpiece and then shut up and think about darning one's stockings. But, Uncle, I read and re-read them, and every time they are new. So bright and fresh and full of great wisdom. Is there any word about him? Have you heard if there are new essays coming?'

'Monsieur Montaigne? Oh yes, something very unfortunate.'

'What? What's unfortunate?'

'Montaigne. The fellow who wrote the essays. I gave you his books, didn't I? They're quite the thing now that Lipsius has come out in favour of them. The French Thales, he called

Montaigne, though he's known to go rather head over heels with his enthusiasms.'

'Justus Lipsius is very wise. I haven't stopped reading the essays since you gave them to me. Nothing like them has ever been written,' Marie spoke severely, correcting Louis's light-hearted attitude. Then she remembered. 'But what's unfortunate, Uncle?'

Louis took a moment to overcome his surprise at being told off for levity by his country niece, before he recollected what he'd been saying.

'Oh, Montaigne, yes. Dead, they say. Just the other day. Killed by robbers, I understand.'

Marie did not take in the meaning of the words, but the sound of them caused the room to swing around as if it hung from a rope. She put her hand down on the floor, to steady herself, while her uncle recalled more of the rumour.

'He was on his way to Paris. Some secret mission, apparently. Carrying messages from Henri Navarre to the King. Some sort of rapprochement. So I heard. But he didn't arrive when he was expected. That was two weeks ago or more. There's talk of brigands. Anyway, they say he was killed.'

A sudden awful noise sawed at the nerves in Louis's temple. A screech, like some creature in the undergrowth caught in the biting jaws of a predator. He pressed his fingers to the sides of his head, and looked for the source to silence it. Marie had buckled down on herself, a huddle, her arms cradling or protecting her head as she rocked from side to side on the floor, the awful cry rising from the concealed centre of her bent-over body.

'Good God, what's happened? Have you been taken ill? I'll get your mother.'

68

Louis threw off his shawls and ran for the door, then ran back and hovered for a moment over the keening form of his niece, not sure if he should leave her, nor what to do if he stayed, then fled the room in search of Jeanne or someone who could help him. He was no good at all with sudden illness of such an alarming sort. When he found his sister-in-law ('Come quick, come quick. Some frightfulness has happened . . . The girl is having a fit . . .') he lagged behind her as she sped to the drawing room, calling at the top of her voice for Louise to come with preparations. She arrived to find Marie collapsed now on to her side and heaving with monstrous sobs, groaning and gasping great sighs of anguish.

'What is it, child?'

Jeanne pulled Marie up into a sitting position and held her there, loosening her clothes, and patting her increasingly hard on the cheeks to get her attention. The girl was quite out of control.

'What have you done?' Jeanne shouted at Louis when he told her what seemed to have occasioned the collapse. 'You encouraged all this reading foolishness. You gave her that wretched book. And now you bring the news that her marvellous Montaigne is dead. God forgive me, but I wish he had never been born. You've turned the child into a useless invalid that I'm going to have to look after for the rest of my life . . . and then, when I'm gone what will happen?'

'She'll come round. I'm sure she will. Her admiration just got a little out of hand.'

Jeanne looked at her daughter howling on the floor and then up at Louis. Louis acknowledged the severity of his niece's response.

'How was I to know she would get so excited? I know lots of people who read books and like them, but they don't lose their minds. It's not normal.'

About that they were agreed.

They carried her writhing and wailing, with the help of several servants, to her room and struggled to put her to bed. She appeared to be unaware of anything or anyone except some terrible agony within. Clearly, the madness had returned in some new and dreadful form. It had been ecstasy, now it was desolation. It took a remarkably strong decoction of hellebore to get her eventually to sleep, and even then she sobbed and moaned as if trying to escape the herbal oblivion back to the searing and longed-for reality of her pain.

· The journey to Paris was postponed. Louis waited impatiently at Gournay, missing the excitements of the city and anxious to get back, but he felt obliged to stay with his sister-in-law while Marie continued to behave so alarmingly. Madeleine was married and away, only the servants, Marthe and Léonore were in the house to help Jeanne. Marthe took very little interest in her older sister, well or ill, and Léonore was not much help apart from insisting on kneeling at Marie's bedside in prayer and explaining in the intervals to her sister that she must give herself over entirely to God's mercy and then all would be well. Jeanne began to worry that her youngest daughter's health would be broken by her intense prayer and evangelical campaign. Louis felt he had no choice but to remain at Gournay during the crisis in order to provide an element of calm in this house of hysterical women.

But the crisis did not pass. Jeanne and Louis began to worry that it was not a crisis after all, but that the girl's mind was permanently lost. When she was not dosed into a struggling delirium, she lay in her bed weeping tears she couldn't possibly any longer have after so many had already fallen, or stared intently at the ceiling at nothing that anyone could see, occasionally convulsed by sighs that came from a depth no human being could possess. She ate only what was spooned into her mouth and never spoke or paid the slightest attention to people talking to her or entering or leaving the room. Indeed, it seemed as if she had no notion that anyone else existed.

After a few weeks Marie had still not altogether come round, but she had returned from the other world she'd inhabited entirely alone and out of reach. Now she was dull and passive. There was a boneless sort of acquiescence about her, as if you could put her in any position and she would adopt it until you rearranged her limbs. She did whatever practical activity she was told to do. She accompanied her uncle on walks, her sister to the convent to be prayed over by the nuns, her mother to the kitchen while Jeanne maintained a one-sided conversation with her about household matters. Louise chattered to her about life in the village when she put out her clothes and brushed her hair in the morning, though she never got any reply. Marthe continued to ignore her. No one mentioned books or literature of any kind. When directly addressed with a question, Marie answered in an unengaged monotone with as few words as it was possible to convey the answer without being impolite.

'I am not cold, thank you.'

'No more soup, thank you.'

'Yes, I would like to sleep, please.'

It even began to worry Jeanne that she did not once in those weeks spend any time in the library, or even approach it. Her hands and the pocket of her pinafore no longer carried one or other volume of the *Essays* with her wherever she went. What she might once have greeted with relief only signalled the desperate condition of her daughter whose infuriating wilfulness had now been replaced by its complete opposite. It was entirely possible that she might even agree to a marriage in her present condition, but who in the world would be found to marry her as she was now? Jeanne conceded that whatever mood she was in she had an unmarriageable daughter.

It was decided to send her to the convent and Jeanne went to see the Mother Superior to make arrangements. But Sister Julian shook her head.

'We can't accept her as a novice in her condition, Madame. She must be able to devote herself to the Lord and be a full member of the community. From what we have seen, when her sister brings her to see us, she is practically incapable of looking after herself. When she's better, we'll welcome her with open arms. Perhaps she needs taking out of herself. Travel, they say, is very good for an excess of melancholy.'

Not even Christ, it seemed, would marry her. It was decided to go to Paris after all. It would at least be a change for those who were looking after Marie, and Louis suggested that she might see a physician who was very well thought of in his circle. In any case, spring was about to arrive and the world was bright with sudden leaves preparing to unfurl in the brisk air. A ride through the countryside where everything was renewing itself might shake her out of her miserable condition.

'Shake is right,' Louis said, remembering his ghastly frozen coach journey to Gournay from Paris in January. 'The city will perk her up. Nothing like Paris for lightening the spirit.'

Louis's spirit felt lighter already at the thought of going home, back to civilisation.

Paris might have been Gournay-sur-Aronde for all that Marie cared. She remained in the small apartment her mother had retained when they left the city, and would have spent all day with her hands folded in her lap if Jeanne and Léonore had not bullied and cajoled her into going out every morning for a walk. Louis insisted on taking her to see his physician who asked her what she was feeling while he took her pulses. She replied in an obedient voice.

'Nothing.'

'But what hopes do you have for your visit to Paris, young lady?'

'None. There is no longer any hope. I have been abandoned. My soul is dead.'

The physician turned to Louis and raised his eyes.

'Hellebore, I think . . .'

Louis shook his head.

'She's dosed daily.'

'Then senna. It scours the blood, lightens the spirits, shakes off sorrow – a most profitable medicine. Taken in a little wine. And perhaps, as an upward purge, laurel. Fifteen berries in a drink makes an effective potion. It's a common enough remedy but I find it does the trick. Humour is required too. Amuse the girl, get her laughing. *To humour the humour*, you see?'

He chuckled at the English joke he had made a good many times before, but which never failed to tickle him. It failed to tickle Louis, however, who sat beside his impassive niece.

'Monsieur, if we could make the girl laugh we would hardly be here.'

Marie was purged upwards and downwards for several days, which prevented her from taking even the brief morning walks she had been managing. The laughter did not come. At night the apartment echoed with the sound of Marie's weeping while her family snored its way towards morning.

And then one afternoon the world came back, the light returned and life became possible once again.

Louis rushed into the drawing room, hardly acknowledging Jeanne, Marthe and Léonore in his eagerness to get the news to Marie.

'My dear, he's alive. He's alive and in Paris. Your Montaigne. There now, does that make you feel better? He was attacked on his way to Paris. They took his money, his clothes, everything, and then were taking him deep into the woods to kill him – so they say – when the chief of the robbers stopped them. Monsieur Montaigne so impressed him by his calm demeanour and his ability to discuss his dreadful situation with the men who were taking him to his death that he was released and all his goods returned to him. Remarkable, eh? So they say. And that was why he was delayed. Not dead at all. In fact, he arrived in Paris yesterday.'

Marie watched her uncle's face with great care. She was disinclined to believe this fairy story. This everything-turning-out-all-right ending to the most terrible news of her life. Not even her father's death had caused such black emptiness to fill her being. Indeed, her father had left her a library in which to live, and in truth, she felt it was a bargain well made. Montaigne had left two volumes of his essays, but it would not do. The *Essays* pointed to the man, to the soul behind the words, and Marie's soul required contact. If he was dead, if the soul was no more in the world, then her soul was lost, too. It withered, atrophied at the certain prospect of a blank future. She would not allow Uncle Louis to warm the ashes without making quite certain that he wasn't dosing her with another kind of hellebore. But he was not so good at dissimulating. His relief, on her behalf, was real, she saw. What was dead had returned to life. Montaigne was alive. He was in Paris. She was in Paris. Marie's soul gathered itself together and began to flame with a future in which there was another like herself to share their being in the world.

She ran to her room and began immediately to write the letter to Montaigne that she had composed in her mind hourly since first reading the *Essays*, and which had continued, cruelly, to recite itself in her ear ever since his death had been announced.

The worst, when it makes itself personally known to you, can be supported, Montaigne had discovered long before he lay on his deathbed in September 1592. Pain, of course. Death, when you are certain, even if mistaken, that it has arrived. And death when, like now, certainty is unnecessary, and not just his own soul's understanding, but the hushed voices, the strained, fearful yet impatient faces, the intonations of the priest, all announce that death has already wrapped its shroud around his physical being. It turns out, like the pain of the stone, that too can be borne. Indeed, the arrival of the worst after so much time spent imagining and awaiting it, is a relief. Nothing in the world is worse than the anticipation of the worst, not even the worst itself. He would, naturally, prefer that neither pain nor death were inevitable, but there is much about life that he would prefer to be other than it is. It is not events, however dreadful, but imaginings which are the monsters that destroy our composure. Reality when it arrives in all its blank horror is simply to be faced and acceded to.

What *is* intolerable, even in the teeth of death, is the recollection of foolishness. Youthful foolishness, an old man forgives himself. Call it wildness. And the wisdom or softness of age allows a little wistfulness for the drive and energy of one's youth. His body, he had always permitted to have its way, up to a point. It cannot help itself, and once it was old it could not help itself in a far less enjoyable way. He gave it licence to enjoy what and when it could, while it still could. But the mind is another thing. When the mind is foolish after so long in the world, when it plays tricks on itself, lies to itself, forgets itself, then there is shame in recollecting.

It's strange how only his foolish old man's delusion comes back to taunt and shame him at the most important moment of his life. This time of reckoning, he had always imagined, would be a balance sheet to calculate what must in most lives be roughly equal columns of virtue and misdemeanour. Veering always, he'd supposed, towards misdemeanour, but in very few cases, surely, grossly disproportionately so. But now he finds not the proportions changed, but that his recollection of what in anyone else he would smile at and understand troubles him greatly. Just a small thing, a few months, intermittent at that, in a long and busy life.

Of course, he can see how it came about, the why, but that he should have been so unalert then, that, with all his experience, he had behaved like just another foolish, deluded old man. But why not? What else should he have been? What miracles unseen in the world of ordinary men did he expect of himself? Yet in the midst of pain and death, for all the world as if he had nothing else to engage him (the future of his family and the estate, the saving of his immortal soul, the nature of the eternity that he was soon to fall into), he lies here and cringes at a past moment of poor judgement.

The letter arrived when he was exhausted and ill in Paris. He had in front of him delicate negotiations for the life and death of France between the most powerful men in the country, none of whom really trusted him. Put yourself in the middle of warring factions as a peacemaker and the most likely result is that both sides will ally for just long enough to trample you to death. Moreover, the third volume of the *Essays* was about to be published, and they were bound to cause extreme responses. He had in those final essays given up all pretence of good rhetorical argument and immersed himself in an examination of his own self, body and soul. In that last volume he gave himself away without reservation to whomever opened the book. Perhaps deliberately, he had not thought very clearly about its publication while he was writing it. Suddenly, the idea that strangers would have him to misread at their will appalled him. He had given to anyone and everyone what, on principle, he never gave to those he knew. Perhaps not even entirely to La Boétie, to whom he thought he had unlocked himself completely. And then there was the sense that the coming book would be his last. That there would be no new volumes, only additions to what was already written. He had by 1588 finished his life's work. His mind was as worn out as his body, and he was deeply weary, but even so he sorely missed the energies and excitement of both.

The letter renewed those energies. Naïve, passionate, and amusingly pompous. Yet for all its wordy over-dramatising, the writer, a young woman, had seen exactly what his growing purpose had been in the *Essays*. He had not received before any indication in all the praise that came to him, that the novelty, the uniqueness of the project he had started to undertake had been grasped.

But he could not in his present state of dying think of any more excuses. He had received a gushing letter from a very young, adoring woman who was presently in Paris.

Young people daydream. Who can say when it stops, but it does. It was 1588, and in the four years since she first read the *Essays*, Marie had created, as the young do, highly detailed reveries concerning their author and herself. He lived in the south, more than a month's journeying away from Picardy so there was very little likelihood of their ever being in close proximity, and the chances that such an illustrious man of such an age would take an interest in a very young woman of no education in the provinces were too small to be worth consideration – these realities made it all the more vital that Marie's daydreams were convincingly and realistically elaborated. It was impossible to imagine that she would travel to Bordeaux, there was no reason for her to go there, and by the same token, Montaigne would never happen to be in Picardy. Paris was the only possibility. Fantasy, to satisfy, must be at least minimally feasible otherwise it is just aggravating. She thought about ways in which they, both happening to be in Paris, might come across each other. Her uncle, Louis, was the only likely go-between. He would hold a party to which she and her mother would be invited. At this event Louis would introduce her to Montaigne, his guest of honour, and she would see his polite lack of interest alter as she impressed him with her love and understanding of his work. (That is, her love-and-understanding of *his work*. No other possible connection between them was conceivable to her. Marie was never aware of any darker desires. 'I will have no other husband than my honour and good books,' she repeatedly told her mother, the world and herself.)

It was a good enough fantasy, until she imagined all the other people attending the soirée; the most talented, clever and glamorous people in Paris. How could she hold his attention? Could she open her mind and heart in front of others? Might a young woman from Picardy speak in such company and make herself heard, do herself justice? No, it was better to write to him of her understanding so that Montaigne would not be distracted by her youth and lack of sophistication. A letter gave her time to compose her thoughts carefully and gave Montaigne time to consider them. Her words would speak for her as his did for him. A letter would help to equalise the great gulf of age and experience between them. Words would not confuse the issue as her physical presence would. Which issue was that they were twin souls.

And then the news that he was dead.

Only he wasn't. The ashes of her reverie warmed and came back to life.

It was curiously difficult writing the letter. She had imagined it so many times in so many versions that she found it almost impossible to choose just one. Each word she inked on to the paper narrowed down a little more the infinite possibilities of what she might say. Increasingly, she believed that only one of those unwritten versions was the Right One, the one that would convince Montaigne of their extraordinary predestined connection. The fear of writing the wrong letter almost paralysed her hand. She was up all night, the words refusing to leave the inky tip of her nib. But it had to be done. She had to make the judgement and produce a real letter. Her reverie (after a slight hiccup) was coming true, detail by detail, making it even more strangely like her daydream. She forced herself to commit words to paper, only the shadow she felt of the real letter in her head that simply would not flow on to the page. The perfect letter remained bright but unfocused in her mind. Nonetheless, first thing the next morning, before she could write another thousand versions, she gave it to Louise to take to Montaigne's lodgings.

'I would count it the greatest honour of my life, the greatest honour that I should ever receive were I to live to the age of Methuselah, if you would agree to a meeting between us. I dare not hope, but I am in Paris and available whenever it might suit you . . .' she wrote. It was inadequate, expressed nothing like the admiration she felt. She spent a wakeful night hoping desperately for a note inviting her to even the briefest of meetings before she had to leave Paris. The truth was that in some part of her she did not entirely believe that her letter (not even the 'perfect' one) would be enough to persuade him of their remarkable affinity. How many letters must he get from admirers? How could she be sure that he would see by her words that she was different? She did not doubt her difference, only his capacity to perceive it from a mere letter. Without admitting it to herself, she steeled herself for a brief note thanking her for her letter and interest and regretting that he was too busy to bother with a silly girl of no consequence. Of course he would not be so rude, he was a noble gentleman, but that is how she would have understood his polite rejection of her suggestion that they meet.

Montaigne knocked at the door of Madame de Gournay's Paris apartment the next morning after he received the letter.

'Le Seigneur de Montaigne for Mademoiselle de Gournay.'

Louise knew the name well enough. No one living in Marie's household those past four years could have failed to recognise it. If the King himself had come knocking Louise would not have been more struck with wonder and awe. He had come to her, without warning, quite impetuously, the very next day. Either her mistress was quite wrong about this fellow's greatness, or standing there on the step he was paying her a remarkable compliment and Louise, along with the rest of the household, had quite underestimated Mademoiselle Marie. What could there be about the young woman who had caused Louise constantly to raise her eyebrows and sigh with impatience, who she had helped to dose into reasonableness, that warranted a visit from such a man?

She barely remembered to ask him in to wait in the drawing room before picking up her skirts and running like a wild child up the stairs, two at a time.

'Mademoiselle, Mademoiselle . . .' she whispered, in what was more like a scream under the breath. Her voice was freed from constraint after she knocked and entered Marie's room.

'Mademoiselle,' she shrieked. 'He's *here*. He's *here*.'

He had come to *her*. First thing in the morning after he received her letter, he was downstairs wanting to make her acquaintance. It was the one scene she had never imagined: that he should seek her out.

She was respectably dressed for the day ahead, her hair had been braided and twisted into a bun at the back, her short curls at the front forming a framing frill around her forehead and temples. In spite of the sleepless night, Louise passed her as fit to be seen after a pinch or two of her cheeks, and Marie had only a brief twinge of wishing for a finer, more elegant dress, a face just a little more . . . before remembering that it was as an intellectual comrade and fellow spirit she was to meet the man she admired more than anyone in the world. Only the souls mattered. He had recognised that by his presence downstairs. She straightened her back against her inner trembling and walked down the stairs. Two days ago Montaigne was dead; now he was waiting for her in the drawing room.

You might think that great fear would have to be overcome by great courage, when, after wanting something so passionately, after loving the signs of someone so much for so long, you at last stand in front of the door you have only to open actually to be in their company. Yet when dreams do come true they turn out never to have been dreams, never delusions, never mere wishfulness. They are just the truth you have seen, queuing up waiting for its time. A dream when it comes true reveals itself to have been necessity all along. Opening the drawing-room door was easy.

He turned from the view through the window to face the door as she pushed it open and walked into the room. In the turmoil of a moment of destiny she saw – a much shorter man than she had imagined, a little portly around the stomach, rather skinny in the calves. His wide domed forehead continued hairless to the top of his bald skull circuited by short grizzled hair. His face narrowed from broad cheekbones, the effect increased by his somewhat sunken cheeks, framed in a full clipped beard that came to a neat point. His small mouth was almost concealed by a somewhat drooping moustache. His nose, disproportionately long and broad, was not at all classical. The eyes dominated, great damp orbs, containing warm brown pupils, the top arc of which were concealed by his heavy, folded lids. They were notably vivid eyes that had not aged at the same rate as the rest of him, set in weather-worn surrounds, and at the instant he turned their gaze towards her they shone with an intense anticipation. His clothes were fine and fashionable, so much so that Marie, provincial that she was, couldn't understand the slightly sagging stocking and draped cloak as anything other than the carelessness of a man of the mind. He was an older man, as she had expected, but perhaps a little older and tireder looking than she had imagined. The flesh around his neck and jaw concertinaed where his ruff pressured it, and on his left cheek there was a small warty lump. Loops of dark soft skin hung beneath his admittedly bright eyes. He was not exactly her pictured Montaigne who lived behind her own eyes when she read the *Essays*, and watched her approvingly as she took in his words. Nonetheless, it was in fact him, and after her first confused glance, she recognised him. He was here. He was Montaigne.

Whether or not she observed it, there was a brief moment after Montaigne's initial glance of anticipatory admiration, and before he hurriedly lowered his lidded eyes. His excellent manners rendered his thoughts invisible almost immediately. If she did catch a fleet unfocusing of the eyes, a momentary fall of the corners of his mouth, a slight sinking of his shoulders, a general loosening of the tension of high expectation, she did not allow it to make any more impression on her mind than she did her own simultaneous perception of him as physically other than she had imagined. La Demoiselle de Gournay required her thoughts to be on a much higher plane. She would not have permitted any understanding that his were any lower.

What physical signs of disappointment had manifested themselves in his demeanour, vanished in an eye-blink. In less time than it takes a heart to beat he broke into a smile and stepped forward, taking her hand.

'My dear Mademoiselle, I hope I am not inconveniencing you. Your enchanting letter made me ill-mannered with impatience to make your acquaintance.'

'I'm very . . . I'm honoured, Sir,' she gasped out, astonished that anything like appropriate words spoke themselves as his moustache brushed the back of her hand.

But now, after this initial success, whatever she had retained of her mother's teachings on social conduct abandoned her. Suddenly, seeming to have taken leave of her senses, she grasped the hand that her own rested in, locked it tightly between both her hands, pulling it towards her breast, and peered with that unnerving, direct intensity of hers into her visitor's face. Polite society may have been, as she constantly informed her mother, hypocritical with its stupidly ritual observances, but the manners she had been taught to use in public encounters also had the purpose, and not only in her case, of erecting a formal barrier that prevented physical and social ungainliness from being too evident. The rules for interacting with strangers might have made her, on first acquaintance, almost the equal of those whose natural grace and ease in the world barely needed rules. Had she curtsied, lowered her eyes, sat neatly on a distant chair with her hands in her lap, answered formality with equal and appropriate formality as laid down by convention, she at least would have ensured her visitor's comfort and seemed to him much like any other young woman. Not beautiful, not elegant, as Montaigne had not been able to prevent himself from envisaging his youthful female admirer on receipt of her letter, but at any rate not startlingly strange and awkward in her speech and movement, or slightly unhinged in the way in which her eyes alternated between avoiding all contact with his, or worse, bored into his face, unblinking, her neck jutting forward to intensify the diamond-hard, demanding stare. She turned her gaze on him now, her neck at full stretch, interrogating Montaigne's face as if it were a distant shoreline that was finally coming into view. She breathed heavily and crushed his rather small, soft hand between her surprisingly large ones, pressing it against her bosom as if she were squeezing the boiling emotions in there into submission. She was alarming. A force quite as fearful as the sight of the robbers in the forest of Villebois bearing down on him. Very remote, it is certain, from the attractive, personable and highly intelligent young woman that Montaigne had thought he was going to meet.

Not that what she had to say was not intelligent, highly intelligent, both in the letter that had brought him to her, and now, as, barely stopping to breathe, she poured out her admiration and analysis of his writing, all the while punishing his hand between hers. But the passion, the stridency, forthrightness, the excessive articulation with which she poured out her thoughts alarmed and distressed him. He also found himself irritated by the faintly offensive assumption she made that never before had he had such a comprehending reader. Concealed within the overpowering expression of her admiration and gratitude towards him for his work and for coming to see her, there lay also an insistence that he recognise and be grateful to her, his perfect, his only true reader.

He had come to be charmed and praised by a bright and beautiful young woman, for a tonic to his depleted spirit. But this over-ardent, awkward girl did more than disappoint and disturb him, she caused him to recognise and regret his old man's vanity. He experienced that teetering moment when you are so close to the lost past of not having done something that you now regret, that for an instant it feels as if you can reel back the act to make it never have happened, and be free again to make the wiser decision. Yet what's done is always done; desperate wishes have to give way to that knowledge.

He gently but firmly started to withdraw his hand from her iron grasp and suggested they sit. Marie could hardly bear to let go, but she opened her clutching fingers and, instead of taking the chair several feet away as he'd intended, she dropped like a dead weight on to a footstool next to the chair on to which he had retreated. She leaned towards him, her torso stretching forward at a sharp angle, and planted her feet wide like a man. With her elbows on her thighs, her hands were free to express the airy subtleties of the words that almost failed her but at the last moment between hasty breaths gathered momentum and raced to be said.

'. . . a Socrates . . . an Epaminondas . . . and I saw at once, even in the early essays the boldness of your project. That no one has attempted such a . . . such a . . .' her fingers splayed apart describing the enormity of his accomplishment. 'In all of France, not in the world, no one since . . . Aristotle . . . such a combination of learning and understanding . . . created an entirely new form, a . . . master work . . . not even Plato, not even he had a firmer or more remarkable mind. Where today are the minds that can think and write as you do, with such clarity, such purpose—'

Montaigne interrupted, though he had almost to shout to stem the flow.

'You flatter an old man, my dear. But there are, I can assure you, at least thirty men in Paris right now with minds very much better than mine.'

'If they were truly wise they would be here, worshipping at your feet, as I am,' she exploded, forgetting in her idolatry that he had come to her. 'You can only say such things to hurt me. Why are you so cruel? Paris is a city of fools going about their foolish business while a god has come among them . . . Who could appreciate you in these paltry times? The ancients must weep not to have had you with them . . . Oh, Sir, from the moment I opened the first volume of the *Essays* I knew, just knew that I was in the presence of greatness. It was essential that we meet, such was the sympathy between our natures. We belong, twin minds, twin hearts. It was immediately clear to me. My mind was fashioned in order to read your work as it should be read. Your words were written so that they could waken my heart to its soul's companion.'

He could no longer quite suppress his irritation.

'I have not been entirely overlooked. I had a letter from Lipsius in Leyden, admiring my volumes.'

'But it is only right that he should bow before you. He's a great philosopher but even he knows that he is not your equal.'

'Child, that's nonsense. You are over-exciting yourself.'

Marie, who had spent so long sitting alone in her father's library among her mute books, could not contain herself. She had no idea how to encounter a person, this living, fleshed man who was the embodiment of the paper and leather and words she had committed her life to. She had never had to prove her worth to books. She hadn't ever had to make them take her seriously. She did not know how to make her words mean enough, or to make them different from the same words that others used when they were being merely polite. The physical and mental problem of engaging with the being called the writer who was yet another person in the room was more than she knew how to manage. The powerlessness of her words to convey and convince left her only demonstration to show the writer the truth of her claim to be a worthy companion.

'You think I'm exaggerating? You think I'm just flattering you?' Her heart pounded and took control of her, mind and body. She jumped up, kicking the footstool away, and stood with her feet planted wide in front of his chair, looming over him. She was quite beyond the words he began to speak to reassure her and try to calm her; beyond her own reason. She knew only that she must prove herself.

'Look,' she cried, and reaching behind her head, pulled out the long silver pin that kept the braid of hair rolled against the nape of her neck. 'I'll prove it to you. I'll prove my seriousness, and my constancy. I'll prove my love and admiration for you and your work.'

As she spoke, she stabbed at the inside of her forearm repeatedly with the pointed end of the hairpin, until, to Montaigne's horror, rivulets of blood flowed freely down to her wrist and dripped to the floor from the tips of her fingers. 'I devote my intellect to you . . .' she cried, now in a trance of classical drama.

'I dedicate my blood and my life to you. I am your lifelong disciple. Where you go, I will follow . . .' the drama taking a biblical turn. 'Teach me, make me your pupil, your disciple . . .'

As soon as his astonishment allowed him to move, the terrified Montaigne was on his feet trying to snatch the bodkin out of her hand without getting himself stabbed and they struggled together, intellects lost to the bodies that performed their dance, until at last, as if exhausted, her hand fell open, the weapon dropped to the ground and Marie collapsed limp against his chest. Both of them rested for a moment. He held her upright, his arms straight out under her armpits, and after a moment to catch his breath he called out for help.

Jeanne and Uncle Louis were out making visits on which Marie had refused to accompany them, rejecting the common social round, but Louise was not very far away. She rushed into the room, was surprised but not overly so to see the gentleman's predicament and then ran to get water and bandages. She returned and between them they laid Marie on the couch. Montaigne fell back into his chair, shocked and distressed.

'It's all right, my lord,' Louise said, trying to comfort him while washing the blood from her mistress's arm. 'She gets very het up. You mean a lot to her. You can't imagine the fuss she's been making about that book of yours, and then she thought you were dead, and then you weren't, and now you're here and it was too much, I suppose . . . She's not used to, well, other people . . .'

Marie came round on the chaise longue. She held out her hand to Montaigne.

'You see how overcome I am by your presence. I beg you . . . I beg you . . .' she began to sob.

Hearing the rising emotion in her voice, he rushed to take her hand.

'What is it, my child? What can I do?'

'Take me as your apprentice. Teach me, let me learn from you. It is all I ask.'

'But I'm in Paris on a mission, and then I have to return to Bordeaux. What would you have me do?'

'Be my father!' She imprisoned his hand again between hers.

Montaigne was silenced by the suggestion.

'I am an orphan. My father died when I was a small child. But you, you are the true father of my soul. Be my mentor, my wise parent, my teacher. Call me a daughter.'

'Adopt you?' he gasped, the words spoken only to express his astonishment.

'Adopt me,' she began to weep, seeing that such a thing was possible, overwhelmed at the idea. 'Yes, adopt me, beloved Father.'

He was ready to do almost anything to appease the crazed girl and get away from the terrible mistake he had made. But to adopt her was asking too much.

'I can't adopt you, my dear. I have a wife, a daughter . . . without consulting them . . .'

He saw her face distort with despair at his rejection of her. More tears welled up and she fell back with a cry of anguish that clearly presaged another bout of madness. With the brilliance that comes of desperation he came up with something.

'. . . but I would be honoured if you would agree to become my *fille d'alliance*. A daughter of my intellect. A more equal relationship than that of mere father and daughter, one that

recognises the connection between our minds, and yet, considering the gap in our ages and so on, a formal relationship that
would not cause . . . gossip. We must on no account endanger
your reputation, my dear.'

'Really? Will you really allow me to be your *fille d'alliance*?'

'Yes, yes.'

'Do you promise?'

'Of course. I promise to acknowledge you as my *fille d'alliance*. Now calm yourself.'

Marie heaved back several sobs while she considered his pro-
posal. It was an extraordinary offer. An offer which proved to the
world that a twenty-two-year-old girl was a worthy and admired
student and companion of the mind of the greatest intellect in all
France, in all the world, of all time.

'I'm not worthy of such an honour, Sir,' she whispered.

But Montaigne did not doubt that she would accept it.

Almost certainly Marie would have seen and heard no more of
the great writer if, after making his escape from her in Paris, he
had been able to conduct his business and return south to his
château in Guyenne. The title of *fille d'alliance*, a real and noble
relationship in other circumstances, in these was nothing more
than the words he devised in desperation to make his escape from
an hysterical and downright dangerous admirer. He was a man of
his word, but under the circumstances in which they were
spoken, that particular promise could surely be made and forgotten. When he finally took his leave of her after that first
meeting he had no intention of seeing her again, nor, when she
wrote to him, as he must have guessed she would, of replying to

the deluge of her daily letters. Who knows what might have become of her if this had been what happened. Something, obviously, but what, who can say?

Montaigne's new *fille d'alliance* wrote immediately to him that very afternoon of their meeting and though she waited in vain for an answer, she continued, confident that he would nod agreement as he read, to send him her thoughts on his work, detailed descriptions of her opinions about literature and language, her plans for a literary life, complaints about the constraints her mother and contemptible convention would impose on her if she let them, and, of course, her passionate but pure feelings for him. She was not especially anxious about his silence during the next three or four weeks because she knew he was busy with secret meetings and negotiations while the army of the Duc de Guise came ever closer to the walls of Paris, and on 12 May, the Day of the Barricades, actually took the city as the King fled with the Estates-General to Blois. Even the singularly focused Marie could see that Montaigne's attempt to avert war by travelling to see the King with messages from Navarre and Guise might take precedence over answering her repeated avowals of devotion. Each of which began *Beloved Father*.

For all her precocious appreciation of Montaigne's writings, Marie overlooked those passages in the *Essays* in which he openly acknowledged his reluctance to shoulder more responsibility than he was bound to, his insistence on reason over passion, his distrust and disapproval of wild imaginings and excessive behaviour, his grave reservations about the intellectual capacity of women in general, and his devout commitment to the unrepeatability of his one great emotional attachment. None of this would have made a careful and thoughtful reader imagine that Montaigne would be inclined to seek out the company of Marie de Gournay after their first melodramatic meeting.

But there are conditions under which the distastefulness of an experience dissolves if there are needs potent enough to override the unpleasant memory. Already depleted by his long and dangerous journey to Paris, and by no means improved, as he had hoped, by his visit to Marie de Gournay, Montaigne was under further pressure from the delicate negotiations that made him a pawn between three powerful and dangerous men. Then there was the publication of the third volume of his *Essays*. What writer is not emotionally unbalanced by the publication of a new book? In June, a month after his distressing visit to Marie, a revised edition of the *Essays* came out, with an additional third volume of entirely new essays which concentrated as never before on the whole being of their author. No one, it was said, had ever been so bold, so personal, or mingled abstraction with the anecdotal in such a way, and there was considerable disapproval from the polite classes and established intellectuals of Paris and the rest of Europe.

Just when the Catholic League led by the Duc de Guise took command in Paris, Montaigne suffered an excruciating attack of the gout, though gout had been one of the few diseases he had not previously been a victim of. Then, on 10 July in mid-afternoon, still in bed with the pain in his left foot, he was seized by the League's militia and led off on his horse to the Bastille, by way of a reprisal for the arrest of a Leaguer in Rouen by King Henri's forces. It was a brief imprisonment, to be sure. Catherine de' Medici, the Queen Mother, and not a woman easily crossed, interceded with Guise, and Montaigne was released at eight o'clock the same evening. Even so. It was the first prison he had seen from the inside, and his release was spoken of even by himself as 'an unheard-of favour'. Just a few days later he was taken ill again, but this time with a virulent ague, or the gripe, or perhaps a jail fever incubated during his few hours in the Bastille. Whatever it was, the doctors despaired of his life and for several days he was on the very threshold of death. According to his friend, Pierre de Brach, who sat at his bedside, he faced his end as calmly as a man with a terminal fever can. He was ready, he said, submitting serenely, perhaps with some relief, even, to the inevitable. But death didn't take him. Another improbable escape. His third in as many months. The crisis passed and he remained alive, but wrecked in body and spirit. He was left utterly depleted, physically weak and dangerously vulnerable to the melancholia that had always threatened to corrupt his carefully nurtured but fragile balanced temperament. He was a man approaching old age, who, quite aside from the persistent agony of his stone, in the course of the past two months had suffered an excruciatingly painful new disease, been hauled off to prison, and finally been overwhelmed by a debilitating fever that took him as close to death as he had ever been, except perhaps for that moment in the forest, just weeks before, when the brigand chief had ordered his men to take him into the trees and slit his throat, before suddenly having a change of heart.

He needed as much as any human being could need to recuperate his strength. There was no possibility of making the long, dangerous journey home to Guyenne in his weakened condition, and though Brach ensured that he got all the physical care that was available, he was in a stinking, sweating, occupied city remote from the southern air of his country estate, being looked after by servants. He was weak, fearful and bereft of comfort, and, though he despised the profession, when the doctor asked him if he could not spend some time in the fresh summer countryside air somewhere easier to get to than his far-off château near Bordeaux, he found that just such a convalescence was all he longed for. To be away from the noise and filth of the city, near trees and water. To walk beside a river. To be peaceful and cared for enough to begin the slow, considered work of amending the *Essays* in preparation for their next edition. He imagined a country retreat where quietly, peaceably, he might read over his previous thoughts and add to or qualify them with a word here, a phrase there, a sentence or two where needed. What greater pleasure than editing an existing text of one's own? Altering, expanding, simplifying, making clearer or confusing an argument. And in between, taking easy walks in the bright air, with a soft breeze, birdsong, well-trimmed shrubbery and paths that returned him to his study or his bed when his enfeebled body needed to rest. His dark, ornate quarters in Paris, that hot, politically dangerous summer, offered none of this.

In his nightshirt, careless of the proprieties in the heat, he wandered through his apartment, imagining being in this somewhere else. His eyes came to rest on the pile of sealed letters from Mademoiselle de Gournay which had mounted up on a side table since the second one he'd opened and let fall unread. He picked one at random from the middle of the pile and broke its seal. Perhaps the intensity of her over-decorated, high-flown language, and her underlying demand for his special regard did make him wince and hurry through her sentences, but he learned that she had returned to Picardy, and, unfolding more letters, in every post included an invitation to spend whatever time he felt able at her château, through which the gentle Aronde sweetly flowed, and where, she assured him, he would be free to spend his days only as he wished: working, walking and resting from his exhausting attempts to reconcile the warring kings and princes of France.

It is widely known that the memory of pain diminishes over time and according to need. It is not only pain: we forget difficulty and distress in just the same way. When we need what we want, our minds work on behalf of our hungry will. Needing comfort and rest as he did, why shouldn't even Montaigne's great mind have hazed away the memory of Marie's infantile ravings and overwrought behaviour when they met, and his eyes slipped unseeing over the unoriginal language and thought in her letters, and taken in only her admiration and devotion to his work and himself, and the promise of a balmy, well-tended convalescence in the mild Picardy countryside?

For most of July, and all of August and September, Marie experienced the coming true of her boldest, most improbable daydreams over the past four years. He went to her in Picardy. Montaigne was in the house in Gournay, needing her care and her assistance. Jeanne was astonished by the arrival of their visitor. Her daughter's mad ravings had come true, and this man who was known all over France and further, according to Marie and more reliably Louis, was gratefully and gracefully accepting their hospitality. Though she tried to see Marie in a new light, Jeanne could not persuade herself that it was either her daughter's social graces or her looks that had drawn him here. Marie remained ungainly. She walked with a mannish stride, her shoulders rounded, her chin taking the lead, without a graceful line in her body. Her cheeks had grown less angular, plumper, but womanhood had not softened the effect of her protuberant eyes, the small, prim mouth and pointed narrow chin. She looked like a plain young woman waiting to grow old. It was certainly not her beauty that had drawn the illustrious and noble gentleman to their château. So perhaps, Jeanne concluded, Marie was right if not modest about being able to understand his work better than anyone else.

Why was he not in Paris with all the cleverest people in the land? All those wasted hours in the library when she had failed to learn a woman's duties had taught Marie to read a book, and that was enough to bring its author to them. It seemed to Jeanne to say very little about the character of authors that they were so available to whoever had time to bother to read and admire them. Still, if her daughter had grasped what others had failed to grasp, she supposed she ought to be proud. But what was the use of it? It was an honour, of course, but aside from that? In practical terms? He was an old man and married, with a daughter of his own. This 'fille d'alliance' that he had offered her and Marie spoke of so much, was all very well, and at least a respectable justification for his presence here, but what future did it offer Marie? It didn't mean he would provide for her, and he certainly wouldn't marry her. It was an honour, doubtless, and it might make Marie very proud, but where did it get her? There was no actual benefit to a woman of such modest means from being judged intellectually able by an intellectual man. Could she become a writer of books, and make a living from it? She was a woman. A woman without a fortune of her own made a living only by marrying, never by poring over books in a study. Still, he was very personable, the Seigneur de Montaigne. His manners were impeccable to all of them, and Jeanne had never seen Marie so happy, or even happy at all. She had a glow about her, which, added to her youth, made her mother almost see how she could have been appealing, if only she did not peer so as if her eyes were on stalks, and clump clumsily about. Perhaps her devotion and attention to his every word and need was enough for the Seigneur, so far from home and sickly. Perhaps, in gratitude, he might come to see her in a different light. A man can forgive a great deal in a woman who adores him. But now Jeanne found herself guilty of daydreaming. She knew that nothing useful could come of this. At the very best, nothing decent or respectable could come of it, and she doubted that the Seigneur was the sort of man to keep another woman . . . it was in any case unthinkable what she was almost thinking. He must eventually return home, and Marie would revert to her old unpromising life in the library, a confirmed spinster unless she could be persuaded that having achieved her dream of meeting the great writer, the convent was an excellent place to spend a tranquil life of recollection. Perhaps, after all, this dream come true might allow her to be sensible at last.

At first Montaigne kept almost entirely to his room. He thanked Madame Jeanne, Marthe and Mademoiselle Marie for their hospitality, but it was clear that the journey from Paris had drained his already meagre resources. A doctor was called and his manservant put him to bed.

'Bedrest and care is what I advise for you, Seigneur.'

Montaigne knew that, it was why he was here. His already poor opinion of the medical profession reached a new low with this prescription, but it gave the women of the household the authority to insist he remain in bed and allow himself to be looked after. He had no more than a formal desire to argue.

After several days, when he was rested and starting to feel more like himself, he considered the present situation for which in his exhausted state he had volunteered. In those moments of surprise and alarm at what he had done, he remained calm by asking himself what was so terrible about being taken care of, and being given the chance to recuperate in pleasant surroundings, required only to listen to an enthusiastic young woman expatiating on the thoughts of the classical masters on such subjects as life and death. Even the memory of her stabbing herself seemed less grotesque, or at any rate more understandable. She was just a child. It *was* extraordinary that a young woman, deprived of a proper education, as he had not been, should have learned to use the marvellous machinery of a library to teach herself to love books and reading, to want to write herself, to master Latin to a very creditable standard.

The more he thought about it, the more he realised how admirable this young woman was. He was ashamed but could not in good conscience fail to admit his disappointment when he found her less pleasing to the eye and to his taste in companionship than he had let himself assume before their meeting. It was, of course, natural, both the assumption and the disappointment, but his wish to flee even before she had said or done anything was nonetheless regrettable. He should have managed something better than that. He was ashamed, too, of having neglected her letters, and of his cowardly offer to make her his *fille d'alliance* only in order to escape from her uncontrolled enthusiasm. How could she not have been over-excited, under the circumstances? Her library had come to life and paid her a visit. How would he behave if Plutarch suddenly announced his presence at the door, and begged to make his acquaintance? With considerably less decorum than he had expected of her. With wild excitement. He had been appalled at her, an inexperienced young woman of twenty-two, for not having the gravitas and subtlety that even a sophisticated, worldly old man would find hard to achieve in similar circumstances. In fact, wouldn't he be delighted if his own daughter displayed such an interest in writing and writers? Or in him. And he realised, also, that he was angry with Marie for not being the wise old man that his true and lost friend would have become, the wise older man he had been for him while he lived. That he could have dreamed, even unwittingly, that this young girl would not only supply his aesthetic (and possibly sensual) needs, but that she might fill the hungering vacancy left by La Boétie, only showed how poorly his mind had been working when he received her letter in Paris. He had grabbed at a mirage, ready to see any flattering babble as offering him what he knew he could, and perhaps should, never have again. How ill equipped he had been for normal social relations, let alone the delicacies of forestalling another bloody war.

He understood that he had to fulfil his promise to her of an intellectual alliance while he rested in her care. In return for her devotion, he might gently tutor her during their conversations, while he continued to get back his strength. What she lacked was a teacher, someone who could lead her towards the right and balanced approach to books and what they contained. Why should a young woman not aspire to an intellectual life just because she lacked the social eminence and grace of Marguerite de Valois or Diane de Foix? If she was destined for spinsterhood, as she was by her own and her mother's account, and as he could clearly see was likely, why should it not be a spinsterhood in the library? She could translate Latin texts, and perhaps, with a bit of discipline, she might write adequate poetry and correspond with other women of letters. He saw that he could possibly mould the raw material of her enthusiasm for his work into something she might usefully make a life out of. To begin with, she could help him with the amendments for the next edition of the *Essays*. He was starting to feel ready to do a little work. Her assistance would be good for both of them.

Marie's life now revolved around him. She and he began the day early in the library at Gournay, a poor thing beside the tower full of books in Montaigne's château, but with a flurry of effort on the part of the servants, none of whom had previously been allowed in by Marie, it had been aired and cleaned and polished into a very serviceable place for the writer and his assistant to get down to their work. They sat at opposite sides of the table with an inkwell and a stack of loose paper between them, and he scratched his notes on to the disbound pages of the newly published edition. Sometimes he pushed it across to her and sat back, or paced around the room, dictating additions for Marie to write in the margins, or if they were longer on to a leaf which she then pasted beside the appropriate passage. Sometimes Marie lay awake at night relishing the thought that some of his manuscript would be in her hand. This great man's worked-over manuscript, which must undoubtedly be studied by future generations for as long as the world lasted or the pages survived, would bear an amendment in her handwriting contrasting the militancy of one man with the restraint of another in the essay in Book I entitled 'Same Design: Differing Outcomes':

'I know another who has unexpectedly improved his fortune by having taken quite contrary advice . . .'

'Who are they?' she asked him while the ink dried.

'It's a state secret, my child, but if you swear not ever to divulge it . . .' She nodded vigorously, solemn eyed with the honour of being burdened with state secrets. 'Very well: Navarre is the one and the Duc de Guise is the other. But I won't tell you which is which or your life might be in danger.'

It took another moment and a closer look at his face before she thought that perhaps he was teasing her. Nevertheless, just in case he was not she gravely assured him that she would never reveal anything he had told her to a soul. Not even if she was tortured. Not ever. But beyond even the satisfaction of possessing this confidence was the thrilling thought that the sentence she had written in her own careful hand in the margin of the page would continue to exist, side by side, next to Montaigne's printed and handwritten words. It was a posterity of sorts. Even though, after both he and she were long dead, there might be no way for other readers to know who had written the alternative hand, it was the silent, secret proof in the world now and in the future of a place in the illustrious work of Montaigne for La Demoiselle de

Gournay. More immediately, it was proof that her dreamed-of life devoted to books had commenced.

They took regular daily walks along the river path. At his request, she waited back at the house while he took a solitary stroll in the mornings, but in the afternoon, once the sun had grown cooler, she accompanied him along what she called 'Monsieur Montaigne's Promenade'. The phrase made Montaigne smile. She had renamed the path they took on their walks along the river's edge (the river path as it had been) after him. While he took his private mid-morning turn around the gardens and wooded trails of Gournay, Marie stood at the library window, watching him disappear from her view and return refreshed, ready to work on until they took some lunch in the dining room, always after Jeanne, Marthe and Léonore had finished theirs, so as not to distract him from his thoughts. Afterwards, he had a nap, required by his doctor and appreciated by the patient as an extra period to be alone. When he woke, they returned to the task of editing, and then, in the late afternoon, Marie and Montaigne walked together along the path that led to the river, and followed its course for a while.

It was the time that Marie most treasured. They talked together. She asked him questions, put points to him, and drank in his answers, though always a little bemused by the light-hearted way he seemed to approach the serious topics she brought up. Usually the subject of their conversation arose from whatever they had been working on that day.

'Why did you make the change from "that monster Caligula" to "that villain Caligula"?'

'One should always avoid insulting the innocent,' he said lightly.

The space between Marie's eyebrows narrowed.

'But Caligula wasn't innocent. He was a wicked tyrant.'

Montaigne made more effort.

'I meant that monsters are innocent. I didn't want to insult them by comparing Caligula to them.'

Marie's brows remained knitted. He elaborated.

'A monster is born, or is a sport of nature that we in the ordinary majority happen to think strange. It is not by definition, nor by will, bad, only different. A villain, on the other hand, chooses his villainy.' He paused and glanced at her, then added, 'A monster need not be a villain.'

Marie's face cleared as she grasped his point.

'Oh, yes, I see.'

'But who knows, my dear, perhaps I'm wrong. How can one be sure that even villainy is purely a man's free choice? Now, you've worried me, perhaps I might be doing Caligula an injustice.'

'Oh no,' she rushed to reassure him, stopping and placing a hand on the sleeve of his doublet. 'I'm sure he was a very terrible man. Suetonius is quite definite about it.'

Montaigne smiled a little wistfully.

'Just a poor joke. Let's leave Caligula a tyrant and keep the monsters blameless.'

Montaigne knew well enough by now that Marie had no capacity for playfulness, but it was deep in his nature to play. Playing was his way to think, and possibly too her solemnity provoked in him the wish for mischief. He had the education and confidence, perhaps also no option but to indulge it.

*

One day at the height of summer Montaigne and Marie took their regular afternoon walk and Marie brought up the subject of love.

'Exemplary love, of course.'

Bearing in mind Plutarch's views on the distinction between love and marriage, she wanted to know what he thought of a story she had read not long ago that took a different view, yet nonetheless had a high moral purpose.

'It's just a little novel, and therefore not serious, as you and I know, and yet, as I read it, I couldn't help but feel that it dealt with great themes – loyalty and devotion, selflessness, betrayal. Aren't all these subjects essential to the development of the human soul? And so why shouldn't we take such a work seriously, too? It concerns a princess who runs away with the man she loves rather than obeying her father, the king, who has arranged a marriage for her, according to his need for an alliance, with someone for whom she could never feel anything.'

The sun was hot still, but occasionally a light breeze blew. Montaigne felt it now, a cooling breath of air against his face. It was delightful, and he waited for the moment it took to pass, before answering Marie, closing his eyes to intensify the pleasure until the thick heat returned.

'Surely it's the duty of a daughter and a princess to obey her father and king?' he said. 'What has love got to do with marriage? If she were a wise woman she would have married as she was told and made the best of the man she loved in some private corner of the palace.'

Marie worked hard to conceal her disapproval at such duplicity, to say nothing of the disturbing image the private corner brought to her mind. She wished he wouldn't make such jokes and tried to draw him back to the seriousness of the topic under discussion.

'The only honourable way to live is to be true to yourself, isn't that so?'

'Certainly not. The honourable thing to do is whatever is best first for your country and then for your family. You are confusing being true to yourself with indulging yourself. What became of this wayward young woman?'

'She was betrayed by the man she loved, the one for whom she had given up everything.'

'Ah hah!' A knowing nod of the head suggested that he was not at all surprised.

'They were shipwrecked on the shore of another land . . .'

'As they deserved.' A small smile played around the corner of his mouth.

Marie's face set stubbornly against what she was fairly certain was his levity, and she continued her story.

'A nobleman of the land where they were washed ashore fell madly in love with the princess. And the young man showed himself to be faithless. He became entranced with the nobleman's sister . . .'

'The wretch. Like all of us, I'm afraid. Men are not to be trusted, none of us. That is the lot of women. More importantly, love is not to be trusted. Whatever next? I hope you're going to tell me that they have a double wedding and all is well? But I suspect that the princess's disobedience will have to be punished.'

'Yes, yes, of course,' Marie agreed heartily, not hearing the ennui in Montaigne's voice. 'Of course, she must be punished, and yet, there is nobility and glory in it.'

He was gazing now at the opposite bank of the river as they walked, almost certainly not visualising the awful quadrangle Marie continued to describe. 'The nobleman thought mistakenly that the princess and her lover were married – they would have been, naturally, both being well born, but they had not had a chance to do so since they ran away – so the nobleman decided to kill the lover to make the princess free to marry him.'

'Goodness, was there no easier way? This seems to me unnecessarily to complicate an already knotty problem.'

This time she caught his tone, and glanced sharply at him. He looked contrite.

'Please, continue.'

'The faithless lover, however, offered the princess to the nobleman in return for his sister, so the killing wasn't carried out, but the princess overheard the conversation between them, and realising that she was vilely betrayed by her beloved decided to pretend to love the nobleman . . .'

'I'm dizzy with the labyrinthine byways of the human heart.' Montaigne clasped a hand to his brow.

'It is more like heartlessness.'

Montaigne let out an encouraging laugh at what might almost count as a jest if it had not been spoken more in the corrective tone of a schoolmistress.

'And so? I suppose that it doesn't end happily for all at this point?'

'And so she agreed to marry the nobleman, but only on the condition that he prove his love to her by promising to kill one of his servants who, she said, had insulted her.'

'Oh dear, I see multiple tragedy ahead.'

'And great nobility, Monsieur. The princess wrote a heart-breaking letter to her lover and that night took the place of the doomed servant in her bed. Her lover came at last to his senses after reading her pitiful farewell. He ran to her, but she wasn't in her room, and searching the palace he finally found her horribly mutilated dead body, murdered, as she intended, in mistake for the servant. He was overwhelmed with shame and remorse and there and then took his own life.'

Marie was quite breathless with consequence.

'I suppose they were laid to rest together in the same tomb, by the wicked but penitent brother and sister who were shown the error of their ways?'

'Yes, exactly. That is just what happened.'

Montaigne sighed deeply, and wiped his overheated face with his lace handkerchief. The breeze had dropped.

'This, then, is the story of a disobedient young woman who lies to several people, and takes revenge on her two lovers by making one kill her, and the other find her dead and kill himself? In fact, a devious act of murder and suicide by sleight of hand.'

Marie gasped.

'No, no, not revenge, certainly no murder is committed by her, and suicide is completely the wrong way of looking at it. She *sacrifices* herself.'

'To what end?'

'Because she has been betrayed. Because her love is like a rock. There is nothing left for her in life. Her love was true and it will never die, no matter if the object of her love fails her. It shows us the eternal nature of true love.'

'Can love live on without a beating heart to keep it alive? A

109

sacrifice must be to some purpose. What is achieved by the sacrifice?'

'Those who misused her and betrayed her are taught to see the terrible thing they have done, by her nobility in sacrificing herself for their redemption.'

'A rather circular argument, I think. The redemption we have to take on trust – I don't hold out much hope for the next pair of lovebirds shipwrecked in the land of the nobleman and his sister. No, revenge and suicide are paramount in the story. A woman's way.'

'What else can women do when they are not regarded as men's equals?'

'Quite. But would you have the sexes equal, now? If I were you I should settle for women being men's superiors, as they are everywhere I look.'

She ignored this; even she could tell that he was mocking. As least she thought he was.

'How can you not see the honour and grandeur of it? Then I told it incorrectly.'

She looked so downcast that Montaigne was once again sorry he took her seriousness so lightly.

'My dear Marie, I think these grand melodramas overwhelm the *true*, by which I mean *everyday* nature of human beings' dealings with one another. A serious young mind like yours needs to make a more considered exploration of the way of the world. Sentimental literature is exciting but deceptive in its concentration on human drama.'

'But there's so much passion and beauty in the story. It has such power.'

'Quite so. Read them for entertainment if you must, but perhaps the kind of passion and beauty and the powerful feelings engendered by novels are not the best way to proceed for a serious young woman who wants to be accepted by intellectual society. As for truth, it needs a sober, quiet search to find it. Truth offers very little excitement, I'm sorry to tell you.'

'Yes, I see,' Marie said, trying very hard to. 'It must be written with greater moral force. Its higher meaning must be elaborated over the simple story. The readers' attention must be drawn to the consequences to those who break the rules of family and nation even when doing so with the purest motives.'

Montaigne merely murmured and pointed out a flight of geese rising in the sky over the Aronde. He was a little disappointed.

Marie was more disappointed than she understood. In her eyes, Montaigne could never be wrong, but there was some vital part of her which was gloriously, she could almost say physically, uplifted by the story of the sacrificial princess. In a different sort of way, her response to reading it matched the excitement she had experienced reading the *Essays*. She could perfectly well see that there were irreconcilable differences between the narrative drama written by Taillement and the remarkable, philosophical works of Montaigne. Yet, reading each of them, she had experienced the same exhilaration which began to flow and pulse through her, until at last she was brought to a feeling of having burst her physical bounds. The something lurking darkly but marvellously within her, that Marie had been dimly aware of since a child, was let loose by both readings to become inextricably one with the surrounding dancing light of the world. Just as the dusty and limited library of her childhood became a place of glory when she found herself working in it with Montaigne, so in reading the Taillement story just as much as the *Essays*, she took leave of her small interior confinement and discovered herself out in the vastness. She had hoped that by telling Montaigne about Taillement's story, he would explain to her that her similar response to it and to his own essays reconciled the two, as different but equally vital food for her being. But he suggested to her that her response to the story was of lesser value; juvenile and emotional, not moral and elevated as she still believed it to be. And still, convinced though she was of Montaigne's rightness in all things and wanting to please him at any cost, she found it impossible to extricate the one sense of elevation from the other. She was reluctant to let go of the unaccountable pleasure her reading of the story gave her, or lose the many moments, hours even, she had spent recalling, even reliving, the narrative and its parts, especially those thoughts about the princess whose sacrifice for love, as well as her betrayal, actually sent delicious thrills around Marie's body and made her crave its retelling. She would sink into the drama of the story like one who, waking from a delightful dream, discovers she has the ability to drift back into it and relish it over and over again.

There was little of this narrative addiction actually in the essays she so admired. Just dry accounts of some classical hero or other set into an argument, or an alarmingly candid description of the writer's personal and physical predilections. She had read and passionately admired the work, but the excitement that had caused her mother to slip hellebore into her food came as well from the private times when she contemplated the man himself, the writer, the person who had infiltrated himself into the words, whom she summoned into her dreaming presence with as much sensuous delight as the delicious moment of the faithless lover finding the bloodied corpse of his princess.

Oddly, to her understanding, though it was wonderful beyond words to have her hero and mentor actually present in her house, working on his masterpiece with her, walking daily beside her, she found that in moments of repose, before or after sleep, day-dreaming as she watched the clouds sail across the sky, she still *imagined* Montaigne coming to her, offering her his friendship, his intellect, his love, as if he were not already there in the house. It was not the memory of the work they had done together, or the conversations they had had that day that played in her sleepy mind, but the same reveries of him and her together and discovering each other that she had conjured in those days before she actually met him, when it was perfectly impossible that they should ever be in each other's presence.

Montaigne stayed in Gournay for more than three months, working on the new edition of the *Essays* and allowing the northern summer sun to warm his bones and settle his blood. He was fed and looked after and he appreciated the attention he received from Madame and the two Mademoiselles de Gournay. He had become fond of Marie, but no less wary of her passion and her longing for a kind of solemnity that he abhorred. He saw her need to be to him what she could never be, and then when she sensed its impossibility, to be something else she could never be, that he would never allow her to be. There was only room in his life for the one true lost friend, and if, by some extraordinary accident, there might be another connection such as he had had with La Boétie, it was clear from the first, and clearer with every passing day, that it could not be La Demoiselle de Gournay. He was sure enough that it could never be a woman (though he was always open to surprise and correction) but he was quite certain that it could not be a young woman, and perfectly convinced it was not Marie, for all her admirable qualities and good intentions. This reality, she seemed not to have come to terms with. She clung on to the title of *fille d'alliance* as if it was an actual adoption, and as if it was an adoption that meant even more than an actual adoption. Yet he wanted to thank her, to encourage her. She was remarkable in her way, and he had taken a great deal from her and felt the better for it, physically, at least.

One morning, not long before he left, he showed her something he had written the previous evening, after everyone had gone to bed. It was an addition on a separate piece of paper that he had pasted in almost at the end of the essay 'On Presumption' in Book II. She hunched over the page and read the new words:

I have taken pleasure in making public in several places the hope I have for Marie de Gournay, my adopted daughter, whom I love indeed as a daughter of my own. If youthful promise means anything, her soul will some day be capable of the finest things. The judgement she made of the first Essays, *she, a woman, in this century, so young, alone in her part of the country, and the good will she devoted to me simply on the strength of the esteem she had for me before she even knew me, are particulars worthy of special consideration.*

She read it two or three times. When she finally looked up, her prominent eyes were oddly dull, and her lips pressed tightly together, but she said, 'I could never have hoped for such an honour. That I should have a place in the *Essays*. My name. Publicly acknowledged as your adopted daughter.'

He had perhaps only imagined a tinge of disappointment in her eyes, because she began to hiccup great sobs and reached for Montaigne's hand, as he hurriedly pulled out his kerchief and sat her down.

'No, no, it's nothing in comparison to the wonderful care you have given me. And your assistance with the *Essays*. Please don't cry.'

She pressed his hand against her bosom which rose and fell

115

dramatically. He watched her carefully in case she reached up to her hair, and wondered if he should call her mother. But abruptly the tears ended, she straightened her back and looked up directly into his face with an almost steely glare as he stood above her.

'I will never forget your faith in me, Beloved Father. I will devote my entire life to making sure that I do not disappoint you. With the confidence of such a mentor behind me, I cannot fail to achieve everything you hope for me. I won't let you down.'

She pressed his hand to her lips. After a moment or two Montaigne eased it back into his own possession.

'Well now. I think it's time for my walk. I am delighted that you're content with my addition.'

He had made another alteration the previous night which also had to do with his feelings of gratitude towards Marie, though this one he didn't show to her. There was a passage in the recently published third volume of the new edition, which she would, of course, have read, in the essay 'On Vanity', musing on the loss of his friend La Boétie:

I know well that I will leave behind no sponsor anywhere near as affectionate and understanding about me as I was about him. There is no one to whom I would be willing to entrust myself fully for a portrait; he alone enjoyed my true image, and carried it away.

Several days earlier, having come on this passage, he thought about Marie and her claim to his friendship and her devotion. For whatever reason, he had added after 'for a portrait': *and if there*

116

should be any, I repudiate them, for I know them to be excessively prej-udiced in my favour'. The same night that he added his elegy to his adopted daughter, he re-read this other passage with his amend-ment and sat over it for a long time. Then he took his pen, dipped it into the inkwell and carefully crossed out the entire printed pas-sage as well as the handwritten addition. It was one of his very few crossings-out. Monsieur Montaigne was not an unkind man.

He was well enough by November to continue with his peace-making mission. It was time for him to go to Blois to discuss with the King the possibility of an alliance with Navarre and a peace treaty with Guise. Marie could hardly support the idea of losing him and their perfect days together. As his departure date came nearer her morning eyes grew ever more tear-reddened. He agreed to visit her again briefly on his return south from the Estates-General. He promised her that they would stay in touch. Letters, and yes, perhaps she could visit him one day, though the journey at present was too dangerous for anyone, let alone a young woman travelling by herself. It was nothing, nothing, she assured him, she would go through fire in order to be with him again, to sit beside him in his tower, the two of them working together, to assist him in any way she could. And she was certain that his efforts at making peace between the warring factions would prove successful. How could they not, when the wisest man in France, in all Europe, including Erasmus, including Justus Lipsius, was adviser to the parties? In such an altered France, without warring armies overrunning the countryside, the journey from Picardy to Bordeaux would present no more than the ordinary difficulties of travel.

Nonetheless, she must make no travel plans, he insisted, without first consulting him by letter.

Montaigne left Gournay for the King's Court in Blois on 23 November. When he arrived he found to his pleasure the likes of Etienne Pasquier and Jacques-Auguste de Thou with whom to discuss his writings and the state of France. He spoke privately to Henri of the advisability of making a peace with the Duc de Guise, and His Majesty listened carefully to what he said and agreed. A month later Henri had Guise assassinated.

His mission having failed, Montaigne made the long, arduous journey back towards Bordeaux, to the château in Guyenne, to his tower. He was too urgently in need of arriving home to break his journey at Gournay. He sent a letter with apologies, adding his gratitude and admiration for Mademoiselle de Gournay who would remain for ever close to him in his memory. He thought it was necessary now to stay in his own study and concentrate for whatever time remained to him on consolidating his real life's work. He was sure that she would understand. He was back in Bordeaux.

Marie was in Gournay with her mother, Marthe and Léonore, just as she had been when she believed her beloved Montaigne to be dead, went to Paris, found him alive, and spent three glorious months with her resurrected new-found father. The battle between Marie and her mother about her future re-commenced immediately. It was as if the trip to Paris and the summer and autumn of walking, talking and thinking with Montaigne had never happened. Had the coming true of her dreams amounted to nothing? Did her mother not see now that she was different? That her life was to be different?

'How are you different? I will tell you how you are different from other women of your age. You are still single, a no longer so young single woman of twenty-three, with barely enough of a fortune after your siblings take their share to keep you fed and clothed, let alone to manage the upkeep of a household, and none of the domestic skills to help you to live a little more comfortably. You have no education. You live in the provinces. A fine nobleman came and recuperated with us for three months. Now he has gone. You do not have a husband. How will you spend your life?'

'As Montaigne does. Writing.'

'Can't you see that what Montaigne does, a man with wealth and the ear of kings, is not a model for you to copy?'

'Why not? He will be my sponsor. With Montaigne's recommendation I will be able to publish books and they will be read. I've already discussed with him a book I intend to write. I'm writing it now and he will spread the word. He admires me. I am admired by the greatest writer in the world. To have the support of such a man is to be more than a single woman.'

Jeanne raised her arms to the heavens.

'You're a fool! You looked after a sick old man far from home, just as a wife would. You took his dictation. You listened open-mouthed to his words of wisdom. He allowed you to walk with him once a day. Does that amount to admiration enough to launch yourself on the world as a woman alone and live as a writer?'

'I am his *fille d'alliance*. He says so in his book. When they read him, they will read of me. I will devote my life to learning.'

'It is not what a woman does.'

'Marguerite de Valois does it.'

119

'That shameless tart? All France knows about her carryings-on. Forgive me but even that life isn't open to you. You have neither riches nor beauty. Anyway, she is not a woman, she is a royal princess.'

'To be the *fille d'alliance* of Michel de Montaigne is to be better than a princess.'

'Does it make you an independent man? Or will he leave his money to you to enable you to read and write your life away? Will he take you into his household? Will he provide for me when his *fille d'alliance* is scratching words on to paper while I shiver and starve in old age? *Fille d'alliance*, indeed. Foolish, deluded girl. You are no longer a child. You are on the verge of not even being young. You will be a cold and hungry old maid. That is how you will be different.'

If she ever had, Marie no longer cared what her mother said, or took notice of her complaints. She was her new father's daughter now.

She began her novel the night she and Montaigne had talked about it, and finished it just three days after he left for Blois. She wrote in a fury of energy that dampened the vast sense of loss at her mentor's departure, but also expressed the excitement of actively beginning the life she intended to lead. She had thought hard about his comments and come to understand Montaigne's reservations about the outline she gave him of Taillement's tale to be his suggestions for her own superior version of it. He had said that such a story didn't suit her intellectual ambitions, and she took this to mean that simply to tell the story *alone* would not do her justice. He wanted her to work to her greatest potential, to find a method that merited her telling the story that moved her so deeply. And, lying awake the night after their conversation, she had, as she knew Montaigne wished, found an answer. She would produce a version that blended the dramatic story with the high moral seriousness that would be a fitting first book for the daughter of Montaigne. He, of course, did not write or read novels. But his words had inspired her to write the story and include her own voiced interpretations of its greater spiritual and social meanings. It would be a concealed essay on love, fidelity and moral certitude. A young woman could perhaps publish a novel (especially if she were supported by a great writer), whereas it might be thought presumptuous of her to begin her writing career with essays, for all the encouragement she received from the inventor of the form. It would not be so very different from Montaigne's technique of relating stories from classical authors and using them to meditate on important topics of philosophy, ethics and politics. She found the characters and their behaviour in Taillement's story to epitomise sincerity and betrayal, and the drama they acted out was no more trivial than a parable of virtue if set in a refined moral context. The purpose of the story must be explained to the reader so that he would realise there was nothing frivolous about it.

It was dedicated, of course, to Montaigne. It was even named for him. She called it *The Promenade of Monsieur de Montaigne*. The title had nothing to do with the content, but it ensured that people would pay attention, and she knew her father would want to help her in this way. It was prefaced with a letter to the dedicatee.

You well understand, Father, that I name this 'your walk' because when we were strolling along the paths I now think of as your own, I told you the story that follows . . . The reason why I have felt impelled to put it into writing and send it to you, after your departure, to run after you, is to give you more opportunity to see in it the faults in my writing style that you would have missed in my telling of the story, which I did rather hurriedly. Read it, please, and correct it – but I fear that if I ask you to tell me what is wrong with it, you will tell me it is harder to say what is right with it. That can't be helped. If you do not excuse me, you will excuse my youth, and the good will you feel towards me will grant me a pardon, even if cold reason refuses. In truth, if anyone is surprised that, although we are only father and daughter in title, the good will that unites us is greater even than that of real fathers and children – the first and closest of all natural ties – let them try and find goodness in themselves and then perceive it in another, and they will understand that goodness has more power to harmonise souls than nature has. Natural affections have often failed, brothers have made war on each other, even fathers and children, but the most sacred love of Pythias and Damon, whom reason (nature is the ruler of beasts – among men reason must rule) had joined together by reason of their completeness and virtue, was inviolable.

It continued:

Because you said that my intellect was better suited for deeper matters than light-hearted efforts, I have included some of my poetry at the end of the story, not from any attempt to elevate myself but

122

to make sure you do not misjudge me by thinking me a subtler thinker than I really am. It is all one, although I wonder if I am not willingly taking pleasure in simply committing this foolishness to paper on purpose, so as to make you, by chastising me, exercise the power you have over me . . . I kiss the hands of Madame de Montaigne and my sister Mademoiselle de Montaigne, as well as your brothers, Messieurs de la Brousse and de Mattecoulon . . .

She ended the letter with a quotation:

'Nor is there any fear that our descendants will grudge to enrol our name among those renowned for friendship, if only the fates are willing.'

It came from a poem, 'Ad Michaëlem Montanum: To Michel de Montaigne – by Estienne de La Boétie'.

Love at a distance is an agony of waiting. The distance between Montaigne and Marie was almost as great as it could be without a vast uncharted body of water intervening. Her parcel would, if fortune was with it (if it did not get lost, if the carrier was not indisposed, robbed or killed on the road) arrive at its destination in perhaps three weeks. A reply might be expected, if its journey was equally uneventful, in another three, always supposing that it was written immediately. The agony of waiting was accompanied for Marie by an agony of uncertainty. Not just as to whether the packet containing her manuscript had arrived or would ever arrive in Guyenne, but if it had, whether it was read immediately (of course it would be, her father would not put it to one side, but then again, he might be delayed on his journey home, or perhaps be in the city on business or affairs of state when it arrived), and then whether, once read, it would be well received. Marie trembled at this last thought though she had great inner certainty in her ability – Montaigne's seal of approval, his literary fatherhood, ensured that – and she sent off the book feeling rapturous about its accomplishment. She knew it was mature in its analysis of the human narrative, that her language was highly poetic and a rhetorical tour de force, pointing always to the triumph of virtue in heaven if nowhere else, and the punishment of sin. It had amazed her when she read it for the final time. Did I write that? she wondered to herself. It was like being in love, reading her words which were no longer just words but her first complete *work*, written with an authority far beyond her years and experience. And yet, for all her confidence as a self-taught, self-motivated and now mentored neophyte, there was a mysterious, unnameable, discomfort clawing in her upper abdomen, as if some small creature was scraping at her from inside, which began as soon as she sent the manuscript on its way, and did not stop for a very long time indeed.

Three weeks passed, the best three weeks, when nothing could have been expected from her father. The package would not have arrived, even if he had, at the Château de Montaigne. Though even then she was alert every day to the possibility of a letter from him written en route about his journey, to keep in contact with his new daughter. Five weeks passed, and with every following day that went by without a response her internal pain, not unnameable by now, but not named, increased. Ridiculously, she told herself; all the uncertainties of her parcel to him would apply to his answer to it. Nevertheless, she wrote to him daily, telling him of her reading, her thoughts and her plans, offering him further analyses of his essays, and including poems she had written, praising him and members of his (and now her) family. Each letter hoped he was well, that he was not suffering any recurrence of the stone, that his age was not too much of an infirmity. Each letter reiterated her filial love and admiration for him, her only father in the world. Very occasionally she wondered, in passing, if he had received her manuscript and whether he thought it worth mentioning.

Everyone who has loved and waited for what will never happen (and that is most of us, though some wait for much longer than others) knows the convoluted thoughts that serve to ameliorate their anguish. Those desperately reached-for hopes and excuses: the misfortune of wrong timings, of misaligned birth, the contortions of the imaginary yet plausible evidence thought up to assuage the ache and humiliation of not being loved. Even to conceal our love from ourselves. Even, perhaps, to conceal the cessation of our love from ourselves.

Marie felt cheated by having met her soul mate when he was so old, or by having been born too late. If only she had known him when he was a young man, before he was burdened with illness, and with the responsibility of a family. If they had just had the opportunities that equality of age allowed and disparity of age absolutely forbade. She alone – she alone and he – knew how close they were during those few months they had together, how their fondness for each other could have only limited expression because of their circumstances: he being old and married, she being so much younger and a single woman with a reputation to maintain. He was a gentleman, and though in the

Essays he had made it clear that he considered marriage to be an entirely separable condition from emotional and physical love, he would never have thought of disgracing a respectable young, single, woman. He wrote that he did not believe physical love and spiritual friendship could co-exist. And, of course, their relationship was of a quite different, much more serious kind than romantic love, that poor shadow of loving friendship between equal spirits. To imagine that anything of a physical nature could have happened between them was to belittle the depth of their real love. But while the coarser kind of affection had not the slightest place in her life, she had come round to believing that in very rare instances, in the fated meetings between special souls, a combination of passionate and spiritual love was possible. She remembered moments when he had looked at her with a strange intensity such that she had never seen before in another's gaze, seemed to lean into her, and consider her with a mysterious question in those half-hooded eyes that he was surely asking of himself, which made her leap from her chair at the desk and stand staring blindly out of the window, catching her breath – those moments (they passed quickly, as if they had never happened) gave her reason to believe that they were two such rare souls who belonged together, mind and body. They might have . . . in spite of their difference in age . . . the possibility of passion was there, but they successfully, if painfully, resisted. And of course, her beloved father was right to be restrained, to pull back from his moments of intense desire; such an alliance would have appeared to the undeveloped mentality of the vulgar world a lower sort of affection which would seem to lesser souls to have contaminated their pure love. She could only be his daughter, his friend, his beloved friend, his literary companion, who understood him as no one else. It must be enough for her. She understood about sacrifice.

Yet still there was no letter from him. Gradually, as time continued to creep, more weeks, more months, without a word from him, she found a name for the source of the pain inside her, though not necessarily the only or the right one. She identified the pain that never quite left her as her fear that he was dead. He was so old, and hadn't he almost died when he was in Paris? She defined the gnawing anxiety that lived inside her as her finely tuned sensitivity to his well-being, even in his absence. His continued silence told her he was dead. The interior clawing worry, the nameless fear, her own anxious heart, confirmed it. He must be dead. Her excruciating sense of loss when she faced this possibility – no, likelihood – made the prospect of the rest of her life an empty eternity in hell. She could imagine nothing more terrible that might happen to her than his death, but she did not measure her misery against the other possibility that he was alive and had found her manuscript unworthy of comment. That thought remained unnameable.

Then, five months after she had sent off her parcel, in the following year, a letter arrived from Guyenne. He thanked her for her letters and apologised for taking so long in replying. He had been ill, several times, and family matters had kept him busy. He asked to be remembered to her mother and sisters, and was grateful to them all for their wonderful hospitality and to Marie especially for her assistance with the editing for the next edition. He hoped she was well and that her reading was continuing. He sent his warm regards, but said that he advised against her regular suggestion that she come to visit him at the Château de Montaigne. The journey, two weeks at the very least on difficult roads in troubled times, was not one a single woman should take. Even if she were accompanied by her mother, it would only double the jeopardy. It was far too dangerous and too arduous. He regretted it, but forbade her to hazard the journey – her fine future was too assured to take such risks with it. Perhaps, one day, they might meet again in Paris. Who knew? He signed himself her dear friend. He did not mention the novel nor the poems she had sent him.

He was alive still. The unnameable gnawing inside her shifted to blanket her refusal to notice the polite, bland tone of the letter she had so longed to receive. Marie replied instantly, and continued to write every day about her reading and opinions, insisting too that the journey to Guyenne was nothing for such a devoted friend and daughter as she. But she also wrote a letter to Justus Lipsius in the Netherlands, Professor at the University of Louvain, who had published his letters three years before in which, as Uncle Louis told her, he had declared Montaigne 'the modern Thales'. Montaigne thought highly of him too, calling him 'the wisest man of our times' in the *Essays*. Marie wrote to Lipsius, thanking him, blessing him, for his praise of her father and mentor, explaining that his appreciation of Montaigne had helped to persuade those around her that she was not mad when she first read the *Essays* and was overwhelmed by their brilliance. She told him of her meeting with and adoption by the great writer and included an excerpt from her novel. Lipsius, too, was not a young man and he was enchanted by the boldness and ornately reverential tone of the girl. He responded in immaculate Latin, immediately (as immediately as the speed of mail would allow) as Montaigne had done when Marie first wrote to him.

Who can you be who writes to me like this? A young woman? Surely not, from what you write. Is it possible that such a sharp understanding and solid judgement, not to speak of wisdom and knowledge can be found in someone of your sex, and in such times as these? Young woman, you astound me! . . . Do you aspire to climb to the height we men have attained or to climb even higher? Do it, with the approval of God and men, certainly with mine. I cherish you, without having even met you, with an affection I give sparingly, and admire you. What a day for me it will be when I meet you personally . . . You should have sent me a longer fragment of your book. I am hungry to know more of it, and what marvels, like an old miracle remade, a virgin can bring forth . . . *Vale vale aeui nostri (viue tantum) vera Theano.*

She wrote back to Lipsius as soon as she had read his letter, including the rest of her book and a sheaf of her poetry, but once again life's difficulties, in the form of geography and politics, intervened. The merchant who had delivered her first letter to the Netherlands had arrived back in Picardy. When she took him the packet to deliver on his forthcoming trip he told her it was impossible. All communications between France and the Protestant north of Europe had been cut off.

'Commerce has completely broken down.'

Montaigne very occasionally responded to her cataract of letters, writing almost identical responses to his first reply. Polite, charming, distantly affectionate and admiring but strongly advising against her visiting him, and never referring to her novel or her poems.

A year after Lipsius had received Marie's first letter, and not a man to leave any of his writings unpublished, his effusive reply to her appeared in the next volume of his correspondence. Nothing would make Montaigne's very infrequent communication and his silence on the matter of her book all right (except, of course, his death, the news of which she daily feared), but Justus Lipsius, the finest scholar and intellect in Europe, had now publicly praised her work and begged for more. Communications being so slow, and living in the intellectual excommunication of Picardy, it was some time before she found out, but Marie de Gournay's vocation as a literary virgin trembled on the verge of becoming a reality.

Yet even as Lipsius's praise was arriving in the bookshops, and her new-found renown permitted Marie to think of beginning her career as a writer, life turned a somersault and prevented her from taking advantage of it. In 1591, two years after Montaigne had returned to Guyenne, Madame de Gournay's fears of a desolate old age were put to rest when she died suddenly. With Charles away in Italy pursuing his military career, Marthe and Augustin too young to take responsibility, Madeleine married and Léonore now settled in the convent of Chanteloup, Jeanne's hopeless daughter, Marie, became the head of the family and caretaker of the estate. There was no time for reading or writing in the emotional turmoil and financial confusion.

Uncle Louis arrived and looked over the figures, announcing solemnly that the debts were greater than the estate. The war had seen to that, along with some very bad investments made by

Jeanne. When Charles's maintenance was taken into account, part of the money owed on Madeleine's dowry paid and the care of Marthe and Augustin added in (Léonore, at least, was a charge on the convent), there was a pittance left over for the estate and Marie's needs.

But there was a solution of sorts for the family: Louis had spoken to his friend the Maréchal de Balagny, Prince of Cambraisis, and his wife, the Maréchale, and they had agreed, old friends of their father, to take in Augustin and Marthe as well as Marie. Augustin would be made a page in their court and they had a young relative, Pierre de la Salle, who they felt might be just right for Marthe in a year or so. This would release the estate, now owned by Charles, to be sold and provide a dowry for Marthe and a small income for Marie. No one mentioned the need for Marie to have a dowry. She was pleased that they understood that she was destined for a finer sort of life. But she would only go with Augustin and Marthe to stay in Cambrai while they settled in. When everything was sorted out, and she had seen her younger siblings into their new life, she would take an apartment in Paris.

'Live on your own? That's out of the question,' Louis said, sounding almost like his late sister-in-law. 'You may stay with me. You can keep house and be a hostess for my guests. You will meet lots of people. What would you do alone in an apartment in Paris?'

'I'll study and write. I am going to be a published writer, Uncle. Writing is my profession.'

Marie did not think that living alone in Paris was out of the question. Yes, yes, she had never heard of any single woman doing such a thing as becoming a professional writer, and no, she did not need to be reminded that even the very few famous literary ladies had great and wealthy families behind them, and lived in fine houses with large retinues. Nonetheless, that was what she intended to do. With talent and determination, and as the spiritual daughter of the great Montaigne, she would be welcomed into the intellectual set in Paris. Her bravery, her social boldness, her self-belief was, Louis had to admit, astounding. But even so . . .

'A literary spinster? What will people think? And your mother would never . . .'

'I am now in charge. I will never marry. My only husband will be my honour, and I will espouse my writing,' Marie declared heroically. '*Literary spinster* seems to me a noble title.'

'But you can't afford to live in Paris on your own. There is not enough money. You need the financial and social protection of the Maréchal and his lady. At their court you can read and write, but without starving or causing a scandal.'

'I will earn money from my writing. I will get patronage from the Court, as other writers do.'

'But they are *men* and . . . well, their work is known.'

'I am the *fille d'alliance* of the great Michel de Montaigne and Justus Lipsius is on record as admiring my work. Do you think that counts for nothing? They will make sure that I am properly supported and known about by the right people, and I'm sure you will too, Uncle.'

'Yes, of course, I'll do what I can, but it's so irregular. I can't imagine what your poor mother would say,' trying again to encourage the development of a sense of duty or at least guilt from her bereavement.

'My poor mother is dead. What mother would not be proud of a daughter who made her way in life by her intellect, and who was already admired by some of the greatest thinkers in the world?'

Louis doubted that Jeanne's spirit was smiling down on her daughter, and he had an uncomfortable suspicion that the praise she had received from great, elderly men had more than a little to do with her youth and their dotage – he had read some of her poetry, and while it was full of noble sentiments and classical references, it lacked originality, and above all ease of expression. But he had no authority to forbid Marie's attempt to live out her unrealistic dreams. And after all, perhaps he didn't want to. There was something admirable about the girl. Her determination impressed him. Perhaps her work would develop a spark and she might make something of such a life. Indeed, he found he rather hoped so.

It took a long time to organise the estate and pay off the debts. In the meanwhile, holding firmly to her plan to live in Paris, Marie waited in Cambrai. She continued to write to Montaigne and intermittently got a brief letter in return, regretting the death of her mother, advising her to remain in Cambrai where the comfort and protection of the Prince and Princess would provide fine soil for her literary endeavours, and regretting that the world was such that still her visit to Guyenne remained out of the question. And never a mention of *The Promenade of Monsieur de Montaigne* or her poetry.

He wanted to think himself an honest man. And what man, on his deathbed, would not like to think so? But Montaigne couldn't let either of those statements pass uncritically, although his weary mind wished that his present frailty would allow him to get away with it. No, he still knew that there were many forms of vanity. Doubtless there were men who might lie dying, as he was, and console themselves with the thought that they had fooled the world entirely, or secretly corrupted numbers of innocents, or been wholly successful at covertly unmaking the happiness of others. They were not so alien to him as he would wish. He was, he knew, of their sort. His desire to have been an honest, honourable man was not greatly different from those other kinds of self-congratulation. His choice to be virtuous was always a considered decision rather than an urgent need compelled by his inner nature. Those like himself who are not innately good – and he had known only the one who truly was – take that option among the many, if they do, for much the same reasons that another man might decide to be a dissembler or a cheat: they consider it the best way for them to get on in this world and the next. The ones who choose goodness were also less brave, perhaps, using the moral structures that have been provided for them rather than casting out on their own to discover what they might. He was not a radical man. His decision to be good was the result of his moderation, and his moderation was very likely an effect of his cowardice. If he was to be ready to meet his maker; he told himself, if his maker was prepared to meet him, he had to acknowledge the circumstantial nature of his character. *If he was to meet his maker*. It had pleased him all his life to give the nod to the Almighty, but also to suppose that His ways and being were too unfathomable to require him to be more religious than his present society required. He had to confess, as this was a good time for confession, that like Abraham, he saw his future existence, such as it might be, only in the memory of those who had known him in this life, in the book he had written, and lasting, not an eternity, but just as long as those memories were passed down the generations, or the book survived. He could think no further than this in case the trembling from this ague was overwhelmed by another kind of trembling altogether.

For as long as Montaigne was not taken, his one true friend, his soul mate, Estienne La Boétie, continued to exist, like a soul might in God's heaven, in his thoughts. When the moment came – the darkness, his mind's dissolution – La Boétie, too, would be no more. He would be in his widow's memory, and some others who came across him in the Bordeaux Parliament, for as long as they might outlast Montaigne, but eventually, La Boétie would go out like a candle from this world, when their minds too gave up the ghost. So, like all of us, eventually there will be nothing of him left. All of us. Except . . . except . . . there was the book. For that reason Montaigne had planned to publish La Boétie's poetry in his own first volume. That they might be alive, together, between the covers of his book, after both of them were gone to dust. That he hadn't included La Boétie's poetry in the end was the result of circumstances. Political circumstances.

Perhaps other circumstances. But the book, in its three volumes, remained. There was the possibility that the book would survive down the years. If there were someone to care for it. To bring out new editions, to keep it alive in the mind of the world. Didn't Aristotle and Plutarch live on in his library in the tower, and in libraries around the world, so many centuries after they quit this existence? If even one copy of the book survived, neglected in a forgotten corner of a library, it would be something. It might be discovered centuries from now and reprinted. Read again. A resurrection, surely? What more was there to him than his thoughts written down? His body had long ago deserted him. He wouldn't hold on to it if he could. It pained him, let him down, humiliated him. He had no fondness for it, though it had served well enough in its day. But the time of thoughts written down is not so short as mere flesh, or need not be. And if he had to choose, would he dare to admit that he'd take that worldly posterity in preference to he knew not what in the hereafter? Would he dare quite to say so even to himself?

Still, he would like to believe that he had been an honest man regardless of his uncertainty about his motives. That was the form of vanity he had chosen. But here he was, close, very close to the final assessment, and doubts had come to him. Of course, he had been duplicitous where necessary. He was a human being living within the conditions of this world. He had told required lies for the purposes of good politics, good manners, thoughtfulness to others and a quiet time in the marital bed. Those daily lies did not preclude him from seeing himself as an honest man, where honest meant decent, honourable, true. In his writings he had indicated the untruths that a decent man must tell.

But there was something that would not let him rest complacent with his moderate decency and honesty. Something that gnawed irritatingly at the reasonable self-satisfaction he told himself he should be allowed. In all those nearly sixty years, he was truly dissatisfied only with his conduct in that one period four years before. And no matter how he explained it to himself, he couldn't quite rid himself of the accusation that he had been crucially dishonest.

He was ill, he was weary, he was lonely, but none of that should have permitted him to use the Gournay girl as he did. She offered him a place to stay, comfort, nursing and praise when he was weak in body and spirit. She was not a bad assistant, either; listening, taking dictation, pasting in his notes. That he took it all was perhaps forgivable. In return she received, deluded as she may have been, his company, which she desired more than anything in the world. But he was not honest with her when she spoke to him of her ambitions and showed him her work. He allowed her to chatter, without being either a good teacher or a good friend by correcting her where she was wrongheaded or excessive about the quality of her reading and writing. He did not tell her the truth when she showed him her poetry – banal, melodramatic, weighed down with the conventions and language of the past. Even that, he could excuse himself for, though he believed it did her no service. For she *was* remarkable. She loved reading, and had taught herself so much. Her poetry did not impress him, but her translations from Latin were, allowing for a certain pomposity, very creditable. Extraordinary considering her lack of education and encouragement. And that was, so he told himself, why he did not speak his opinion. Surely, she might improve. Her personal work was imitative, how could it not be? With time she might find her own way to write. She had (aside from her admiration for his own work) excellent taste in literature. Either she would see that her own was not good enough, or enough practice would allow her to relax, as he eventually had, and find a style and thoughts of her own. He had not wanted to discourage her, it's true, but it is truer that he did not have the will to engage with her ambition, to tell her what he really thought and spend a part of each day that he stayed with her helping her to improve her own work. He wanted urgently to concentrate on producing a new edition of the *Essays*, and time was limited.

What was entirely unforgivable, however, was that he might have allowed her to believe that they were closer, body and soul, than actually they were or ever could have been. Clumsy little creature with the face of a startled monkey. He was horribly disappointed by her looks when she came through the door in her Paris apartment, with her passionate words and adoration still echoing in his mind from the letter she wrote (in that she was effective or he was shamefully flatterable). And he was horrified by the bloody pantomime she enacted on her arm to prove her devotion to him. He feared that he would be burdened with her as Our Lord was burdened by his cross. He was no martyr. He had intended to dismiss her from his life when he left the Paris flat, but yes, when he needed to recuperate he pushed his physical hopes and mental doubts away and allowed her passion for him to improve his health and well-being.

There were moments in Gournay when he did not make his lack of physical interest in her perfectly clear. The days when almost any young woman who desired him made his manhood swell were long gone by then. He needed a much finer cuisine than she could provide to get his mouth watering. But occasionally he let her believe he might have feelings for her. He allowed his hand to remain in hers without withdrawing it immediately. He held the gaze of those staring, longing eyes for moments more than he should have. He even toyed with the idea of having carnal knowledge of her sometimes, and posed the sheer fact of youth against the plainness of her face and body. Did she not, after all, have the essential requisites an old man might be grateful to be offered regardless of the aesthetics? And though eventually his answer was always the same, he allowed her to think that he was considering disgracing her. She took his rejection of her longing as his gentlemanly refusal to compromise a young woman, and he did nothing to disabuse her.

When he left to get back to his regular life, he resolved, apart from the necessary letter of thanks, to allow the 'friendship' to wither. He had no trouble at all not remarking on the romance she sent him. A trite, dishonest story made far worse by her ridiculous moral interventions. The child had no notion of a mind, her mind, developing carefully over time. Nor really of careful thought and its uses. She spoke of improvement but behaved as if she were already fully fledged as a writer and thinker. Nor did he like the sly title that had no connection with the book but spoke public volumes of her intimate connection with him. But his silence on her story too was an act of cowardice. It would have served her better if he had written to her and told the truth, rather than pushing the manuscript out of sight and thinking no more about it. He did not do justice to her stated wish to improve herself. Occasionally, unease at the deluge of letters which arrived from her and were taken away by his manservant unread to be disposed of, caused him to write a note to her, brief, not at all familiar. His good manners got the better of him from time to time. Or some part of him that did not wish to seem callous to another human being. More evidence of his vanity.

And now, weak and failing once again, though this time without hope of recuperation, he was filled with guilt for his treatment of her, but also for a thought that had crept up on him in the midst of his self-confession, and, in spite of berating himself for his use of her, had given him an idea of using her further. His shame was shamelessly subservient to his desire to last in the world.

His wife and daughter took no interest in his work. Nor did either of them have the education to know how to maintain it. There was his dear, devoted friend, Pierre de Brach, who would work on the unfinished new edition of the *Essays*, but he couldn't expect the man's undivided devotion. He had his own writing, a wife, a life of his own. And he was not such a young man. La Demoiselle de Gournay had none of those distractions, whether she thought so or not, to keep her from devoting her time to his work, and she was young – she would live longer, well into the next century, than Pierre, especially if she remained a spinster, and she could take Montaigne's work with her. If, after Pierre made the important transcriptions, she were to be given charge of finding a printer in Paris, and with keeping the work alive, surely she would jump at the chance? It would give her some sort of income, purpose and status to become the posthumous keeper of his flame. It offered her a longed-for connection which would serve her ambitions well. Already she was using his name to boost her own work. A devotion to Montaigne's work would replace the husband she would never have, the quality work she would never produce, and the restricted life she must inevitably lead. So there was something in it for her, as well as for him and his memory. He decided to speak to Françoise about it, and ask her to send a farewell letter to La Demoiselle as if dictated by him. And yes, he knew how close this thought was to a crime against her. A further crime. He would have liked to think that he was not a dishonest man. But he was, after all, a man like any other.

It wasn't until April 1593, five years since Marie's only time in the company of her adopted father in Gournay, during an especially long silence from him, that the embargo on commerce between France and the Netherlands eased. Marie found another merchant in Cambrai to act as her courier, and packed up all the letters she had previously written and not sent to Justus Lipsius. She also added a new one in which she complained to him about the conditions in France that prevented her from seeing Montaigne.

The desperate times dreadfully hinder the further development of my uneducated mind by depriving me of the joy and learning of my father's presence; he whom I possessed for only two or three months so long ago. It is like a terrible bereavement. It must end at any cost. I don't need to tell you, the defender of the *Essays*, what anguish it is to be deprived of such a beloved friend for almost five years . . . especially for so loving and sensitive a soul as myself . . . It is impossible for me to have known his presence and to endure his absence – all the more so because for all I know with every year I fail to see him, I may be losing half the time he has yet to live. Tell me how long is it since you have heard from my father: it is more than six months since I had a letter from him.

It was more than that, but Marie could not bear to think, let alone write that she had not heard from him for almost an entire year. A month later, a reply arrived from Lipsius.

Virgo nobilis, I have received and read your letters with delight. I long to see you and speak with you, and I do not despair of doing so this summer if I go to Douai or somewhere nearby.

He told her that his health was a little up and down, and without skipping a rhetorical or grandiloquent beat continued by giving her the news she was waiting for.

We are feeble creatures, yet a privileged species and of celestial origin, but chained to this earth. Happy are those who have left the world and are free from it. Your adopted father is now one of them. I bring you this news if you have not heard it since you wrote – I confirm it if you know already: he is no more. What am I saying? The great Montaigne has left us: he has gone above to the ethereal heights. The news came to me from Bordeaux, and as your last letter was some time ago I suppose that you, too, are suffering from this grievous loss. But why think of his end as a misfortune? He would smile at us if he knew we were lamenting. I imagine he greeted death gaily and that he triumphed over her just as she seemed to be vanquishing him. He has departed: we too will depart. Why should we not wish to leave a world so privately and publicly undesirable? I love you, O maiden, but as I love wisdom, chastely. Love me in the same way and, since he whom you called father is no longer in this world, accept me as your brother.

Montaigne was dead.

Actually dead, not just in her imagination and fears. And so just as life promised to begin, for a second time, but this time properly and actively to begin, at the age of twenty-seven and by no means young any longer, it was over, it seemed, for Marie de Gournay.

This time the Maréchale had to administer the tincture of hellebore and put Marie to bed. There may be some, nearer to the end of their life, with much time already lived through, familiar with disappointment, used to so many ordinary days of breathing and performing necessary duties – who find it hard really to feel the despair of a twenty-seven-year-old woman who sees her desired future come to a blank halt. It might seem to them almost enviable not to have to know yet that life goes on, that one goes on.

The dashing (again) of Marie's hopes happened because of her ability to hope so grandly. And even as she mourned the loss of the man she hadn't seen for so long, and of his patronage, there was a small furious corner of her mind working to keep her plans alive. Montaigne had died, but her self-belief remained, wounded, outraged by the setback, but firm and determined like the fierce black pupils of her eyes that gleamed on brightly even when she wept her heart out.

While he was alive Montaigne's relation to her had been tenuous after he had taken his leave of her in Gournay. The few letters, his refusal to allow her – on account of the danger – to go to him in Guyenne, the well-mannered greetings and hopes for her continued health, the absolute silence on the subject of her writings, had all kept the creature that chewed away at her insides fed and watered. With the arrival of Lipsius's letter and his terrible news, the anguish of her unacknowledged doubt at her mentor's silences and refusals began to weaken, to subside. Her certainty about her adopted father's love and admiration was no longer threatened by his absence and a dearth of letters, nor, when his letters came, by his neglect of her work, of the book, her book, her first book, and her poetry, that she sent him to show him what she might be capable of. If there were to be no more letters ever, that was terrible, and her heart was broken, but equally, yes, equally, if there were to be no more letters that disappointed her, that failed her hopes and expectations, then she was free to speculate on what he might have written if he had not been so cruelly taken from her. If she could never see him again, this side of the afterlife, she did not have to face even the possibility that he might not demonstrate the extraordinary degree of love and admiration she could now know with absolute conviction he bore her. It was catastrophic that he had died, her own life was cut off with his loss, and yet, as she lay tossing and turning on her bed, weeping and mad with grief for the father she had so briefly met, who had spent so little time with her, but who had loved and understood her as no one ever had, in that small fearful place inside her the weight, whose existence she had hardly acknowledged, gradually but quite perceptibly began to lighten.

3

For some weeks after she heard about Montaigne's death, she was prostrated with grief, and on the authority of the Maréchale, Louise – who had accompanied Marie with her sister and brother to Cambrai – once again prepared the hellebore. The worst of it was that he had died so far away, and it had been so long before she knew of it. Montaigne had in fact been absent from the world during all those months when she had believed him still to be living and breathing, possibly at any given moment writing her a letter, thinking of her. And there was a precise moment when he had died, in September of the previous year, nine whole months before she received Lipsius's letter. It was a moment she had lived through in Cambrai quite normally, without knowing that in Guyenne he was taking and expelling his last breath. She repeatedly tried to relive that moment. To participate in his going.

She also wondered at the silence in those nine months following his death. She heard nothing from the family, though as his adopted daughter she surely deserved their consideration. Was his death so very sudden that he had no time to bid farewell to his *fille d'alliance*, and offer her a few last words of hope about her future? Marie took steps to find out, in spite of her depleted condition. In the most implacable mourning and heavily veiled, she took a coach to Chartres where she had heard that her adopted father's cousin, Raymond de Montaigne, was to be found. Perhaps he could tell her if her name had been on his cousin's lips in those last hours. But though he was in Chartres, he had not been in Guyenne when Montaigne died and knew nothing about his end.

Marie returned to Cambrai and before re-immersing herself in her prostration, she wrote a letter to Madame de Montaigne, telling her they were, both of them, the most miserable women in France, in the world, to have lost such a husband and father. The world too had lost its only modern sage ('Who truly understands except for you and I that the Socrates of our time is no more?'), but only they knew the greatness of the human being who was lost, since only they possessed the intimate knowledge and understanding of the man himself. (Though, in truth, she felt, but naturally did not say, that Madame de Montaigne was not intellectually equipped to fully grasp the loss of her husband to the world. Her loss was merely emotional. Marie included her in the larger understanding only out of politeness.) She begged her adopted mother to tell her of Montaigne's last hours, if the pain of recalling it was not too great (but then how could it be greater than knowing nothing, and being so far from his deathbed?). She reminded Madame de Montaigne of the esteem in which Marie held her husband's work and how she had assisted him with it and understood completely what his intentions were. How, also, her husband had admired her comprehension of his work. She was aware that Mademoiselle Léonor, charming and loving natural daughter though she was, had little interest in literature. If there was anyone who could take the terrible burden from his grieving widow of trusteeship of the *Essays*, and cherishing the first posthumous edition into print, it would be his equally grieving but intellectually capable other devoted daughter and disciple. She signed herself: Your devoted, grief-stricken daughter.

Another long wait. A very long wait. The winter passed, dead and devoid of future, and another year arrived, a year that Montaigne would not be part of. He was nowhere in the world, and nor, as a consequence, was she. She felt let loose, lost and pointless, in pointless Picardy. It was not until the spring of that year, 1594, that Marie received an answer to her letter. This was the package that contained the copy of Montaigne's annotated edition in his study, which Pierre de Brach had worked on in the months since their author's death, the manuscript of the novel she had sent to Montaigne and heard nothing about these past six years, and the note from Madame de Montaigne. It was indeed a catastrophe to lose such a husband, the widow agreed, and she was moved and grateful for La Demoiselle de Gournay's devotion to his memory. He had died in the manner he would have wished, calmly, without complaint, making his peace with God and taking the last rites as the devout Catholic he was. Madame de Montaigne was very sorry to hear that Mademoiselle de Gournay did not receive the letter she had sent via her late husband's brother, Monsieur de la Brousse, in which she conveyed Montaigne's farewell to his adopted daughter. But letters were so easily mislaid in these troubled times. She hoped, now, that Mademoiselle de Gournay, being so near the capital, would consent to arrange for publication in Paris of the enclosed revised edition of the *Essays*, checked and copied by Montaigne's good friend Pierre de Brach. And, of course, if Mademoiselle de Gournay ever found herself in the locality of Guyenne she should make every effort to visit herself and her daughter.

Marie immediately began to make arrangements to be in the locality of Guyenne, writing by return that she would be arriving to visit 'her family' as soon as she had checked the manuscript (doubtless perfectly revised, but every text can benefit from another eye on it) and arranged for the publication of the new edition of the *Essays*, which, Madame de Montaigne would be pleased to learn, would include a Preface written by his adopted daughter putting the world to shame for its failure properly to appreciate the greatness of the writer, and even, in some cases, criticising him. Madame need have no concern that she would fail to deal with these criticisms with the scorn they deserved and a full exposition of their errors. It pained her that she could not respond immediately to Madame's invitation to go and spend time with her family in Guyenne, but she had responsibilities that could not be put off merely to satisfy her own passionate desire to meet them, and tread in the footsteps of her mentor and father in his very own place of meditation and work. There were things of a family (her other family) nature to clear up, an apartment in Paris to be found and work to be done on the manuscript of the *Essays* as well as the Preface to write, so she would be obliged to remain in the north until her tasks were finished. She was to be expected at the château in the autumn of the following year – 1595 – just a month or two before she hoped to arrange publication of her new edition of the *Essays*. The delay wrenched at her heart, but their meeting to share their recollections of the man, the love of whom made them sisters of the soul, would be all the sweeter for the anticipation.

The package from the widow of Michel de Montaigne marked yet another beginning, the true beginning of Marie's career as a woman of letters. It was a phrase she would often use about herself. 'Speaking as a woman of letters,' she would say before making some pronouncement of an intellectual or literary nature. She would say it in public and she would say it when there was no one else to hear but the cat or a servant. It was not to be forgotten. In much the same way, she referred to Montaigne always as 'my father'. Her tone suggested pride, arrogance even, but it also marked out for herself her right to speak, even if she was only speaking to a cat and a servant. The phrases were spoken when no one was present at all. *Montaigne, my father. As a woman of letters, I must say* . . . It was not only other people she had to convince.

As soon as it was possible after the manuscript arrived, Marie left for Paris, and, with the help of Uncle Louis, found an apartment in the rue des Haudriettes. It was much larger than she needed and too grand, far more expensive to rent and keep up than she could afford, but she explained to Louis, who could hardly disagree, that as a single woman living alone, she needed to have a respectable place to live and receive company. After the family debts were settled, she had barely enough money to survive, but things, she was certain, would get better for the editor of Montaigne. Louis was quite impressed that the new edition, the first posthumous edition of the *Essays*, had been entrusted to her. Unheard-of though it might be for a single woman to set up a household of her own, he relented about the apartment, in any case somewhat relieved to know that no offer of his to have Marie live with him would be accepted. Louise accompanied her to the rue des Haudriettes where she set up her first establishment. The furniture and fittings were somewhat sparse, but Louise made the place as comfortable as possible while Marie organised her books and study in a room next to her bedroom. Before she settled to the task of preparing the manuscript Madame de Montaigne had sent her, she found a printer, and with the promise of good sales from the first posthumous publication of the *Essays* soon to come, he agreed also to print the manuscript that had accompanied them in the parcel for no more than cost. The book she had called *The Promenade of Monsieur de Montaigne* along with the letter she had written to him accompanying the manuscript were to be published together as soon as possible, before the *Essays*. Her first book. A romance with a dedication by the daughter of the great writer to her mentor. To be published well before she left for Guyenne. That settled, the printing under way and booksellers informed of its imminent arrival, she returned to the matter of the *Essays*.

There was no editing work to do, the widow told her. Pierre de Brach had spent many hours in the study in the tower transferring Montaigne's written notes and amendments from the disbound copy of the 1588 edition to this second copy, marked up and ready for the printer. But Marie nevertheless felt it was her duty to examine the manuscript closely from beginning to end in order to be absolutely sure that all was as it should be – certainly Pierre de Brach was a close friend of Montaigne and a fine poet but she needed to be certain that no errors had crept in, no misunderstandings of Montaigne's thoughts that needed correcting. *She* was Montaigne's designated editor and keeper of his book. She had no doubt at all that this was what his last letter to her contained, the one he had dictated to his wife on his deathbed. Madame de Montaigne had not mentioned the content of the lost letter – doubtless making up the parcel had plunged her once again into that first grief at his loss – but the fact that she had sent her the manuscript and asked her to look over it and have it published was proof enough for Marie of Madame's late husband's intentions. It was nothing less than heroic of her adopted mother to recognise her literary limitations and accede to her husband's wishes, though she might perhaps have done it sooner. It was kind of Pierre de Brach to work on the new edition, and understandable that a duplicate had to be made from the treasured copy Montaigne had worked on himself, but if she had been contacted sooner, in the weeks after his death, rather than a year and a half later, she could have travelled to Guyenne and done the necessary collating herself. But never mind. She of all people knew the pain that his loss caused. His widow and his friend could be forgiven for their distracted thinking.

Some weeks after first receiving the package from Madame de Montaigne, she sat down at her new desk in the new Paris apartment in front of the disbound copy of the *Essays* with Montaigne's additions duplicated on it in the margins and on pasted-in slips of paper, and took a deep, settling breath. She put Books I and III to one side and opened Book II, leafing through it until she came to the essay, 'On Presumption'. She continued briskly to turn the pages until she arrived at what she was looking for: the page with a piece of paper pasted in and a cross inked in the margin to indicate where the passage was to be added. It was written in the hand of Pierre de Brach, not, of course, Montaigne's as she had seen it the first time.

I have taken pleasure in making public in several places the hope I have for Marie de Gournay, my adopted daughter, whom I love indeed as a daughter of my own. If youthful promise means any-thing, her soul will some day be capable of the finest things. The judgement she made of the first Essays, she, a woman, in this century, so young, alone in her part of the country, and the good will she devoted to me simply on the strength of the esteem she had for me before she even knew me, are particulars worthy of special consider-ation.

This was her place in the *Essays*, the only place in the entire work where her name was mentioned. He had shown her the acknowledgement the day after he added the words to the essay, just before he left Gournay. She read it over again several times. Why did it give her so little pleasure? He named her his *fille d'al-liance* and spoke admiringly of her abilities and her potential. Yet, when she read it the first time, and again now, she had a dull feel-ing of disappointment. She couldn't understand exactly why. After a moment, with an irritated shake of the head, she put the pages of Book II back together, pushed it to the far edge of her desk, pulled Book I towards her, and settled herself with her quill and inkpot at the ready to read over the entire manuscript metic-ulously, word by word, from the beginning, as was her duty and the greatest honour she could ever have imagined.

Montaigne had not written any new essays after the 1588 edi-tion was published, the one that had come out just before he spent time with Marie in Gournay. That last publication had included the new third book of extraordinary essays, the longest and most intimate, but there he allowed it to rest. He had spent the remaining four years of his life going through his work adding thoughts, qualifying others, entirely changing his mind on some occasions and saying so, or taking off on long tangents which sometimes seemed to be, integrated though they were into the original essays, almost new essays themselves. Second, third and fourth thoughts were inked over much of the white space around and between the printed words of the 1588 edition he worked on. Some of these Marie had seen for herself while helping Montaigne with his work in Gournay, but there were a great many new additions which were made after his recuperative visit to her and before death drew what might have been an endless reconsideration to a conclusion. She read slowly and carefully. Not having the original copy of the annotated manuscript she had no way of knowing for certain that Pierre de Brach had not missed anything. She would have to take it on trust for this new edition, which, she agreed, should be brought out with all speed in order to keep Montaigne's star bright in the literary world. When she made her visit to Guyenne she could prepare the next edition entirely herself from the original source. So, after all, there was not a great deal that needed to be done apart from making certain insertions clearer for the printer.

Several days into her nonetheless careful reading of the manuscript she discovered that the passage he added to 'On Presumption' was not, in fact, the only mention of her. She was still working on Book I, and had reached the essay entitled 'The Taste of Good and Evil Things Depends on Our Opinion of Them', when she found, after some examples of women who considered pain a lesser evil than ugliness or ageing ('*Who has not heard of that woman of Paris who had herself flayed alive merely to acquire a fresh colour from a new skin?*'), an added passage about those for whom pain was overcome by their desire to give greater credit to their word.

> *. . . I personally saw a girl who, to prove the earnestness of her promises as well as her constancy, took the pin she wore in her hair and jabbed herself four or five times in the arm, breaking the skin and bleeding herself in good earnest.*

Marie gasped. She put down her pen and hastily loosened the lacing at her wrist until it opened enough for her to pull the sleeve up and reveal her left forearm. Those pinpricks were still there, pale spots of healed skin memorialised against the darker surrounding flesh. They ran up her arm from wrist to elbow, a zigzag patterning of the passion she wanted Montaigne to understand was without limit. There she was in his pages again. But so distant, so indistinct – as those white spots on her arm were not. '*I personally saw a girl . . .*' She might almost have read it and passed by, so remote, so faceless was this girl, such a blank example, seen and remembered by Montaigne, but as no more than a glancing instance among many to prove his argument. The '*I personally saw*' so much more emphatic and solid than '*a girl*'. A particular girl, in fact, who had stabbed herself to prove her love and devotion to him. Was she no more specific than the vain creature who had had herself flayed alive? Was her action only of interest, not her qualities? How that anonymous, non-specific '*girl*' stung. For a moment before she recognised herself, she pictured a foolish, over-excitable, inarticulate creature, an immature girl indeed, not a serious young woman demonstrating the depth of her mind and feelings, for whom bodily pain was nothing compared to her metaphysics of love. '*I personally saw . . .*' The eyewitness to an excessive, even ridiculous act. She felt the blood rush to her face. Something inside her chest contracted sharply and pulled tight. Then it passed.

She re-read and this time read differently. It was an essay about the variability of the world according to how people perceived it. The woman who stripped her skin to look fresher was a quite different example to the women, the one woman in particular, who offered their pain as proof of their sincerity. Was that not what the martyrs had done? Montaigne was, of course, she realised now, protecting her by making her anonymous, and keeping private the mutual truth of that first passionate meeting when she had stabbed herself, and he, as impulsively, had offered to become her father. He had protected her by not naming her or describing the circumstances that made it much more than a frivolous act, but still that phrase '*a girl*' displeased her. She remained too distant, too undifferentiated. There she was, where she wanted to be, in the pages of his essays, but deprived of her singularity. Deprived of the very special relationship between her and the author. No, she would not want to be named, but . . .

She picked up her pen and dipped it into the ink. After the words '*a girl*' she made an insertion mark, and in the margin wrote '*from Picardy*' so that the printed version would read

> *...I personally saw a girl from Picardy who, to prove the earnestness of her promises as well as her constancy, took the pin she wore in her hair and jabbed herself four or five times in the arm, breaking the skin and bleeding herself in good earnest.*

It simply made his point clearer. Made the girl more real. Placed her as an individual known to the author. It did not violate Montaigne's intentions. Clearly that girl was her. The reader was entitled, in a work that relied so much on intimate knowledge of the author, to the added clue as to the identity of the girl, as well as to the fact that the writer was, in this case, more than a distant, uninvolved observer. '*I personally saw . . .*'

She continued with her reading. Correcting a slip of the pen here, a doubtful grammatical formation there in Pierre de Brach's annotations. Once or twice the point of her quill hovered for a bare second over a printed word or phrase, a bird not quite daring to peck at something unidentified but interesting. Something she thought might be improved, which was perhaps not entirely correct or elegant French, a resounding Gasçonism that sounded alarmingly coarse to her fine-tuned literary ear. But the hesitation always passed without her dipping the nib into ink and making a mark to substitute her word for his. Only Pierre de Brach's annotations were changed and of course not Montaigne's additions, but what she determined were Brach's misguided attempted improvements to or misunderstandings of the copied edits. Things she was perfectly certain were not Montaigne's intentions.

Eventually, she arrived back at the passage that referred to her by name in 'On Presumption'. In some sense she had never left it. She had felt it getting closer, as though the words on the page were moving to meet her while she read through them. Her place in the *Essays*. Where she was recognised and named as the worthy keeper of Montaigne's posterity. She arrived at the place and sat for a long time staring sightlessly through the window in

160

front of her, while the words on the leaf pasted to the page waited on the desk in the silence, mute and prim.

I have taken pleasure in making public in several places the hope I have for Marie de Gournay, my adopted daughter, whom I love indeed as a daughter of my own. If youthful promise means anything, her soul will some day be capable of the finest things. The judgement she made of the first Essays, she, a woman, in this century, so young, and alone in her part of the country, and the good will she devoted to me simply on the strength of the esteem she had for me before she even knew me, are particulars worthy of special consideration.

What she saw through her middle-distance stare was the morning she had sat in the chair beside him and he had shown her the passage. How through the window just to one side and behind them, the one where she stood each day to watch him disappearing down the path for his daily solitary walk, the sunlight slanted in and bathed the page, him and her too, in cold morning light. The rest of the room was in deep shadow, the stone walls still radiating the night's chill. She had been aware of him close and watching her while she read, and when she looked up, there was an expectant smile on his face, as if he had given her a present. Not a rose, brought back from his morning walk that proved he had thought of her while he wandered alone. He had never done such an absurdly emotional thing as that, of course. He smiled like Uncle Louis did when he presented her with a book he had brought from Paris. The chill in the room enveloped her as she read his words about her, and then looked up to see that amused, avuncular smile. It must have simply been the cool of the morning reaching through the light stuff of her summer dress. But there was, she couldn't help remembering it now, a rush of disappointment at the words and his look, as the bright expectancy in her mind and heart as she sat down to read plummeted to an unfathomable, unfetchable place inside her. A precious stone rolling off the edge of a cliff and swallowed by a boiling sea. It was more than she could ever have expected; but it was not enough. Her face clouded and the lines hardened, the mouth small and tight, the eyes a beady glare, but only for a moment until his look of surprise at her response blew the cloud away.

She came back to the present, dropped her eyes to the hand-written text and read it once again. There was something wrong with it. A new recollection brought the passage she had read five years before back vividly, its length, the pattern of the sentences, even particular words. She looked again. It was different. It was possibly shorter than she remembered, and there were certain phrases that she recalled very clearly which were missing in Pierre de Brach's transcription. Had Montaigne's friend diluted the passage dedicated to her? He had changed it, she was certain. Cut phrases out. Had he done it from envy? There was no such acknowledgement of him in the *Essays*. He could not accidentally have left out what was missing, some sentences were quite rewritten in order to make sense of his cuts. Marie was not surprised to discover herself resented and worked against for her special relationship with Montaigne.

It was the first time she grasped the depth of the world's jealousy of their understanding and her position in his life and work. She realised that it would not be the last. She must learn to expect the anger of an intellectual world that saw itself sidelined for a mere girl.

A young woman. A woman given trusteeship of a masterpiece. It was not going to be an easy life being the executor of her father's legacy, and fulfilling the promise of her own work that he saw and encouraged. So be it. Her memory of the passage she first read seven years before now had the clarity of an illuminated manuscript. She took up her pen and dipped it into the inkwell. She worked on the pasted-in slip of paper, adding, amending and crossing out according to the bright picture of the original she held in her mind.

I have taken pleasure in making public in several places the hope I have for Marie **le Jars** *de Gournay ,* *my adopted daughter,* [~~whom I love indeed as a daughter of my own~~] **who is loved by me with more than a fatherly love, and cherished in my retirement and solitude as one of the best parts of my own being. She is the only person I have regard for.** *If youthful promise means anything, her soul will some day be capable of the finest things,* **among others of perfection in that most sacred kind of friendship which, so we read, her sex has not yet been able to attain. The sincerity and firmness of her character are already sufficient, her affection for me more than overflowing, and such, in short, that it leaves nothing to be desired, if only her dread of my death, in view of my fifty-five years when I met her, would not torment her so cruelly.** *The judgement she made of the first Essays, she, a woman, in this century, so young, and alone in her part of the country, and the* **remarkable eagerness with which she loved me and yearned for my friendship for so long a time,** [~~good will she devoted to me~~] *simply on the strength of the esteem she had for me before she even knew me, are particulars worthy of special consideration.*

By the time she had finished, the pasted-in slip of paper was not fit for the printer. Much better, she decided, to make a fair copy. She called Louise and told her to mix up a paste and then took a loose leaf from a sheaf in her drawer and wrote on it in a clear and careful hand, quite unlike the scrawl of her amendments. The paste was ready by the time she had finished. When the ink was dry, she gently pulled away the loose leaf with Pierre de Brach's addition and her corrections and replaced it with the new clearly written one, pasting it carefully over the small mark left on the printed page by the original amendment.

I have taken pleasure in making public in several places the hope I have for Marie le Jars de Gournay, my adopted daughter, who is loved by me with more than a fatherly love, and cherished in my retirement and solitude as one of the best parts of my own being. She is the only person I have regard for. If youthful promise means anything, her soul will some day be capable of the finest things, among others of perfection in that most sacred kind of friendship which, so we read, her sex has not yet been able to attain. The sincerity and firmness of her character are already sufficient, her affection for me more than overflowing, and such, in short, that it leaves nothing to be desired, if only her dread of my death, in view of my fifty-five years when I met her, would not torment her so cruelly. The judgement she made of the first Essays, she, a woman, in this century, so young, and alone in her part of the country, and the remarkable eagerness with which she loved me and yearned for my friendship for so long a time, simply on the strength of the esteem she had for me before she even knew me, are particulars worthy of special consideration.

These were the only two places in the work of Michel de Montaigne where Marie de Gournay inserted herself. In the other thousand and more pages, she attended to his words, making sure they were his own and that they conveyed his intentions as she alone understood them. She was the wet nurse to his posterity. If she infiltrated a little posterity for herself, pointed more directly to the passionate girl from Picardy, and intensified the author's stated love and admiration for his adopted daughter, it was perhaps understandable. His memory and his words were all she had to prove to herself that she was worthy of the remarkable honour of being his editor. If she imposed herself as more beloved than Montaigne's natural daughter, actually differently beloved, it was to give her the authority the world needed in order to accept her as his champion, just as much as to show the world that he was her champion. It allowed her to be ready to write her Preface to this first posthumous edition. It would be clear from Montaigne's own words in the *Essays* themselves that she was the right person to do it and that she had not only his blessing and his love, but also his astonished admiration. Her additions were understandable. They were also the result of an uncontrollable desire to make publicly true what she needed to be true more than she needed the air to breathe.

Marie is alone. It is 1595, she is thirty years old and for seven years her life has been a desert . . . She sits in the tower library she has dreamed of and longed for since Michel de Montaigne left Gournay to return home to his life and death here in Guyenne. On the desk in front of her is the original copy of the *Essays* with his amendments of the past seven years added to the pages in his own hand – the only up-to-date one that exists, now that Pierre de Brach's copy of it has been destroyed by the printer of her new edition. It is disbound, loosely laced and open. She is bent over it. With one hand she is steadying the page, the other hand is carefully manipulating a piece of paper attached to it.

It is easy enough to pull the loose leaf away from the page, gently, so that it seems that nothing violent has happened, leaving behind for posterity just enough evidence of the dried paste that had attached the leaf to the end of 'On Presumption'. It would be seen that he had written something that had been lost – and yet not lost, because Marie de Gournay has published it in the new edition from the copy sent to her with the missing amendments noted. It is an elegy in the midst of the essays, to Marie de Gournay, commending his adopted daughter to his readers, telling of her qualities that put her beyond the usual accomplishments of women, and declaring that he loved her more than a daughter of his own. Her amendment of his addition to the essay in the newly published volume is now the only evidence of the leaf of missing words that could so easily have fluttered away as the pages were turned and worked over by Pierre de Brach while he copied. The paper she now crumples in her hand contains her father's elegy to her. Her destruction of the loose leaf with the original note on it is not a lie, exactly. It is an absence. Her embellishments were made only in order to make her a more authoritative keeper of his flame.

In any case, her additions were true; a truth he had omitted. She *was* capable of friendship like no other woman Montaigne had known. Had they only had the time together, he would have seen that La Boétie was not the only individual in the world capable of sharing the great man's soul. There were two such individuals. Nothing he said about the friendship with the dead old man was absent from her soul's capacity to be his beloved friend. *Because it was he, because it was I.* Yes. But he had been so busy mourning his one true friend that he had failed to find the other, the one he had actually been looking for, writing for. '*I hope that if my humours happen to please and suit some decent man, before I die he will try to meet me . . . If on good evidence I knew a man who was right for me I would certainly go far to find him, for in my judgement the sweetness of well-matched and compatible fellowship can never cost too much. O! a friend!*' He had asked for her. He had found her. Rather, she had found him. Yet mysteriously he didn't hold on to her with all his strength. He had made her his *fille d'alliance*, but, incomprehensibly, not that friend he cried out for.

Yesterday when she re-read those words about his longing for another friend in 'On Vanity', she came across a passage that had been crossed out.

I know well that I will leave behind no sponsor anywhere near as affectionate and understanding about me as I was about him. There is no one to whom I would be willing to entrust myself fully for a portrait; he alone enjoyed my true image, and carried it away. That is why I decipher myself so painstakingly.

She had read these lines before, in Gournay, in this 1588 published edition. As Pierre de Brach had indicated on the copy she worked on in Paris, he had crossed it out. But there was something new to her: before he crossed the printed passage out, he had added a line in ink after the word *portrait*. That was crossed out too, presumably when he deleted the whole paragraph, but it was there before it was deleted, and he must have added it after the last time she had looked at the book while he was in Gournay, because she had never seen it before.

. . . and if there should be any, I repudiate them, for I know them to be excessively prejudiced in my favour.

La Boétie was the true friend and knew the true Montaigne; she was merely excessively prejudiced? But she knew, whatever he said, that the words she had added to the newly published edition, making her his rightful replacement for La Boétie, were not lies, they were simply a truth that had been unrecognised by Montaigne. Yesterday, she had wept at his desk, seeing those words he'd added. Then she had stopped weeping, because hadn't he also crossed them out? It was surely more than a gentlemanly consideration for her feelings. It was a change of mind. One that his death, and the mysterious loss of his dictated final letter to her, had prevented him from doing anything more about. She was convinced. And so, there was nothing more deceitful in taking the loose leaf from the solitary example of his intentions and feelings for his literary executor, and letting her own additions stand than there was in observing his wishes and keeping the other, deleted, paragraph out of the edition to come out next. She would, all the better to preserve his wishes, have taken it away from this Bordeaux copy, had it been written on a separable piece of paper like his elegy to her, and not inked on to the printed page. What was a small editorial deceit in return for, and necessary for, the immortality her attention to his work would give him? Almost certainly she only put the words into the text that he would have put there himself if he had thought to do it, or known that he wouldn't have the time to add them later. Making clear; making things true that *were* true – that could be done. That was an editor's task.

Marie's unquestioning faith in words made sentences on the page truer than events that happen in the world or the things that happen between people. She had taught herself to translate Latin into French, and language into life. Language was capable of realising her dreams and hopes. When she read words, her own or others, they became all the reality she needed. Or at least, they gave her a place and a way to live where the wishes and whims of other people, and her own unsuspected limitations, did not turn her life to dust. Words gave meaning to Marie and she came to believe that meaning was only meaning when it was written down. Most especially, meaning was only meaning and the truth only existed once *she* had written it down.

When she received the package containing the manuscript of

the *Essays* from Madame de Montaigne, Marie de Gournay became the phoenix. From the ashes of Montaigne's mortal remains she rose up, his memory her sustenance, his spirit her soul, his work her work. Her pen was dipped in the blood of her father and her words winged across the page. The problem was that they were, after all, her words, their wings dark and heavy, and obliged to beat the air brutally in order to remain in flight. It was not enough for her to be reborn from his ashes, she had to be a bird of the air as well.

In the Preface to the new edition which she wrote before she left for her visit to Guyenne, she did not forget to thank Madame de Montaigne for entrusting her with her late husband's work, or rather complying with his wishes. And she did it in her own effortful style. Regretting the absence of letters of praise known to have been written by Justus Lipsius and Lord Ossat, she describes the latter as '*the person in Italy . . . best loved and esteemed by my Father – and I cannot, Reader, use another name for him, for I am not myself except insofar as I am his daughter. It is scarcely a reflection on the diligent search made by Madame de Montaigne that she had not found the letters amongst his papers after his death, when she sent me these last writings to publish . . . Everyone owes her, if not so much gratitude, at least as much praise as I accord her for having wished to rekindle and rewarm in me the ashes of her husband, and, not to marry him, but to make of herself another him – reviving in herself at his death an affection in which she had never participated except by hearing of it – and so truly to restore to him a new appearance of life by the continuation of the friendship that he bore me.*'

Did she wonder what Madame would make of this, or was it written without any other reader in mind but her beloved Montaigne, *her* beloved Montaigne? Was she soaring entirely on the currents of her own self-belief, so that it never occurred to her that her words would be read by other sentient beings? She went on to explain her entitlement to take on the task of ensuring that her father's work was available for future generations. On the doubts the *Essays* raised in some minds about Montaigne's commitment to the Catholic religion she said:

It is I who have the right to speak in this regard, for I alone was perfectly acquainted with that great soul, and it is I who have the right to be trusted on this subject when his book does not clarify it, as someone who has relinquished so many magnificent, rich, and admired virtues, which the world glories in, to incur the reproach of silliness from my fellow women for having nothing to my lot but innocence and sincerity.

She dismissed the inevitable question of her sex in the matter of speaking the mind of Montaigne:

Blessed indeed are you, Reader, if you are not of a sex that has been forbidden all possessions, is forbidden liberty, has even been forbidden all the virtues . . . As for me, if I wish to put my auditors to the sort of examination that involves, it is said, strings that female fingers cannot touch, even had I the arguments of Carneades, there is no one so much a weakling that he will not rebuke me, to the grave approbation of the company present, with a smile, a nod, or some jest, which will have the effect of saying, 'It is a woman speaking.'

So remarkable, her self-belief, and where from? Only herself. There was nowhere else it could have come from. Whatever her flaws, is not that self-belief alone enough to guarantee her greatness and posterity's respect? But, of course, she did have her male sponsor to prove her confidence:

Now one thing consoled me against those who have mocked my relations with Montaigne, or rather who hold my sex or myself otherwise in disdain; that is, that they have infallibly declared themselves to be fools, insofar as they have proved that a man such as Montaigne was one when he esteemed me worthy, not only of a different estimation, but of being admitted as a soul equal to his own in the sort of association ours was, as long as God permitted it. But our kind, because we are slight and weakling, is fittingly the target of the magnanimous courage that exists in that variety of man. Nevertheless, I advise them in friendship not to take on those who are so strong with their pens; you have to kill such people as much as wound them; take away their strength or do not inflame their hearts . . . To offend a rare spirit is to ensure, as if by an act of conscience, that one's fault will be repented. We see how it took Minos to kindle the verve of those chattering Athenians.

But only with the mind of Montaigne could she be so extraordinary an example of her sex:

. . . nature having done me so much honour that, except in the greatest and the least respects, I was wholly like my Father, I cannot take a step, whether in writing or speaking, without finding myself in his footsteps; and I believe that I am often supposed to usurp him. And

the only time that I have ever been content with myself was when,
amongst the recent additions you will see in this volume, I encountered
a number of things that I had imagined in just the same way before
seeing them.

In the rest of the Preface she dealt, contemptuously, with what she saw as a lukewarm response in some quarters and answered further criticisms that lesser minds had dared to make of the *Essays.* They were blind. His unorthodox use of language, his crudely personal references to his body, his waywardness of structure, his irrelevant digressions, were all signs to Marie of the greatness and originality of the man; of work in advance of its time. She championed his every word and battled the dull minds who wanted to keep everything unchanging, who devoted themselves to dull rhetoric instead of vivid, flashing human thought.

The Promenade of Monsieur de Montaigne was published before she made the journey to Guyenne, and sold quite well to an audience with a ready taste for romantic drama. It was not, however, as gratifying an event to Marie as it should have been. Montaigne's now eternal silence about her manuscript encased the success of the book like a caul. It could never be other than stillborn in such an unredeemed state, and she found she could not take proper pleasure in it, even if it briefly gave her a small income. Clearly, she was, as Montaigne had said when she told him the story she intended to turn into a romance, destined to write much more substantial work. She was an intellectual, not a provider of frivolity for idle minds. She couldn't stop herself from publishing it when it came into her hands, nor even from reprinting it, but it didn't bring her the sense of at last having become the kind of writer she longed to be. She decided that it was her name on the first posthumous edition of the *Essays*, and her own authoritative words in the Preface – making her an integral part of his work – that would ensure her entry into the serious intellectual world of literature. She did not send *The Promenade* to Justus Lipsius, but she did instruct the printers to send a copy of her new edition of the *Essays* with her Preface to him as soon as it was available. And, naturally, copies of the *Essays* were to be sent to Madame de Montaigne, her daughter, Léonor, and Pierre de Brach, to arrive a few months into her own visit to her adopted father's home.

Marie was treated with gracious if distant good manners by Madame de Montaigne and her daughter during the early months of her visit. If, indeed, visit was the right word, Marie wondered. Wasn't her true place at Montaigne, in the tower of her mentor? Paris, of course, was important for a public intellectual, but to work in that study, with his books, his view, his desk; being cared for by his widow and daughter, as they had cared for him, and as she cared for his great reputation, surely that was her real place in the world? She said nothing, but she supposed from the outset, even from the arrival of Madame de Montaigne's open and rather vague invitation to visit if she happened to be in the vicinity, that the château in Bordeaux was to be her new world, where she would live out her days (aside from regular trips to Paris) with her new family and in her rightful position. All day Marie worked in the tower, and in the evening she ate and talked about her day with Montaigne's family. They listened politely and expressed what interest they could, considering their limitations. It dawned on Marie that neither widow nor daughter had read more than a few pages of the *Essays*. She understood how badly she was needed, while he was alive, and certainly now he was dead. Who else could take care of the heritage of one of the greatest minds of France? Nonetheless, Françoise and Léonor were of him and therefore deserving of her consideration.

In December the new edition of the *Essays* with La

Demoiselle de Gournay's Preface was published in Paris, and by the end of January 1596 copies from the printer arrived in Guyenne for Madame and Mademoiselle de Montaigne, as well, of course, for Marie herself. They expressed their delight and gratitude to Marie for the book she had made ready for publication, which they turned about in their hands, exclaiming over the tooled calfskin, and opened, admiring the frontispiece and glancing at several of the pages, declaring it to be a fine production, just what they had hoped for, and entirely worthy of the memory of their husband and father.

Marie was pleased to be so appreciated. She took her copy to the tower the following morning and placed it on the table beside Montaigne's annotated pages that she had been spending her days poring over for the next edition. For the entire day she did nothing but leaf through the new volume, imagining others in Paris and all over Europe doing the same, and seeing her name, *La Demoiselle de Gournay, fille d'alliance of Michel de Montaigne*, at last in print, his editor and author of the nineteen-page Preface. She had become incontrovertibly an intellectual, a writer, a public critic and thinker. The evidence was the book she held in her hands, whose pages she turned throughout that day. It was material proof that an ill-educated girl could will herself into the life of a female professional intellectual that she dreamed up for herself. An impossible life. But her life now. She found 'On Presumption' and turned to the final page, resting her eyes on the paragraph near the end:

> *. . . loved by me with more than a fatherly love, and cherished in my retirement and solitude as one of the best parts of my own being. She is the only person I have regard for . . .*

At the age of thirty-two, a spinster without the wish for or the prospect of marriage, approaching middle-age, Marie de Gournay's life was settled, at last, now, to her complete satisfaction.

There were loud footsteps on the stone staircase. The servant who brought her lunchtime bread and cheese and refreshing tisanes at intervals during the working day always climbed the stairs with a deferential tread. These footfalls clattered on each step, disrespectful, stamping, without the slightest concern about disturbing the serious silence of the studious occupant of the book-lined upper room. They sounded urgent, echoing upwards, giving notice of the arrival of a deliberate disturbance. A voice soon accompanied the sharp smack of determined steps, carrying explosively up the stairwell long before its owner arrived at the top.

'Mademoiselle! Mademoiselle! Mademoiselle. De. Gournay!'

It was Françoise, but snapping in a tone of frigid anger such as Marie had never before heard it, each word a steely articulation of impending trouble. It was just possible to imagine that an accident had happened and that Madame de Montaigne was alarmed and calling for help, but only until she arrived at the top of the stairs and stood stock-still in the opening, her handsome, lined face adamantine with rage, her lips pursed tight, her burning eyes narrowed to slits of fury, all the better to spit out what was on her mind and focus her glare icily at the woman sitting at her late husband's desk. Marie was looking up from her edition of the *Essays*, startled and cross at the noisy interruption to her satisfying reveries, when Madame de Montaigne arrived at the top of the staircase. There was silence for a moment while the two women stared, unblinking, at each other.

'Mademoiselle de Gournay!'

Marie had no idea what the trouble was, but her anger immediately rose to match the evident ferocity of the other woman. How dare she break into the tower like this? Montaigne would not have permitted it. She would never have dared to come here, to break into his thoughts. And was not she, Marie, now the occupant of the study, no less deserving of consideration? The triumph of having her new edition in her hands, the glow of achievement that grew to entirely fill her being as she weighted the reality of its boards and pages in her hands, and turned again and again to feast her eyes on her name printed in close proximity to his as the maker of the book, all that vast swelling pleasure was destroyed by this invasion of the widow and the challenge in her stony face. Marie deserved her day of private satisfaction. She would not have it broken into by a woman of such limited intellect and appreciation. She reprimanded her intruder.

'Madame, please, I am working.'

The legitimacy of the verb moved her. At last, she could say to the world that it must leave her alone because she was reading and writing, because reading and writing was her *work*. She had the right now to be uninterrupted, just as her father, both her fathers, had demanded privacy and silence while they bent over their books or their accounts. *You must not disturb your father, he is working. Do not make a sound while Montaigne is in your library, thinking.* Did not she too now deserve the same consideration, hushed tiptoeing so that no train of thought would be lost?

'Madame, I am working.'

Madame de Montaigne did not however look even slightly chastened. She raised her eyebrows at the younger woman's impertinence.

'Mademoiselle de Gournay,' she repeated in a dangerously low voice. 'I have just read your Preface. How dare you intrude on my family! How dare you presume to speak of my late husband as you do! I asked you to have my husband's work printed, not to explain it or defend it. As to your claim to know him better than all the world, to have been his soul mate, it is not only vulgar, but laughable. He was my husband for twenty-seven years. We were man and wife, do you understand? You were a girl with whom he was briefly acquainted. *Do you understand?*'

Marie stared blankly at Montaigne's widow. She did not understand, could hardly take in the words, let alone make sense of them.

'And I am not alone in my distress. Today I received a letter from Justus Lipsius telling me of his shock when he read your Preface to the *Essays*. He says it is a disgrace, and a deep embarrassment and distress to him that he should ever have trusted your judgement, let alone publicly praised you. It was partly on his recommendation that I entrusted you with the simple, practical task of finding a printer in Paris. He says he deeply regrets his error and begs my forgiveness. You have gone too far with your presumption, a great way too far. This new edition must be destroyed. My husband's work is made ridiculous by your idiotic, self-important, silly words. You are a very foolish and conceited woman. What is more, I cannot understand why you are, as you call it, *working*. You have not been asked to do anything further with my husband's book. I will write to Pierre de Brach and ask him to produce another edition as soon as possible, without the absurd and insolent Preface of yours, so that the work will be as my husband would have wished, and his spirit can rest in peace. There'll be no more of this *adopted daughter* nonsense. My husband and I had just the one child. Please put this library back to the exact state in which you found it, Mademoiselle, and make your arrangements to return to Paris as soon as possible.'

So daydreams burst, like a toy tower destroyed by a sudden downpour of rain, revealed as paper not stone, a child's plaything, a merely imagined simulation of reality, not at all a rock-solid place of safety and retreat with a controlling view of the world. The woman writer stood in the remains of the derelict toy tower, exposed by the storm of the adult world as nothing more than a self-absorbed child playing a private game of make-believe. A child just old enough, just aware enough of the world to be ashamed of being caught out at play, of having been seen to be telling herself stories about being one of the grown-ups.

Even as she opened her mouth automatically to defend herself and her Preface, to insist to Madame de Montaigne on her exceptional closeness to and understanding with her late husband, a cataract of shame engulfed Marie. It was the certainty, the confident adulthood of the widow's manner, just as much as the terrible words themselves that drowned her ability to respond; the assurance with which Madame spoke of 'her husband', the easy authority with which she described Marie as 'foolish' and 'laughable' instantly dissolved everything Marie had believed about herself just a moment before. And the condemnation by Lipsius was unbearable. Her words of self-justification died before they ever reached her lips, not being the words a foolish, inconsequential child could say to a securely superior adult who saw her with such worldly, knowing eyes, and dismissed her absurd fantasies with such cruel and brisk finality. This was not at all the Madame de Montaigne whom Marie had urged her readers to forgive for failing to find vital letters, who could be forgiven because at least she had the insight to know that Marie de Gournay was the only true executor of her husband's wishes. This was not the woman who merely lived in the château of her husband's tower. And what of the great Lipsius who had once praised her keen understanding, her solid judgement and her wisdom?

Marie de Gournay turned scarlet and inarticulate with humiliation. Her sudden, shocking embarrassment at this new vision of herself as these others saw her, her horror at the prospect of being exiled from her rightful place in the *Essays*, turned all her confidence about her place in the world to liquid shame and despair, surging through her, burning and seeming to shrivel her viscera. She stood up at the desk, clutching at herself, folding her arms tightly around her torso to contain the anguish. Her foolishness ate away at her, sharp, acrid, stopping her breath, as how she appeared in the eyes of Madame de Montaigne, Lipsius, and all who read the Preface, became horrifyingly vivid to her. She saw how she was seen by others and saw herself too in the same suddenly unprotected light. She was, after all, merely ridiculous. The walls of Montaigne's tower could hardly contain such a piercing howl of dismay as uncoiled from the anguished interior of the devastated Demoiselle de Gournay.

*

This time it was Madame de Montaigne who called for the helle-bore to be administered to an inconsolable Marie. Her boneless collapse and inarticulate wails of apology and shame took her adopted mother completely by surprise. She feared for Marie's life, so terrible were her cries and the hammering of her fists against her temples as she writhed on the floor of the study. It was a fit, surely. However aggrieved Madame de Montaigne might be, she did not want the woman to die in front of her. She was, now that her husband had passed away, a devout Catholic who met with her confessor daily. She couldn't have this torment on her conscience.

She ran to the window and shouted at the gardener below to call a servant, to prepare some tincture of hellebore, to get the physician from the local town, to hurry, hurry and bring help to take Marie back to the house and put her to bed. The gardener and Madame got Marie down the dark spiralling stairs, half-dragging her while her screams of self-disgust, her babbled apologies, her avowals of shame, remorse and vast, heaving sobs of horror at what she had done to the precious memory of Montaigne and to his family echoed through the tower and out into the courtyard, causing the hens to scatter in alarm. Madame de Montaigne had meant to convey her severe displeasure at the dreadful Preface, she had intended Marie to regret her presump-tion, to apologise and repent her foolishness and leave in disgrace, but she had not expected a complete and catastrophic capitulation into remorse and madness. Françoise, horrified and frightened by Marie's response to her rebuke, was unable to turn on her heel as she had intended and leave the woman to stew in her own embar-rassment, after which she would return chastised to Paris and leave her late husband's work to those who had the talent, experience and gender to act with suitable decorum. This was not at all what she had envisaged. Instead of retaining an icy distance until Marie disappeared from their lives, Françoise now found herself nursing the woman whose impertinence had so enraged her back towards the margins of sanity.

Marie was quite delirious with remorse for several days. The smallest move in the direction of rationality caused her to remember the catastrophic perception Françoise's words had given her of herself, with the result that she retreated immediately into a dazed and whimpering condition that drowned out such intolerable thoughts. When she finally came back to herself, weak and disturbed by the slightest light or noise, she needed Madame de Montaigne constantly at her bedside so that she might apologise over and over again in a small, wounded but urgent voice, for her gross insensitivity, her youthful foolishness, her ignorance, her disgraceful behaviour and lack of judgement, until the flood of regrets threatened once again to return her to a state of delirium.

'Madame, I am so ashamed. There will never be enough apologies to you and to my beloved Léonor for the embarrassment I've caused you both. Each of you dearer to me than my own family. There is no one in the world I admire more. How will I ever go out into the world again? I am a laughing stock, a joke, and I have dragged you and my dearest, dead, adopted father into the mire with me. You can never excuse me. There can be no forgiveness, never enough remorse, no apology sincere enough . . .'

For the sake of her speedier recuperation, Madame de Montaigne repeatedly forgave Marie, understood her explanations, and even expressed regret for seeming to have made more of it than the minor error of judgement required. In fact, in search of her former peace, and discovering that she valued that above her honour or even the memory of her husband, Madame de Montaigne apologised to La Demoiselle de Gournay for her outburst in the tower, insisting that she should not take it to heart, a grieving widow says things she does not mean, overstates her case. She had never read the wretched book her husband had spent so much of their married life writing. She had opened it once or twice, but found nothing in it to interest her. Indeed, her priest told her that His Holiness was not entirely pleased with certain passages that veered dangerously towards blasphemy, to say nothing of the crudeness that he had heard tell of. Actually, the book had caused her considerable embarrassment. It was her duty to have it published, Pierre de Brach had explained it to her, but she vastly preferred to be the widow of the former Mayor of Bordeaux than of the writer of a mere book – and a very long, dull one at that. Yes, she had thought Mademoiselle de Gournay a little forward in her belief that she knew her husband better than his wife, but about the book she cared very little, really. She wanted nothing more than to get her daughter married and to retire into a life of constant prayer and preparation for the life to come.

She had to get the girl to calm down and be ready to leave. Rushing her would only delay that.

'My dear, you must rest and recuperate your strength. There is no hurry, very little. Take as long as you need.'

The subject of the Preface or of Marie's arrangements for returning to Paris were not mentioned again. Whatever had happened to Madame de Montaigne's hot anger when she read the

Preface or her pique at having been usurped by a deluded upstart who had insinuated herself into her family, the task of getting La Demoiselle healthy had now become her priority.

Very gradually Marie regained something of her former strength, although she lost no opportunity to reiterate her apologies. Madame continued to assure her that it was nothing, she must forget it and feel perfectly at home. Doubtless, she would want to return to Paris when she was completely recovered. The last suggestion caused a brief relapse.

'Oh no, no, no. I can never show myself in Paris again. I will be a public laughing stock. Paris is impossible. I must hide myself away. If it were not the deadliest of sins I would do away with myself. I will put myself behind convent walls and put an end to my absurd thoughts of reading and writing. It is just as my mother said. She was right. If only I'd listened, so much unhappiness and shame would have been avoided. I will take the veil and spend the rest of my days praying for forgiveness.'

The tragedy of this future caused Marie such distress that Madame de Montaigne immediately vetoed such an idea, fearing another collapse.

'Nonsense, my dear. You will remain here with us. There's no need to go anywhere.'

'But the . . . the Preface?'

She could hardly articulate the word.

'Well, it was an error, but why don't you work on a new edition and the Preface will be forgotten when it is printed.'

'Work here, on the manuscript in the tower?'

'Of course.'

'But Monsieur de Brach?'

'I'm sure you will do a fine job. Pierre has his own work to do.'

She must not mismanage the situation again, and having the girl here doing the new edition without her outrageous Preface would be safer than allowing her to go back to Paris and start to think herself Montaigne's true reflection again. In any case, the fact was that the *Essays* meant very little to her. Her life was now devoted to God. She would do her duty by her husband, but how long would any edition of his book last? It would be forgotten soon enough, while the Kingdom of Heaven would last an eternity. Let poor Pierre de Brach attend to his own life, write his own poems. Let what doesn't matter run its course.

'You trust me?'

'Now that we have an understanding. No, you mustn't think of leaving until you are strong.'

'You are truly a great woman, a great soul, in every way worthy of the honour of being the wife of Michel de Montaigne.'

If something of the hot anger rose again in Madame's gorge, she suppressed it in the name of the Holy Catholic Church and peace sooner rather than later.

'Thank you,' she said, heading towards the door.

'I'm sure his great spirit is smiling down on you.'

'Very possibly,' murmured the widow as she closed the door behind her.

But things were not as they had been before in Guyenne. For all Madame de Montaigne's assurances that she might stay, Marie never felt perfectly at home in the presence of Françoise and Léonor. There was a distance that either she had not noticed before, or which had developed since the incident in the tower.

The anger never re-emerged, but there was no doubt that she was not completely in their confidence, not entirely a member of the family. She continued to work in the tower on the new edition, but whatever Madame had said in the midst of her fear for Marie's sanity about remaining as long as she wished, now the immediate threat of her breakdown was past, the open invitation was not repeated, and increasingly things were said that suggested it was expected she would be making her way back to Paris once the new edition was ready for publication, and that she would be staying there.

'You must be missing your literary friends.'

'How relieved you will be when you return to Paris with the new manuscript to be back home at last.'

'Ah, we are such dull, country company for you. Never mind, soon you will be back with your intellectual friends.'

All her passionate denials of wishing to be anywhere in the world but where she was were received with blank formality as mere politeness.

'How kind you are.'

'What tolerance of our poor company.'

There was never the slightest suggestion that she should return to Guyenne after she took the prepared manuscript to Paris to be printed. The dream of a life in Montaigne's tower receded. And perhaps after all they were right. Once she had made good her minor error of judgement with the publication of the new edition minus the Preface, the literary world would forget, as it did, and her own work would be all the justification she needed to lead the life of an intellectual. Guyenne was no place for her. Hadn't Montaigne felt the need to leave his tower and travel around Europe, to mix with the more sophisticated world of the Court?

She wrote to Justus Lipsius, apologising and begging him to ignore her Preface, enclosing a copy of the *Essays* with the offending pages sliced out. But she reminded him in her letter 'I was his daughter, I am his tomb; I was his second being, I am his ashes.' There was no reply. She tried to convince herself that his letter had been held up or mislaid. Such a great man would make allowances, she had no doubt. And so many important letters went astray, who should know that better than she? She worked on in the study, her agitation quite soothed, and prepared, though there was no hurry, for her return to her proper life in Paris.

When she eventually left Guyenne, sixteen months after her arrival, Marie put the unpleasantness of the Preface out of her mind. She only returned to the rue des Haudriettes for long enough to arrange a trip to the Netherlands where, hearing of Lipsius's praise for the remarkable Demoiselle de Gournay, and his recent repudiation of her not yet having become public knowledge, she was quite feted by the intelligentsia of Brussels, Antwerp and Flanders. She returned to Paris just as the brand-new century began, buoyant and filled once again with her own promise. Her collapse of confidence at Guyenne had quite gone, massaged away in the Netherlands. She had overreacted to the hysterical cruelty of Madame de Montaigne's accusations. No wonder her husband had sought a life of solitude. It was another new beginning for the Demoiselle, or rather it was another instance of the same beginning that had been repeating itself in her life since she first read Montaigne. This time however was to be the final repetition.

She republished her romance, *The Promenade of Monsieur de Montaigne*. Not only did she now not need Montaigne's approbation to publish it, but as well as adding further expositions on the high moral seriousness of her heroine and the joy of sacrifice, she appended to the end of the novel the full text of her Preface to the *Essays* which had caused so much recent distress, and which she had cut from the following edition in order to appease Madame de Montaigne. Included in the book, as well as the novel about which Montaigne had had nothing encouraging to say, and in addition to the introductory letter addressed to him, her contentious defence of his work, with its description of their special closeness (his ashes, his very self). She locked together ever more firmly – front and back – her first published writing and her revered adopted father. She was possessed by a powerful confidence that now was her time.

In readiness for her new beginning back in Paris, Marie bought a carriage, and to go with it a horse and two servants to care for and drive it to the various soirées and salons she planned to attend. She also employed a young woman who played the lute, to help her drive away her melancholy, she told her Uncle Louis, though it seemed to him that her sadness was more a matter of the current style, in the manner of Montaigne's wrinkled stocking, indicating a mind with far deeper things to consider. In spite of his alarm about her finances, Louis watched her creating her proper place in Paris with amazement: she was bursting with energy finally to become herself. Even her movements, staccato as ever, now seemed to be small explosions propelling her forward, always forward, towards what was unstoppably her future. She spoke rapidly, barking out words that tumbled over each other, getting lost in the next sentence, as she gave instructions and got everything ready to burst on the literary world of Paris. To do so, loath though she was to waste her time with such fripperies, she had no choice but to possess the right kind of household with the right constituents. She had to attend the salons that really mattered, to be what was expected (inasmuch as she was capable of so being) and most importantly, to create her own salon, where people would come to eat, drink and talk about the latest books, poetry, plays and ideas, to add to the gossip, and to see and be seen.

The King's sister, the shameless but undeniably brilliant Marguerite de Valois, had just returned to Paris from her elegant imprisonment in the Auvergne, and her new household was the talk of the city. Such goings-on, unmentionable behaviour, but there was no one who didn't crave an invitation to the literary evenings at the Hôtel de Sens, where poetry and drama and unorthodox fashion held all Paris in a fascinated trance. Marie did not hope to equal the salon of La Reine Margot, and certainly had no plans to emulate the immoral activities that were said to be encouraged by her, but she knew she had to be a part of that social circuit.

Money was the only problem. All those household expenditures took a terrible toll on Marie's very limited income, and even began to eat into her capital. But it was, she insisted to Louis when he nervously brought up the matter of money, an investment.

'The only way I can make a living as a writer, a *woman* writer, is to receive a pension from the Court. I've got to have the right people know me and visit me, so that when they're at the palace they'll bring up my name and my work, and persuade Their Majesties that my presence would grace the Court and be of value to the cultural life of the country. That's how it is, Uncle.'

A writer makes a living by making the right friends, she told Louis, as if the way of the literary and fashionable world was mother's milk to her. To do that, a little money had to be laid out to make the conditions such that the right people would want to patronise her salon.

Louis listened, somewhat surprised by his newly worldly niece. But he had grave doubts that it was possible for an impoverished spinster to make a writer's living, and even graver concerns, given the blank plainness of her clothing and inelegant manner, that she was fitted for a life in fashionable courtly circles. He had read the disastrous Preface and the over-written romance, and doubted that her writing talents would sufficiently overcome her limitations of personal style to encourage a groundswell of opinion enough to persuade Their Majesties of her importance to the cultural life of France.

'But, my dear, I must tell you that your money is running away fast. There is a great deal owing and nothing coming in. Yes, yes, I know you have hopes of something from your novel and the new edition of the *Essays*, but your reputation is not yet settled and it won't keep up with all this expenditure of yours. Your capital is dwindling, rapidly.'

'Yes, exactly,' she told Louis impatiently. 'It's when the tide is going out that it's most necessary to embark on the journey. There is no other way.'

Louis did not look convinced. She was disappointed in her uncle for being so faint-hearted. She explained the facts of the world to the elderly man.

'Only the other day His Majesty presented Desportes with his very own abbey at Aurillac as a gift in return for a single sonnet that he wrote which the King admired.'

Louis opened his mouth to speak and then shut it again. Marie continued in his silence.

'Of course, I have no wish for such riches. I don't want an abbey. All I want is a small pension, just enough to add to my income to allow me to live a modest life. To do that, I need friends at Court, and friends, Uncle,' she confided, for all the world as if she were the most accomplished of social beings, 'are made by offering hospitality. Yes, you can say that I'm spending more than I can afford, but it's a necessary risk to take. I must have a carriage. How can I go about Paris picking up the mud and filth of the streets on my skirts? That means a horse and someone to look after it, and a driver. Louise is leaving to go home and look after her father, and I'll have to get someone else. And one new maid will hardly be able to manage all the catering and cleaning and clearing up required for regular entertaining, on top of my daily needs. But, all right, I'll try to manage with just one. Perhaps the lute player is a luxury, but it is so soothing to the spirit, and it will be especially so after all the jarring social inter-course, when the music will help to clear my mind and direct my thoughts towards the words that I need to express.'

Louis gave up, but suggested that under her pecuniary cir-cumstances he thought she might have to do without the inspirational lute at least until she knew what size pension His

Majesty would honour her with. Marie listened impatiently to her uncle's excessive caution, and what she suspected was his lack of faith in her future, but she needed Louis and his literary friends at least at the beginning, to get word of her soirées around. She brought the conversation to an end.

'Very well, Uncle. I will do without my lute player.'

It could well have been the first and only compromise in Marie de Gournay's life.

4

Louise returned to Picardy to look after her aged father, relieved to get away from the horrors of the city and her demanding mistress. Uncle Louis found a replacement for her. A literary acquaintance told him about a small merchant, Pierre Jamyn, a supplier of paper and ink, who had died recently of a sudden fever, leaving a destitute fifteen-year-old daughter. Nicole Jamyn's mother had died in childbirth, along with the infant, when the girl was six, and there were no other relatives, nor any inheritance after his debts were paid. She was urgently in need of a domestic position.

Marie agreed to employ her when Louise left, partly because she needed a maid and she was assured the girl had kept her father's house as well as doing all the provisioning and cooking for him, but also perhaps because she was taken with the idea of passing on some of her own hard-won learning to a youthful, empty mind. To take an unformed girl into her house whose thoughts she might mould would complete her transition to her new status as a literary figure approaching middle-age. A new century had just begun and she had finished her apprenticeship; it was time to be a mentor herself.

When she first entered Marie de Gournay's household, Nicole Jamyn had no idea that such a life could be lived, not by anyone. Her youth and ignorance of the world and Marie's wish to pass on her knowledge made her more than just an employer. Marie explained herself and the world to Jamyn, for her education, but also because there was no one else she could say such things to. Who would not have smiled at the idea of the awkward and socially inept Marie de Gournay passing on her worldly knowledge? She needed to have an audience beyond her own mind for the plans and stratagems she devised in order to sound plausible to herself. Jamyn was not, of course, expected to have an opinion, but to listen and learn. And she did, she cherished the moments when her new mistress spoke of the wonders of literature (and of her father, Monsieur de Montaigne, the greatest writer France had ever seen), and explained to her how the sophisticated world of Parisian intellectuals worked. Jamyn didn't doubt for a second that everything was precisely as Marie said. She was, to her, so educated and wise, and set on an unimaginably heroic course. The girl could hardly make out any difference between her mistress and La Reine Margot about whom people spoke in excited whispers. It was true that her new mistress was not beautiful – time was beginning to nip at Marie's prim face and stringy neck – and that her clothes were chosen solely for warmth and comfort, that she was comically graceless in her movements with a voice sharp as a knife's edge. But Nicole was not a pretty or graceful child, though she was large-boned and round, her face plain with lack of definition, where her mistress had been gaunt, angular and sparrow-like. In any case, it was Marie's mind, and most of all her confidence and conviction, that placed Jamyn metaphorically and actually at her feet while she listened to La Demoiselle's plans to be something the young girl had not imagined possible, could not have conceived before she met her – an independent woman who earned her own living by reading books and writing. To know such a thing might be possible was to be admitted to the secret nature of the world.

The girl was not unused to sitting and listening. Her father, though not educated except by himself, had spent many hours teaching her how important it was to be a reader; that books and writers were essential for knowledge and for a proper life. In fact, while her father lived, Jamyn was given a better education than her mistress had received. Until he died and left her an orphan, Pierre Jamyn had taught his daughter what he would have wanted any son to learn. He was not noble or wealthy but of a low-middling place, yet he valued and sought knowledge, and was independent-minded enough to wish a daughter of his to develop her mind as would have any son. He had no library, though, nor even the slightest of fortunes to pass on to her. What he had left at his death went to pay debts, even his few books, and though Nicole could read and write, she was alone in the world and had no choice but to go into service though it was not a future that her father had imagined for her. But Jamyn had never considered the writers themselves, how they lived and thought and worked, nor the extraordinary notion that a woman might become one and be respected among the finest minds of Paris, even admired by one of the finest writers in all of France. Her father's gift of a respect for books and what they contained now enlarged and opened up to offer Jamyn an unsuspected vision of a way of life that a person with a remarkable mind might lead. She could not imagine how she, so unfortunate in losing everything, could now have been so lucky as to find herself here, in the service of one at the centre of what mattered most to the father she so mourned and missed.

From the start, Marie made the assumption that young Jamyn was illiterate; uneducated as any girl of the lower orders would be, and unable even to teach herself to read, as Marie had, for lack of a library. In the first weeks, Nicole Jamyn did not correct her mistress; she was too nervous to speak up for herself, thinking it not her place to contradict, and not wanting to interrupt or stem the flow of Marie's glorious and unheard-of plans. Jamyn was content to listen wide-eyed, believing that she was learning everything there was to know about how the life of the mind could be lived. She did not doubt any of it, and certainly did not mind waiting to receive her wages for a month or two. Marie herself said that it was unacceptable to judge a person by the size of their purse. And wasn't her mistress feeding and housing her; wasn't she teaching her so much? Had she expected a regular wage from her father?

Yet time passed, the weeks into months, the months into a year or two, and still Jamyn, although she had grown more confident around her mistress, remained silent about her ability to read. Sometimes, it simply becomes too late to tell the truth. Certainly, it was impossible by the time a couple of years had passed and Marie was embarked on her attempts to teach the girl how to read. For an hour each day, in the evening after supper, Marie sat with Nicole, and taking her copy of the *Essays* explained about letters and words and sentences and tried to show her young servant how she might read them for herself. Nicole watched her mistress's finger moving along the page with wide eyes that seemed to indicate an intense effort at concentration, but which actually concealed her embarrassment and discomfort at being able to read Monsieur de Montaigne's prose perfectly well (apart from understanding the Latin and Greek quotations) herself. The more often she sat in silence during these lessons, the more impossible it became to tell Marie the truth. But why had she not spoken up sooner, in the period after her initial shyness, when it would have been perfectly easy to explain and have her reticence understood? Jamyn certainly asked herself that question, because she knew well enough that the excuse of it being too late was not the whole, or even the real answer to the problem.

There was another fashion, as well as for melancholy, at that time, which Marie de Gournay began to investigate in the hope of improving her increasingly dire financial condition without cutting back too much on the necessities for an appropriate social life. Not only Marie, but kings and princes and some of their more intellectually curious courtiers, as well as oddballs, itinerants, tricksters, criminals, magi, dreamers, medical men, philosophers, astrologers, adventurers and artists, were all following the ancient master Hermes Trismegistus, and mixing, heating and murmuring over their crucibles. All peered intently into their alembics to see if they had succeeded in turning base metals – lead, tin, iron, copper; minerals – phosphorus, sulfur, arsenic, antimony, vitriol, cinnabar, pyrites, orpiment, galena, magnesia, lime; salts – potash, natron, saltpetre, kohl, ammonia, alcohol, camphor; acids – sulfuric, muriatic, nitric, acetic, formic, citric, tartaric, and aqua regia – into gold, the philosopher's stone, the dancing water, the elixir of life, the universal panacea, the quintessence. They were variously searching for the secret to feeling better or being younger, wiser, more powerful, richer. This last was the great hope of Marie de Gournay, who took up the chemical way in order to sustain the life she was intended but couldn't afford to live.

There were those who searched only for a greater understanding of the world and themselves, using their crucibles and chemicals in much the same way that Montaigne used solitude and words to focus on the nature of the man who used them. Others intended to find out exactly what happened when they mixed and heated their substances, thinking that the changes they observed would tell them something about the laws by which Nature proceeded according to God's instigation of them. Still others sought to remedy ills, both the small everyday kind that caused pain and discomfort in a single life, and the larger sort that condemned all sentient creatures to suffering and certain death. In different ways people searched, thinking that they might live for ever, know everything, change the way the world worked, speak to God, or be God. Some or all of those things. Marie took up the hermetic tradition simply in order to finance her chosen way of life, whatever she may have said later about her low expectations. She was not a believer, not even an adept. She was a follower of recipes, in the hope that she might amalgamate and bubble her ingredients into a regular dish of gold. She no more believed in the process she took up than Jamyn did in the baking of bread. There are those who can throw together flour and water, knead it into a dough, see it rise, knock it back, pop it into an oven and produce a fine, light loaf of the staff of life. Jamyn had became a competent housekeeper for her father, but her cooking appeared to be no more than edible. She and Marie ate to live on her porridge and stews. Her bread turned out dense and tasteless. Perhaps, knowing her mistress to care so little, Jamyn cared only to produce the kind of bread that would be little cared about. Perhaps, as with reading, she had some unacknowledged impulse not to give evidence of her ability. At any rate, she did not believe in her bread, she simply made it and they ate whatever the result was.

Marie did not care about food any more than she did about clothes and it was much the same way with her alchemical experiments. It wasn't so much that she believed she would transmute base metal into gold, as in the *possibility* that she might and how very useful that would be to her ambitions as a writer. Like a dying man who takes whatever vile potion a confident quack offers, in the hope but not the belief that it will keep death from his door, so Marie purchased her equipment and materials and turned one room of her apartment into a laboratory kept firmly under lock and key. Jamyn was never allowed to enter, though she saw the equipment arriving and disappearing behind the locked door. The furnace, an enormous expenditure, great quantities of wood to burn, and the vials of substances, inert, viscous, plain or strange; bowls and bottles, flasks and dishes, taps and connectors arrived for the boiling and bubbling, the distilling, extracting, crystallisation, evaporation, filtration and whatever other marvellous processes went on in the mysterious room.

Jamyn heard small explosions, hissing, clinking of metal against metal, breaking of glass, Marie muttering to herself and sometimes shouting furiously at what she found in her crucible after spending an entire night in the room bringing it about. Frightful choking smells seeped under the door which no opening of windows could quite dispel. And all the while there was the roaring of the furnace, burning up Marie's minuscule fortune.

When she emerged from the room her clothes were often singed, blackened or tattered about the sleeves and hem. Her face and hands were grimy with grease and soot, and sometimes brightly stained in no colour skin had ever known. Once or twice she burst out of the room shouting for Jamyn to bring water, and Nicole got her mistress on to the bed and bathed her eyes, streaming with tears and blood red, while she moaned in pain for an hour or more. Jamyn took it all to be part of the necessity for living her writerly life, though occasionally in the early days of Marie's experimentation she feared that neither of them would survive to see its flowering.

Marie didn't only rely on conjuring money from the air. She busied herself making other efforts to secure herself an income. At the announcement of the forthcoming first child of King Henri and Marie de' Medici, she wrote a long oration, which she had published as a pamphlet, on the subject of the proper education of a royal prince. It was a clumsy version of Montaigne's great essay on education, and even she seemed to wonder what it was she had to tell the royal couple. *'As for the education of children in general, it is a much treated subject, but that of the Royal children of France, and from the point of view that I consider it, is perhaps not exhausted.'*

This woman who had educated herself, who really knew something about a child's hunger for knowledge, her capacity for learning, her insistence on finding her own place to belong in the world, informed Their Majesties that they had to provide an education for the Prince in order to form in him a good moral character. The Prince must learn self-knowledge and proper conduct. A royal child must be taught ethics by a learned tutor.

Instead of writing what she had to write, what was hers alone to write, she produced a menu of banalities that could whet no one's appetite.

Jamyn read it secretly and was uneasy.

In any case, the pamphlet didn't have the effect she had hoped for. If Their Majesties ever set eyes on it they must have dismissed it along with all the other unremarkable attempts to curry favour. There was no recognition of her effort in the form of the pension that Marie so urgently needed. Still, all was not lost, she told Jamyn. Her name had been brought before Their Majesties, who might recall it when she was spoken about by those who attended her literary evenings.

Marie de Gournay's salon began at last, and with the help of her uncle and some of his friends, all Paris, at least most of those who mattered, did indeed attend. Curiosity, and the possibility of another fine evening of good food and amusing conversation, brought them to her door at the rue des Haudriettes, at least for the first month or so. On that first evening people arrived with high expectations. For weeks Marie had been organising and arranging the seating, the food, the lighting, and preparing topics for discussion and quotes from Montaigne to be debated if the *conversazione* should flag. But she did not have an elegant bone in her body. Jamyn observed the preparations and purchases. It was clear to her that neither her mistress's eye nor her understanding were true. Everything that seemed to Marie right was at best slightly wrong. She entirely overlooked charm and comfort in her attempt to get her apartment to accord with the way she thought it was supposed to be. She strived for appearance, grasping nothing about atmosphere or of the underlying principles of hospitality and pleasure. Jamyn tried to ignore these insights, telling herself it was none of her business, and in any case who was she to make such judgements of her socially and intellectually superior mistress? But she couldn't escape the pricking thoughts. Marie bought plentiful food for her social evenings, but of the cheapest sort from the most dubious purveyors. What does it matter, she told Nicole impatiently, when the girl looked anxiously at the stringiness of the fowls she brought to her. Just cook them, they will be fine. Marie seemed to believe that the point of cooking was to render everything identical in looks and taste, no matter what the quality of the materials. She took her understanding of cooking from her alchemy. To her, it was the application of heat that transformed the inedible into that which could be eaten. Since she did not take pleasure in food herself, how was she to know? Neither could she imagine that anyone else cared more than she did, being oblivious not just of what there was to care about, but also of the differences between her own desires and those of other people. Since she was not naturally sociable or hospitable, she thought only about the result to her welfare of the eating, drinking and talking that she proposed. Cheap wine was wine, was it not, and so it would do. Chairs were to be sat on, so people would sit on them, even if they were ugly and uncomfortable. Plates and glasses served their purpose and prevented food and drink from falling to the floor. What really mattered was that her guests should go away and tell each other and Their Majesties how clever and talented the Demoiselle de Gournay was, how she wrote and debated like the ancients. What had the taste of the food, the softness of the chairs, or the quality of the china got to do with that? And she was right. And she was not right.

Only Piaillon's predecessor, Mathilde, did not raise an eyebrow at the poor food. She polished off the ducks that no one could eat, tough and overcooked, sad cheap scrawny birds cooked by a young girl who knew little about the art of cuisine. Nothing went to waste, there was too little income for that. Marie and Jamyn ate what remained, and Marie was very satisfied with the savings she made from all the leftovers. Her guests consumed so little, she believed, because the discussions had been so absorbing. For the rest of the week they lived on the food and drink that Marie's guests had not been able to bring themselves to do justice to for reasons quite different, it was plain to Jamyn watching their appalled faces as they chewed an unhappy mouthful, from her mistress's understanding. But the two women shivered through the week, saving their fuel for the coming soirée. They each wore what clothes they had, bundled in layers, during the freezing winter, and fought off the ice that formed on the windows and over the buckets of water.

Within a few weeks of the beginning of La Demoiselle de Gournay's literary evenings, the regular company had dwindled from the crowded roomful of guests that first night to an uneasy handful of elderly friends of her Uncle Louis and a few other souls who rallied round, moved by her spirit, if not by her work, or lacking invitations to the more desirable salons. But soon the numbers increased again, and groups of elegant, foppish young men about town appeared at the door, always struggling to stifle the high-pitched giggles that Jamyn could hear as she went downstairs to open it. Marie was happy to see that even the young appreciated her salon. They were the most fashionable people, courtiers and rising young stars of the literary world, who would spread the word and get her noticed at the palace. After the weeks when fewer and fewer people attended and Marie was at a loss to know what had gone wrong, she delighted in her new popularity. She understood nothing, while Jamyn, just going about her household business, shopping in the market with other servants, listening to their talk (when they did not shut up at the sight of her), knew why these young gentlemen started to attend their evenings. It had become quite the thing to have been to the Demoiselle's soirées briefly and later, at properly conducted gatherings, to laugh together about the décor, food and drink. Such taste, my dears. To tell each other tales of the hilarious formality and awkwardness with which the hostess announced topics for discussion and the long silence that ensued before she filled it with her own orotund declamations which almost invariably began: 'As my beloved father, Montaigne, said . . .' She did not notice the braying boys wide-eyeing the ugliness of her surroundings in mock despair, or deliberately encouraging her pomposities. 'Oh, tell us, tell us, dear lady', or the deliberate foolishness of their responses to her speeches on intellectual matters, barely able to contain their vicious laughter.

'Plato, Plato, ah yes, Plato, as you say Mademoiselle, a god, a very godlike god. And so . . . godlike . . . in his godlikeness . . . And not, I think, unlike Montaigne . . . yes, yes, as you say, the Socrates of France . . .'

'This platter, Mademoiselle, such a finely crafted specimen. I believe I have seen something very similar, though not as good

I think, in the Louvre. I'm sure Her Majesty will be quite green with envy, when I tell her.'

'Oh, Monsieur Ronsard, yes, he was a frightfully talented fellow. So tremendously modern, so utterly à la mode . . . truly, as you say, the greatest poet that has ever been in the world.'

If Marie heard the scorn in their voices, she never imagined that it had anything to do with the subject of the conversation. She could not imagine laughter at the expense of Plato or Ronsard, let alone Montaigne. Marie found nothing serious funny.

They mocked her poverty, they mocked her untutored taste. Most of all they mocked her learning, hearing in her voice the strained tones of the self-taught, of the single woman in a world of men at ease: the not-quite-sure cadence that transformed itself in her throat into a strident, didactic, excessive presentation of her knowledge to those whose education and place in the world had been for ever assured.

Jamyn could not help but see this going on as she ran around, pouring wine, clearing away, banking up the fire they could hardly afford to feed, showing people in and out. She caught the tone of mockery and hated the clever boys who were so certain about the way things should be, who saw so clearly the faults of those who were not like them. But she also began to feel – she was young – deeply embarrassed for her mistress. No, embarrassed for herself. It was of Marie that Jamyn, the servant, pupil and admirer, was ashamed. She saw her mistress as they did. She found herself looking sideways at Marie, and wondering on those evenings if she was after all the wise and extraordinary woman she had taken her to be. Jamyn tried to stuff such thoughts away when the guests had all gone and she tidied the apartment. She needed her mistress wise and remarkable. She found she could not abide the thought that, after all, she was in so wrong a place with so inept a person. It mattered to her that Marie was what she had first seemed to her to be. Could she have been so mistaken? Did she know nothing about what was valuable in a person? She hated those laughing young men, and although she despised them as a mere mob with no individual minds of their own, it also in some deeper way pained and alarmed her to see them mock the woman who had taken her in, and whom she had believed the epitome of sophisticated knowledge and understanding. Jamyn did not want to admire a fool. She did not want to be in the service of, devoted to, a laughing stock. She was ashamed of such thoughts, of course. But still, even years later, when it was all settled in her mind how it was between them, the same rush of anger and uncertainty rose in her at the idea that she had spent her life and love on so laughable, so self-deceiving a creature.

They call her *faithful Jamyn* when she sees them to the door, after they have stood at the foot of the bed and made their silent farewells to her sinking, unhearing, unseeing mistress, indecorously dying. It is not terribly sad for them, she is an old woman, eighty in a day or two, though she will not know it even if she survives that long. It is no great tragedy when the old die, it's said. The few visitors who come are not so much grieving their loss as paying their respects, though perhaps that is not quite the right word in most cases. Perhaps they are marking the passing of an era, and acknowledging the loss of the final connection of their time to the great Montaigne. Great, Jamyn knows, partly because her mistress ensured he would be so. But she supposes Marie would be gratified to be connected still to him and exultant to be taking the last vital link to him off with her to her grave. She gave him to them and now she is taking him away, leaving behind his work, but only in the form that she has had control over since his death. Perhaps, after all, she has won.

Jamyn has read them: his essays and her writing. Marie never knew. When she was out, Jamyn read the books on the shelves and whatever happened to be lying at the top of the confusion of books and papers on her desk. When you are so close to someone you have to make an effort to understand their passions. Writing was Marie's passion, and Montaigne was her passion. Jamyn took it to be her business what they wrote. She needed to know, also, if

Marie was what she said she was, or what they said she was. To love someone means to know them. What she knew about her lady was that she couldn't be taken at her word. Her truth was a very personal affair.

His writing was quite different, Jamyn saw that immediately. He sounded like himself, though she never met him. She gathered a lot about him, browsing his essays. He gave a lot, offered himself up, it seemed, to his reader. She could feel how she herself, were he alive, living somewhere reachable, would be pulled towards the author of those words, feeling his familiarity, sensing a common understanding between them. It was a remarkable way to write. She can see how her mistress responded as she did, being as young and sheltered as she was.

They call her *faithful Jamyn* and they are not wrong. She is faithful. As a servant and as one who loves, she is faithful. She is faithful to Marie de Gournay as she is faithful to herself. Marie has been her life for forty-five years. 'Servant and companion,' Jamyn says to people when they ask. 'My servant' was how Marie referred to her. 'Dear Jamyn' occasionally. 'Idiot' often enough. 'My lady' is how Jamyn thinks of her. How can she not see it through to the end? Not that she expected to outlive her mistress for all that she had twenty years on her. No old woman ever seemed so robust until she was suddenly taken with the ague eight days ago. She stamped around, heavy-footed, with her head down, charging at whatever she deemed to be her business. Jamyn also did not expect her mistress to die first because she could not bear the idea of a life without her. It was essential that she believed her mistress would outlive her. Ten years ago she made a will leaving everything she had to Marie. The lawyer laughed when Jamyn scrawled her signature on the document.

'There aren't many servants who leave all their worldly goods to their employer, especially not when they're younger than their mistress.'

Jamyn didn't respond to his raised eyebrows, but put her coins on his table, thanked him and left. It wasn't much, some savings she put by on those occasions when Marie paid her a wage, before and after the times when there was barely enough money to keep the two of them, and Piaillon, fed. And some linens Jamyn had bought and put away when she was first taken into Marie's employ, a girl of fifteen, an orphan, half-supposing herself to be like everyone else (except La Demoiselle, of course) and that she might one day have the need for some kind of dowry. The bequest only gave her mistress back what she had given to her servant. Jamyn had nothing of her own when she took her in as her maid. And God knows how Marie would have managed if Jamyn had died before her. The few sous and linens she had accumulated were Marie's whether she was alive or dead. For some years now they had been using Jamyn's sheets, since the old ones had worn to rags, though Marie didn't know it; and the money she left her mistress is now a good deal less than she bequeathed – there were times they would have starved without it.

It was selfish of her to want to die before her mistress, she decides. She and Piaillon will manage as best they can.

By 1608, though the mockery continued, Marie de Gournay had produced four more editions of the *Essays* and established herself as Montaigne's editor, no matter what the world thought of her taste or her personal writing. The work on memorialising her adopted father, and reminding the world that she was his chosen daughter and editor never stopped, Madame de Montaigne having become increasingly other-worldly and unconcerned with her dead husband's future. The editions came out with only minor changes and copies were sold, enough to pay for printing of the next one, at least, with the extra financial help of those she badgered to keep the great man's work in print. Marie wrote and published poetry, made translations, received her guests, mixed her noxious potions in the locked room, and the years slipped by, but Montaigne was always on her desk, always being pored over and always being edited. It was her life's work, of course, but also still a preparation for her life's work. And in spite of all the scorn that was heaped on her, Marie very nearly achieved her goal. Finally, Marguerite de Valois, either for laughter or from kindness of heart, summoned the Demoiselle de Gournay to attend her literary evenings at the Hôtel de Sens.

Jamyn found her mistress overcome, like stone in the middle of her writing room, pressing the note to her face, breathing in the rare scent of Marguerite de Valois, and all that she meant to Marie.

'At last, at last!' she cried, seeing Jamyn standing uncertainly in the doorway, and holding out the beautifully written invitation for her servant to see.

That royal lady, a woman alone, an intellectual, a writer, a leader of thought, one to whom Montaigne himself had dedicated an essay, now wished for Marie de Gournay's company. Marie could hardly imagine a more successful outcome of her social evenings at the rue des Haudriettes.

Not even the prospect of an evening at the most fashionable soirée in Europe caused Marie to wonder for one moment what she would wear. Her dark plain wool, only best dress, was what she wore for the occasional attendance at the opera, for visits to anyone who was not socially beneath her. It was the dress she had, it was the dress she would wear. Not one second of thought was to be wasted on such matters. La Reine Margot wanted the company of the Demoiselle de Gournay, and that bore thinking about day and night. Her reputation had reached just the right person, the most cultured woman in France, recognised by Montaigne himself, who had recognised from others' descriptions of her, another such.

She became a regular. Jamyn thought that Marguerite de Valois must have been as moved by Marie as she herself was. Jamyn, even with her doubts, did not believe that Margot encouraged her mistress just so that she could join in the laughter, though doubtless Her Highness did laugh at the ungainly Marie and her pompous self-importance. Jamyn thought better of Margot than of those young men who had whetted her appetite for the queer old maid. Certainly Marie would have amused the company as she went about oblivious to her real effect, speaking of high-flown intellectual matters in her dowdy dress and chewing absent-mindedly on the most refined sugar-spun delicacies as if they were root vegetables.

She was by no means impressed by the company.

'Oh, such foolish fellows for the most part,' she told Jamyn, 'and some of the behaviour, well, I couldn't possibly tell you about it. No, don't ask me, there are things I cannot bear to think of.'

But of Vénus Uranie, as Margot called herself on those evenings when she proposed discussions on the equality of the sexes, or the true nature of human love, Marie had nothing but praise and admiration.

'I will not listen to vile gossip,' she declared, 'the woman has a very fine intellect and a proper respect for knowledge. If she is a little lacking in decorum, well, she has had such terrors to live through, she cannot be entirely blamed.'

And of course she had been good enough for Montaigne. The unforgiving Demoiselle de Gournay relaxed her usually inflexible moral judgement in this one special case. Marie became a sort of pet, laughed at but adopted, at the gatherings at the Hôtel de Sens, but Jamyn was sure Margot also knew that she was both remarkable and in her unknowing way tragic.

Better even than her regular visits to the dinners and literary evenings, she was given the freedom of the fine library in the Hôtel de Sens, and later at the new residence in the rue de Seine. It was even finer than Montaigne's collection of a thousand books in his tower, and vastly better in number and quality than the small library her father had left her, in which she had learned to dream of a strange and impossible future. She had a library once again and spent long satisfying days in Margot's rooms full of words, living with the books and their contents as she had as a child. It was perhaps the happiest time of her life, apart from those weeks in Gournay when Montaigne had allowed her to sit beside him and permitted her to share in editing the *Essays*. Jamyn was glad for her mistress. La Reine Margot was wild and wilful and doubtless as scandalous as she was said to be – roaming the streets and taking any man who caught her eye there and then, they said – but she did well by Marie. Am I, Jamyn thought, to begrudge anyone whatever kind of love they need? Margot even gave Marie a small pension to supplement her dwindling income. And plainly she must have spoken to her brother, because finally, at last – *at last* – Marie was summoned to the Louvre for an audience with Their Majesties.

It was perfection; His Majesty was so gracious, so intensely interested in her life and her work, Marie told her wide-eyed servant.

'I spoke to him about my pamphlets and my poetry. And of course, about my knowledge of Montaigne. He knew everything. He nodded and was exceptionally complimentary about my work. I think I can say that we got on famously.'

Her face was bright with royal attention when she returned home and told Jamyn what had happened at her audience with Henri IV.

'It will be all right now,' she repeated, over and over. First to Jamyn, then to Mathilde the cat, then to herself, letting the relief wash over her.

Jamyn was as relieved as her mistress. If there was going to be a proper royal pension, that was excellent. No more scrimping and cutting back. Warmth, decent food, better clothes, less worry and fear. Her mistress could write to her heart's content, publish, discourse with the fashionable and perhaps, Jamyn thought, if she didn't need to petition for favour she might write differently. As time passed, reading him, reading her, when Marie was out of the apartment or asleep, it was impossible to deny that her mistress borrowed her language from a ready store, while he translated his thoughts carefully into the words that more closely represented them. Over the ten years of her service, Jamyn had become an attentive secret reader, and her increasingly discriminating understanding taught her heart to sink at the heaviness of her lady's verbiage. She was sure that the child Marie had told her about who sat in her father's library had been the true writer her lady thought herself to be. But Jamyn couldn't suggest that she reach back to that love of words she had had, and to the recognition she had felt when she read Montaigne with his marvellous ease with language. Jamyn couldn't do that because she still held that she was illiterate, and also because there was no moment in the past ten years when Marie offered the possibility of her servant speaking to her as a friend. At best, as now when she returned excited from the Louvre, she would talk to her as if she was a small child being told about the unknown and, to her unknowable, wide world, or she would simply talk to herself aloud, letting her eyes rest on Jamyn's face. Jamyn's response (at least until she understood that they would be together until the end, no matter what, and that nothing would ever change between them, and so became as sour as her mistress) was confined to repeating 'Yes, Mademoiselle. No, Mademoiselle. How wonderful, Mademoiselle' and the conversation, such as it was, would end with Marie telling her to 'run along, child' as if Jamyn had been keeping her from important work with her idle curiosity.

Back then she longed for her mistress to speak to her, to tell her things, to light up with the pleasures of success, or just to acknowledge her presence. She had grown to love her mistress. Though the reason was not easy for her to understand. Because she had no one else to love? Because the anger Jamyn began to feel at Marie had to be balanced by something benign, as the sourness started to seep through her body and threatened to eat it away? Or because we love who we love and she could not help it? That would account for the hatred she also felt; not the other way round.

What was so difficult for Jamyn to understand about her feelings for her mistress was that the more she came to love her, the less amenable she was to becoming her protégée. In the same proportion that her feelings for her mistress grew, so she concealed her mind. She refused to let the older woman be her teacher. She did not just fail to tell Marie that she was a more than competent reader, she presented herself as intellectually wooden, and remained stubbornly resistant to what her mistress loved most in the world. Marie gave up on the girl, but had become used to her. Jamyn doggedly refused the one gift that Marie had to give, and withheld the one gift Marie would have wanted from her. Deliberately withheld. Sometimes she had to dig her fingernails into her palm to stop herself from responding with interest to a poem or idea her mistress read aloud to her. She read only in secret; her work, his work, and sometimes other things she found in the bookshelves, but she never let Marie know. Her refusal to give her mistress anything but her devotion was adamant. Yet Montaigne, who loved Marie not at all, had given her almost everything she craved.

Montaigne's love had been engaged only once in his life, however many times his passion ignited. In that he was like Jamyn, but he was luckier to have had his love recognised and returned. He had mourned the brevity of his relationship with La Boétie and wondered if the few years that belonged to the two of them had not emptied out the meaning of the rest of his life.

Since the day I lost him I only drag on a weary life. And the very pleasures that come my way, instead of consoling me, redouble my grief for his loss. I was already so formed and accustomed to being a second self everywhere that only half of me seems to be alive now.

Jamyn and her mistress were not loved at all by the only loves of their lives. Not for the briefest of times. Jamyn was not loved by her, she was not loved by him. Both of them eventually were haunted by Montaigne's four perfect years. He toyed with the idea of wishing them away for the pain their loss gave him, while Jamyn and Marie, not having had them, would have settled for just a moment of such ideal mutual affection. But at the same time, Jamyn, and, she suspected, her lady, understood only too well about the lifetime of void that had to be suffered by one who had experienced and lost a true beloved. For Jamyn there was something worse. Montaigne, losing his other half, settled down eventually to be his own other half in the *Essays*. Perhaps he even needed the death of La Boétie to allow him to discover how to be the kind of person his friend encouraged him to be. Before La Boétie died, Montaigne was restless, unsettled, lacking a sense of purpose. His friend's death and his own despair pushed him into the back room where he learned to write himself into the world. And Marie, lacking Montaigne's genius, nonetheless made a profession for herself out of him, an unheard-of profession for a woman, after his death. Stunned into immobility while he was alive yet no longer in her presence, and then, once he died, free to be the keeper of his flame, to make her life around the bonfire of her love for him. And Jamyn? Jamyn lived with her loss while her love called her to stoke the fire, wash her clothes, run errands to the printer, eke out her poor living to provide enough to keep them fed. She could not mourn and rise up with the image of her lost love burning in her mind and heart. Marie was present all the time, demanding and dismissive all day, and at night upstairs and separate and not so separate. Jamyn did not lose her beloved as Montaigne and Marie had.

Now, very soon, like them, Jamyn would be left alone in the world, without the one that makes the world have any meaning at all. No wonder she made her will in Marie's favour, determined that she would die before her mistress. What would she do, after all the silent, withholding years when the new silence meant only that there was no one to refuse to reveal herself to? Tidy up Marie's desk and papers and hand them over to the loyal Monsieur Costar. She had never had the heart, or whatever it was, to speak on her own behalf. She would remain as she had been formed and accustomed: faithful, mute, obedient Jamyn.

Because, she thinks with a grim laugh that almost breaks into the world, I was I and she was she.

Yet what if Marie had been able to write without the anxiety about money and the terrible criticism? Jamyn wonders if perhaps then it would all have been different. But she doubts it. She has to be realistic, as she has always been, apart from that small isolated place of love that lives untouched in her. Nothing would have been different. Not their relationship, perhaps not even Marie's writing. She has such pointless thoughts at the end of a lifetime of how things were.

Things were to be, it turned out, as they had always been. A month after Marie de Gournay's audience with Henri IV, he was assassinated by a young man called Ravaillac, and the light went out of his life and her eyes. Indeed, all France was shocked and horrified, but it is certain that no one was more disappointed than the Demoiselle de Gournay. The new and final beginning of her life turned out to be just a hope that lasted no more than a few pitiful weeks.

This old crone, the tiny bag of dying bones wheezing in the bed, whom Jamyn only has to stretch out her arm to touch, though her mistress probably wouldn't know it, was never beautiful, but she was not so plain as they all made out. Startling, awkward, not pretty. They meant that. And her manner; her mannish stride, her jutting head on its stalky neck, that voice strident as a starling fending off the competition. Not pretty, not sweetly soft. Unsoftened, they meant, by love, or at least unprotected from scorn by not having a husband who knew her place and kept her indoors. In any case, to the young Jamyn she looked the way she looked, and was the way she was; while they mocked her looks and her character and Jamyn had her moments of embarrassment, she nonetheless loved her mistress. And now, far from young, knowing, it feels, everything, she loves her still. Even Jamyn finds this hard to understand.

She looks at the diminishing scrap of body dying here beside her, toothless, sunken-eyed, what flesh there is falling limp in empty folds and strangely, alarmingly grey, and it has no effect on the fact of her love for her mistress. Perhaps it is because love is now an almost lifelong habit. There is nothing special about it. It is an ordinary fact. It simply comes to Jamyn, this love she has for Marie, without the need for thought. It does not *come* to her at all. It is the why of her life, the substance, like the gristle between bones, that has kept her here in her mistress's presence, and in the world, these past forty-five years. But when she thinks about it, she's no longer sure what she means by 'loving her'. It drops into her mind like calling Piaillon 'beautiful one' falls from her lips, though she too is no beauty. Nor, Jamyn is at moments surprised to find, is she distraught at the sight of her, so lessened, so dying. Loving Marie is a large stone inside Jamyn's chest. She lives with its weight and it brings her neither joy or sorrow. That is its habitual nature. Featureless, not a feeling of delight, not even really a burden, but an inert blockage filling the space inside her. When did love become a habit? And before it did, what was loving her? Before it was like the sun coming up and going down, day in, day out, needing no thought or comment, what did the love she had for Marie feel like? Before Jamyn was a stone-filled old crone herself, when love made demands on her, rather than requiring nothing more of her than to sit still and wait, to clean up the faeces and urine without disgust or pity, what can she remember of its quality? Suffering that felt like actual pain; yearning that turned to hunger; humiliation; hope without conviction, no peace, no joy that she could remember, and always, she thought, *always*, an accompanying rage, running below all the other feelings like an underground source, a fast-flowing stream of black bile. Had she loved her? Did she love her? It had better be so. She had better believe it to be so. Whatever it was, and whatever it is now, she will choose to call it love.

She remembers, once again, the first time she went to Marie with her love, or her need, like a shudder skimming her dry bones. There were many times, and they were all much the same, but she recalls the first time when she chooses to remember. She was mortally frightened. She feared for her life. She never felt any certainty, was never quite sure, not even the last time, though she doesn't remember that particular occasion so clearly, recent as it is. But the first time, she stepped out over the edge of her life. There was everything to lose. All she had. She'd already lost everything and had got something of a place in the world back during the ten years of being with Marie. That's how Jamyn knows she must have loved her mistress. She risked not just her love, but her livelihood, her home, her security, her hope. Everything. Her mistress housed, fed, protected and clothed her, even tried to educate her. All that might have disappeared in an instant. And more, something more than loss, that she can't quite think about, which has no exact name.

She was still quite a young woman of twenty-five. It had come over her gradually, over months, years probably, like a sweat breaking out which you hardly notice until it overwhelms you and you find yourself drenched. It originated in her dreams and then into the half-awake moments when she was barely alert to who or what she was. Soon, it seeped into the cold grey light of dusk and dawn, in the seconds before she slept and after she woke, so that, caught moving from one state to the other, she couldn't help but know what she was thinking, feeling, doing, wanting, even if she didn't or couldn't define it. She can't imagine that it came to her easily, without a battle to keep herself ignorant of it. She did not know of such things, nor had she thought such thoughts before.

It must, at first, have been no more than a young woman wanting. She believes she remembers that. That large sense of something beyond her but within her reach that was hers for the having. And a need for having. Since her father had died there had been no one close to her. She arrived as a servant in Marie's apartment in the rue des Haudriettes aged fifteen, and now she thinks back, dumb with misery at the loss of the only person she had ever been close to. She had cherished her father so much, and perhaps feared losing him as she had lost her mother, that she hadn't chosen or dared to spend time or thought on anyone else. Marie de Gournay was a rare spirit. So bold, so fearless, so ready to take on the unthinkable. How could so young and fearful a girl fail to fall in love with such a woman? She can't recall ever having daydreams about love and marriage, though her father sometimes suggested that one day soon he would have to find her a husband. She didn't want one. She wanted nothing to change. She loved living with him, waiting for him to finish his day's business and settle down with the meal she'd cooked, to talk with her about the book they were reading together and the stories he heard from his customers and suppliers from other places. Or bold new ideas he had heard tell of. He talked to her as if she were his shadow, as if he were talking to himself, but then he would remember their situation and remind her, and himself, that she had to have a future.

'No, I want to stay with you.'

This worried him.

'But I'm teaching you these things so that you can take them out into your life. When I'm gone . . .'

And her heart turned to ice. The 'out into' her life and his loss were one and the same, and intolerable. Her kind, tired, intensely curious father was precisely who she wanted to be with. Nor did the possibility of loving a man who was not him ever occur to her. She did not watch young men of her own age with any interest, although girls around her posed and got that look as if they were regarding themselves in a glass whenever any youthful male came into view. She thought them idiotic. They embarrassed her, with their simpering *girlishness*. She wanted to sit and talk to people, to know what they knew. Romance, desire, love in *that* way, did not occur to her. At any rate, she did not feel any physical yearnings for the boisterous and handsome lads that strutted around the area. Nor for the girls. She can't remember any physical yearnings at all. The love she developed for her mistress came to contain desire, but desire was not initially fired by anything physical. They were right, those fine men who mocked her, Marie was no beauty. First, Jamyn loved her, and then she thought, if that is the word, to involve her body in the love. Eventually, she burned. Though the desire only ever flowed in one direction. Her mistress's precisely regular breathing carefully attested to that, night after night.

Eventually, one night, ten years after she first entered her mistress's service, she woke yet again in the dense blackness before dawn cradling herself with one arm wrapped around the opposite shoulder and the other arm pressed between her thighs. Her cheeks were damp but she was not actually crying. It was that terrible winter, right in the middle of it, so very cold and grim, a freezing winter, and the King had been assassinated, too, just weeks before. She felt the icy air on her cheeks and forehead and her breath cooling on her lips as it left her – if she could have seen, it would have clouded in front of her face. The rest of her body was wrapped in woollen blankets, but not so well that her skin couldn't register the frigid temperature in the room. She knew she had been having those dreams. She felt the residue in her belly, and the sense of loss at waking too soon.

They had moved by then to these poor rooms at the top of the house in the rue de l'Arbre Sec, much meaner and smaller but also much cheaper than the previous elegant apartment that her mistress had pretended she could afford to run. Now, with the death of the King, all hope of a royal pension had gone, and they went to the meagre new apartment. Marie slept, as she does now if it can be called sleep, in the bed opposite her desk in this attic. Jamyn slept in the room below, her bed in a recess separated from the scullery by a curtain.

Jamyn got up, intending she thought to use the pot under the bed, but instead found herself feeling her way up the stairs, guiding herself sideways, hand over hand on the rope that served as a banister. She might have lit the piece of tallow she kept by her bed, but she hated the smell and wanted the density of night to continue. By then she had come to know the tiny apartment well enough, running up and down the stairs a hundred times a day, fetching and carrying as her mistress called and requested hot water to sip, a bite to eat, a message to be run, Piaillon to be taken away when he fussed her as she worked, trampling over the pages of her book in search of her full attention. Jamyn knew the stairs that creaked, the width and undulation of each tread, and which crack every icy draught blew in from. But in ten years, in either apartment, she had never made the journey upstairs at night after her mistress had retired. She never called for anything more once Jamyn had taken up her hot milk and carried Piaillon down the stairs to spend the night with her. She could only guess whether

her mistress had good or troubled nights by the creakings of the floorboards above her bed that sometimes woke her when Marie paced about. She never spoke of her nights when the morning came, though Jamyn would see that she was more or less rested by the dark circles under her eyes and the excessively pinched look of her mouth. For most of those early years she slept well enough. Only when the world began to savage her did her midnight pacings keep Jamyn from her own dreams, and as time went on they both increasingly lost sleep to the vengeful, furious thoughts that had Marie marching up and down at all hours of the night.

Jamyn lifted the latch to her mistress's room and the wailing noise the door made when it opened would have woken a stone. She knew the sound well enough, but in the dead of night, it was remarkably loud. Alarming too because it reminded her that she had never before entered this room at such an hour when her mistress was asleep. She had a second to freeze and ready herself for a flight downstairs, but her body was moving forward through the open door even as she considered a retreat. Her mistress showed no sign of waking. Jamyn realised that she didn't know if she was a light or heavy sleeper. She supposed heavy. The breathing didn't change as she listened to its pattern for a moment: a sharp intake of breath followed by a long, soft growl, the bare suggestion of a snore. She found her way by habit to the bed to the right of the door, opposite the window through which, unlike now, no moon was visible. She touched the edge of the blanket, felt the rough fabric rise and fall for a moment and then her eyes adjusted a little to the darkness and she saw that Marie lay on her side, turned away from her. Jamyn held her breath while with infinite care she lifted a corner of the blanket and slipped under it, making herself a phantom of delicate undisturbing movement. She lay on her side, hardly breathing, her face towards Marie's back, right at the edge of the narrow bed, her feet curled back away from her mistress's body because they were icy and she feared that if they touched her Marie would wake. Jamyn was barely covered by the blanket; not just her feet, but her whole back was exposed to the freezing air and she cautiously pulled her nightdress down over her knees and calves to get what extra warmth she could. After the intrusion she had already made she tried to keep a distance between their bodies, in spite of the narrowness of the bed and the temperature in the room, in terror of a bodily touch waking her mistress and being found there. Marie's breathing had changed. Without Jamyn noticing when, the sharp inhalation and snore had disappeared and her breathing had become more even. She had not moved and there was no indication that she was awake, but on later occasions Jamyn came to believe that the quieter regularity of the rise and fall of her chest was more like someone breathing *as if* they were asleep.

She did not move nor did the rhythm of her breath alter, when eventually Jamyn gathered the courage to touch her. She dared to do no more than lightly place the palm of her hand on the upper part of her mistress's thigh and leave it to rest motionless on the thick stuff of Marie's nightdress for a long time. Perhaps half an hour later, she extended her arm further and let it fall gently from the elbow down in front of Marie's body. Again she stopped, and when there was still no movement, no change in the breathing, she softly, very tentatively, pressed the side of her hand, gloved by the fabric of Marie's nightdress, between her thighs, and slowly let it relax, palm up, on her mistress's lower leg. And so Jamyn remained, lying almost as she had when she woke hours before alone in her own bed, one arm out of the way caressing her own shoulder and her other hand clasped close between warm flesh. Except that the hand was tucked between her lady's thighs rather than her own, and the rough cotton of her nightdress kept their flesh apart. She did not sleep. When it was nearly dawn, she reversed the slow connection she had made, got up in slow motion, and crept downstairs to her own bed. The next morning when Jamyn brought up the morning cup of coffee, her mistress showed no sign of having had a disturbed night, and the day passed quite normally.

Once Jamyn had established that it was not just a peculiarly heavy sleep that had kept Marie from waking that first time, she spent part of the night in her mistress's bed two or three times a week. Gradually, she grew bolder and although every move she made was slow and cautious, like an underwater dream creature, she found that lifting Marie's nightdress did not disturb her. She held her mistress *there*, in that warm, private, unheard-of, unimagined centre. And she held herself too, with her other hand, softly rubbing herself to a gentle pleasure, a thickening of blood in her thighs, though not to anything more disturbing, and eventually very delicately massaging both of them simultane-ously, each of her hands finding a warm damp spot to soothe. And her lady never woke or never missed a breath.

So the years passed. The day years, the night years. Jamyn became an old woman, too. She was increasingly a companion as well as a servant, though Marie would never have acknowledged it. As Jamyn understood more about her mistress, she feared her less. As she learned of her mistress's need for her, as she knew she had become a necessary habit for her mistress as much as her mistress was for her, Jamyn lost her early reverence and fearful obedience. She had her moods, developed her own way of doing things and came eventually to respond as gruffly to her mistress as she was spoken to. Finally, long after that first night, it was clear that nothing would change. They were a habit with each other. The never-mentioned night-time visits continued. There was no need for fear or caution, only a need to pretend that nothing was happening. The visits stopped just a few weeks ago, when La Demoiselle could no longer rise from her bed or separate the day from the night. But in all the time before, those thirty-five years, though Jamyn grew physically heavier and more clumsy in her movements, and less cautious in her touchings, Marie de Gournay's breath remained perfectly and agonisingly regular.

No one could have accused Marie de Gournay of not working hard at increasing the effects of God-given catastrophe in her life. The death of King Henri, you might say, was not her fault. Well, no, but there was a woman, the servant of a Catholic lady, who claimed she had overheard talk about a plot to assassinate the King. She waylaid Marie in the street and told her what she suspected . . . heaven knows why, but perhaps, La Demoiselle having let it be known around town that she was now the King's favourite, this woman, La Coman, found her the easiest or perhaps the most recognisable person with, as she thought, the ear of the King, to get hold of. But it was said that the woman had given birth to a child out of wedlock and then deserted it, and the Demoiselle found out. She was also known to be continuing a wayward life. Marie, her head so high in the moral firmament, dismissed La Coman as a reprobate, socially unacceptable and therefore not worth listening to, and so said nothing to those who might have warned the King, not wanting to be thought of as consorting with such creatures. But others, too, ignored La Coman, who was later arrested either because of her lewd behaviour, or to shut her up for fear of the consequences if she told what she knew. No, the death of Henri IV was not Marie de Gournay's fault.

What was her fault was the step she took that established her, for the rest of her life, as a laughing stock, at the very least, to those whose respect and admiration she needed and felt she deserved. Just weeks after the death of His Majesty she produced a pamphlet. It was in two parts: the first bade farewell to the King in her most ornate prose, declaiming at the young assassin as he raised his hand: '*O parricidal assassin, what frenzy drives you on? What are you about to do? Strike the Lord's anointed? The grandson, the son, the heir, and the father of a thousand others anointed of the Lord? Will you render the mourning country an orphan and a widow who stretches out her arms to you and cries out for mercy?*'

And so on. Perhaps Her Majesty would have appreciated the thought, if not the lip-smacking drama of it, but the second part of the pamphlet was relished by no one. The country, so recently free from decades of religious strife, was enraged at the act and convinced that Ravaillac was encouraged, even assisted in his crime, by the Jesuits, who were deeply mistrusted, having some years before been implicated in an attempt which failed that time to kill Henri. The King had only the year before revoked the edict that banned the organisation from France. At this moment of national fury, Marie de Gournay plunged into the national distress with a passionate defence of the Jesuits. Based on nothing more than her *feeling*, and her knowledge of Jesuits – a relative of her mother having long ago become one – she assured all France that they were innocent and that the mistake all but she were making was a result of confusing the Spanishness of the previous failed assassin with his Jesuit connections. He had been a *Spanish* assassin, therefore, not a *Jesuit* one. A somewhat Jesuitical argument. As to this tragically successful attempt on the King, she was simply sure that they were not behind it, quite certain. As far as Marie was concerned, such an assurance from her should have satisfied the doubters. But no one was in the mood to listen to the overbearing no-one-in-particular, Mademoiselle de Gournay, lecturing them on politics and religion, and telling them that she alone knew they were wrong.

The fact that she did not consider this response, nor anything else about how her pamphlet might be received made Jamyn wonder whether in her heart she did not believe that anyone would actually take her writing seriously in the real world, or, whether she truly was convinced that her arguments were impregnable and that what she had to say about anything would, by virtue of the respect she was due, daughter of Montaigne that she was, bring people to their senses – or her senses. More likely the latter, Jamyn thought, her lady being her lady. She supposed both conditions were possible. Marie was so remote from her own doubts that she could act with total conviction while some part of her floundered unrecognised in a morass of uncertainty, without any noticeable discomfort. She was perhaps not unique in this. Perhaps all writers, sitting alone in their towers, do not deep down believe that anyone reads them or, if they do, pays any attention to what they say, though they speak in marvellously confident voices. Or perhaps they are all sitting alone in their towers, unable to understand or accept that the world is not waiting restlessly for them to explain the how and the why of everything. Jamyn would never know if Marie entirely believed in herself as she seemed to, or if there was a deep, undisturbed, well of doubt or at least secret confusion – it was likely that only Jamyn's own well of unrequited love made her wish to think that Marie too may have had such a place within her. Jamyn found it hard to accept such absolute confidence as she saw in her mistress, but then, being solely herself, how could she tell? She saw no chink in the faith Marie had in herself, but for all she knew, her lady suffered agonies of fear that she was not who she wanted to be. The effect, however, whether real or performed, was the same.

All those fashionable gentlemen had been waiting for that moment when, inevitably, Marie de Gournay would overreach herself. They had laughed at her salons, and listened to her make too much of her connections with Montaigne, the beautiful and original Margot, and most recently with His Majesty himself; and now, more than ready, they tore into her like the predatory pack that she had failed to understand they were. Her public life exploded into open mockery, and she had no other life she valued. At home, she was just an ageing woman alone, who built a world and her place in it from tales she told herself, her cat and her servant. She concocted herself like the fools' gold she dreamed of producing from amalgamating base ingredients in her crucible when no amount of mixing and heating ever resulted in the real thing and often enough it too blew up in her face.

A pamphlet called *The Anti-Gournay* was published and everyone read it. It laughed viciously at the pretensions to knowledge and interference in matters of public importance of an uneducated woman, worse, self-educated; an old maid, no, 'a thousand-year-old virgin', a withered crone, a shrill, opinionated, argumentative spendthrift, a greedy social climber who had dissipated her entire fortune in vain luxury and the pursuit of magic. Somewhat inconsistently, the writer or writers also made scurrilous suggestions about her relationship with Montaigne. She had thrown herself at him; he had toyed with her; she had been, simply, his whore; and if she was, as she said, his adopted daughter then her sin was compounded by adopted incest. Why would the great Montaigne have bothered with her, a born old maid, plain as a pigeon? Perhaps he was not so great after all; then again, any old man can be forgiven for short-sightedness. Now, because of an old man's blindness, she gave herself ridiculous airs. She was contemptible for interfering in matters she knew nothing about, not just because she knew nothing about them, had less than immaculate Latin and ludicrous social graces, but because she was a woman, and a single woman at that, without the authority of a husband or a convent to hide behind. Moreover she was ugly, a donkey, dressed no better than a peasant, stomped the elegant streets of Paris like a gouty yokel just come to town, and shrieked her wholly unoriginal opinions in the voice of a squabbling fishwife. The sound of sniggering followed Marie everywhere, in the streets and the salons, muffled at first, but then openly as outright laughter as the weeks went by. She said nothing to Jamyn, of course, and scorned to read the despicable pamphlet that bore her name. She continued to behave as if everything was normal, but her salon emptied of all but the most sympathetic souls. Louis did his best to keep his friends attending. And a few individuals she had met at Margot's court loyally kept up their attendance – the Abbé de Villeloin, Colletet, Claude de l'Estoile, Cotin, Costar and La Mothe le Vayer. The discomfort of those evenings was to be seen in the effortful conversations and eyes that refused to connect with each other.

It was the beginning of a new life, once again, for Marie, but this time as a national joke. The pranks began. Satirical dramas on the public stage included barely disguised versions of

Montaigne's whore, Methuselah intacta, or the bumbling blue-stocking constantly tripping up on her shoes and declarations. She was not allowed even the one mistake. The fashionable world needed an ass to ride and refused to set it free. It was to be the long-drawn-out end of her hopes. Like that box full of earthly horrors, or the bag the cat jumps out of, Marie de Gournay had unleashed all the dislike and contempt that male society and self-regarding intellectual pretension can heap on a single, middle-aged woman of no particular breeding or schooling. But who while still a child, faithful Jamyn knew with a renewed sense of the wicked unfairness of the world, had shown a hunger for knowledge, a love of language, a recognition of the most original voice in literature, and as bold an ambition as it was possible to possess.

It had all come easily to Montaigne and she had to work so hard. Whatever happened to her, she had to make happen. What happened to him, he allowed to happen, or didn't demur. Or if he did ache as she did for the same things she did, and worked for them just as single-mindedly, he was more covert about it. His evident ease, her doggedness. It was the difference between them for all to see. In spite of his advanced age he'd tossed his cloak casually over one shoulder like a scarf, wore his cap at an angle, and carefully neglected one wrinkled stocking like a disdainful youth. Yet all the while he smiled, acknowledging the absurdity. She, on the other hand, truly did not know that they, all of them, laughed and raised their eyes to the heavens when she passed them in the street, her brain boiling with injustices or schemes to improve all manner of important matters, while they flapped their hands in front of their faces to disperse the air of hilarity at the sight of her ridiculous, impossible shoes. Even her loyal friend Costar, moved to write an appreciation of her after he visited the deathbed, said that for all her admirable qualities he could not mount a defence of her shoes.

His ease, her inability, went deeper too. Whatever pain Montaigne suffered – of course he had pain, everyone has pain – was cushioned by the unfairness of good fortune. It was not the differences in their wealth, or not that alone. Nor in their education. It was not even simply that he was a man and she a woman, though that difference was implacable. It was that he possessed – had been freely given – the mind, the talent, the originality: everything that was needed to make, and to seem not to try hard to make, what he wanted of himself. She was so exposed, no padding, just the near-transparent skin and bone of her desire chafing constantly against the raw wind and weather of her lack of what she needed in order to be what she knew was her true self. La Demoiselle de Gournay bled and froze for what came so easily to him and did not come to her at all. He can't be blamed for his good fortune. Yet Jamyn couldn't help but brood on how unfair, how miserably unfair it was.

Jamyn had never conceived of herself wanting the impossible, but she was wrong; she thought that her longing to be loved by Marie, to have her love returned, was so much less impossible than Marie's desire to be Montaigne's successor, a woman writing and receiving respect. Whatever you want that you can't have, that is the impossibility of your life.

Marie was horribly shocked. In the first place because they did not agree with her – when she was perfectly certain that she was right. And in the second place because those who had accepted her hospitality, and who she had no doubt were her intellectual inferiors took such pleasure in publicly abusing her. Was she not better than them all? How could it be that this was not acknowledged? Had not his late Majesty so appreciated her company and mind that he had invited her to return regularly to discuss important matters with him? How different her life would have been had he survived. Did not Montaigne himself make her his intellectual daughter? What further marks of respect could there be? It was incredible to Marie that those who should have had nothing but deference for her could treat her so shabbily. This was simply not right, not how it was supposed to be, and she was dumbfounded by the venom in their voices and faces. Not because she lacked venom herself, but because she knew herself to have all the qualities of mind and spirit that put her beyond the contempt of others. This mockery *could not be*.

She went to law to silence the pamphleteers, suing for slander and the possible loss of a future royal pension from Her Majesty should their vile accusations be believed. In court she called her adversaries worse names than they had called her, while demanding the automatic justice due to the daughter of Montaigne and the beloved friend of the late King. The laughter rose to epic proportions, the case was thrown out of court, and the costs diminished her capital to a dangerous pittance.

With so little money coming in already, so much spent in her attempts to run a fashionable household, and now the cost of the court case, she was terrified that she would lose even the small pension from La Reine Margot. At home, she added up figures and added them again with twitchy agitation. The sums never came out right. It became clear to Jamyn that there was no choice but to leave the expensive apartment in the rue des Haudriettes and find something much more modest. Even Marie could see that they could no longer afford the carriage and horses, or the flunkies to drive and care for them. They were got rid of, and the secret room remained locked, no more supplies arrived to feed the furnace or bubble in the crucible. Even so, they were all growing ever thinner on watery soups, scraps of meat, and meagre porridge. The food Jamyn put on Marie's plate and her own became almost indistinguishable from the slops in Mathilde's bowl. The Seine froze that terrible winter – Jamyn couldn't recall being colder before or since. They shivered separately, swathed in layers of clothes and blankets, the servant in the scullery, pacing for warmth, Marie at her desk, with the cat in her lap taking or giving heat, her mittened, pale, chilled fingers enclosing the inkwell, no more likely to thaw than if it was held within a block of ice. Sometimes they sacrificed food for warmth: Jamyn bought a little firewood and the two of them would share the dismal comfort there was to be had from the poor flames that licked feebly at the sticks thrown into the stove. They sat side by side watching the fitful fire, barely feeling anything of it through the layers they were wrapped in, but it was rare enough for Jamyn to sit with her lady like this and she would have had winter go on for ever for more of her mistress's sullen, silent company.

Marie brooded, bewildered by the terrible turn her life had taken, barely noticing the dying flames, while Jamyn thought of nothing, but felt the proximity of another soul, her mistress's silence allowing her to imagine what contentment must be like. Eventually, she had to tell Marie that there was no money left after the rent had been paid. They could not afford even the poorest of food. They had to draw again on the diminishing capital, but it would not last for very long if they did not do something about the level of their living expenses. Marie screamed like a demented creature at her servant. What could *she* do about that? Whose fault was it? Surely Jamyn's for being so wasteful with the housekeeping, and all those who poured calumny on her head and prevented the Queen from rewarding her with a proper pension for her public work. When the screams died down, Jamyn explained sullenly, now a tone she was occasionally beginning to take, that no matter what the reasons, just or otherwise, the fact was that they could no longer afford this apartment. Marie began screaming again and flung the jug of coffee Jamyn had just brought her at her insolent maid's head. It missed. Another waste; though it was a great deal more water than coffee, heating it had depleted their resources even further. Jamyn left the room muttering warnings and sat shivering and waiting in the scullery.

This scene was repeated daily for several weeks before Marie informed Jamyn one morning that she was to find somewhere smaller for the three of them to live.

'I've had my fill of society,' she said haughtily. 'I will no longer entertain the wretches and fashionable fools who have the temerity to call themselves intellectuals. I need a more compact residence where I can receive only the best people in small, select gatherings, and where fine conversation and depth of soul counts for more than foolish delicacies to eat and drink. I will no longer waste my precious time on fools. Go and find us somewhere smaller, away from this thoroughfare of the mindless dandies. I have decided to test the true friendship of my acquaintances with an unfashionable address and plain living and see who is base metal and who gold. I am going to go into voluntary exile from the fashionable world and find out who has the taste and discrimination to dare to follow.'

Hunger and cold had eventually had their effect even on Marie de Gournay's pretences.

They moved to the rue de l'Arbre Sec, to a couple of rooms at the top of a dark, decrepit house. It was shelter suitable for the impoverished, if not the destitute, of the city. A dingy building for those without the means to live somewhere better, in a street that none of the fashionable young men had ever walked down. They took what little of their undistinguished furniture would fit into the new rooms. It stank when they moved in, of time and neglect and worse, and Jamyn scrubbed and re-scrubbed for weeks until either she got the worst of it out of the crevices in the floorboards, or they no longer noticed the sharp smell of piss and poverty – it had become their own. Jamyn made it as nice for her mistress as she could. Her room in the attic had her bed with the woollen mattress and her old table to work at, with a plain wooden chair. There was barely space enough for the one small upholstered chair they kept so that she had somewhere a little more comfortable to sit and regret what her life had come to. Jamyn covered her bed with an embroidered spread she had bought when she was younger from her savings – her trousseau, as she once thought of it. Marie's books were set in close piles everywhere, stacked against the walls, beside the table and the bed, and meandering across the floor, so that to cross the few steps from the table to her bed she had to manoeuvre sideways around the piles, or high-step over them. The tiny room below served as the scullery with Jamyn's bed, just a pallet on the floor, in the recess, her few possessions (those that were not in use upstairs) in a small wooden chest beside it. Between Jamyn's room and Marie's, the precipitous, narrow stairs with the filthy rope tethered at places to the wall as a handrail. Here they settled down to live out the rest of their lives in disgrace, in shame, but according to Jamyn's marvellous and tragic lady in noble retreat from the shameful world.

They slept fitfully in this new apartment. Jamyn's nights were broken by the sound of her mistress's heavy shoes pacing above her head, tramping back and forth, back and forth, not slowly, in a thoughtful, meditative rhythm, but snapping to and fro in a great nervous rush, towards, it seemed, some destination for which she was late. And while she pounded the length of the room and back, she kept up a monologue, her ratcheting shrill, indignant voice, only slightly muffled by the floorboards, answering her persecutors and threatening them with the full force of the law, her pen, God, the shade of Montaigne and Her Majesty's displeasure. Marie, who had usually slept so soundly, the sleep of the justified, remained awake and active in those first weeks and months, until late into the night. During the day, she barked her orders at Jamyn, called her fool, ignoramus, simpleton, idler, useless idiot, misbegotten orphan, parasite, and Jamyn for the most part still held her tongue, waiting, waiting for time to pass and for . . . something . . . eventually from her mistress, while she made her food, tidied her room, took out the slops, fed and comforted the cat who suffered as much as she did, but was better at avoiding the book or inkwell which, in an access of temper, Marie hurled at one or other of them. Jamyn understood her despair. She shared it. Marie's despair was Jamyn's. And she had a despair of her own, too.

It was during this beginning in the dreary accommodation to their new openly impoverished life, that waking up to find the floorboards had finally gone silent and certain that Marie was at last asleep, Jamyn had made her first terrified journey up the stairs and crept into her mistress's room in the dead of night. There, always tentatively, to the sound of Marie's uncannily regular breathing, Jamyn took what comfort she could, and in the process, lost all last remaining hope.

Oh, she knew well enough that her mistress felt her touch, that she was as awake as her maid was. Jamyn no more wanted her mistress to acknowledge what was happening than Marie did. Of course, that is not perfectly true. With all her soul she longed for Marie to turn towards her and put her arm around her body, to let her know she felt something, to allow Jamyn to whisper her love and have it heard as she stroked her, instead of barely breathing while her heart and body ached for the closeness and lack of it. And yet Jamyn held her breath, she maintained the fiction that her mistress never woke, never knew she was there, never felt Jamyn's fingers stroking her papery thighs and penetrating her virginal cunt and gently rubbing her own, to give herself what comfort she could get.

As the hope faded and Jamyn's unacknowledged night-time visits became a habit, they sank, the two of them, into a mutual bad temper. Time turned Marie's dreams into delusion, and Jamyn's died altogether. Montaigne had turned his despair into playfulness. Sometimes Jamyn thought she might have known playfulness when she was young, but as the years went by she came to match her lady in temper. She wondered if their mutual severity had not become a form of playfulness of their own, but the weight in her chest made her dismiss the idea.

Increasingly, with the passing years, Jamyn gave up her silence during Marie's tirades, and shouted back, muttering complaints, calling her mistress a deluded, demented old fool and worse, though the privilege of throwing objects remained the mistress's alone. Jamyn knew her place. But finally there was no more deference in her. She no longer held her tongue in the hope of hearing what she needed to hear in the silence she created. Jamyn complained continually while she did her tasks, taking time to hear her own voice. She grunted ill-tempered curses when she opened the door to visitors. She allowed herself to be as irascible as her mistress. Jamyn's aches and pains, her neck, her back, became the equivalent cause for angry mutterings to Marie's persecution by the vicious tongues that wagged against her. Jamyn accused her mistress of taking her for granted, demanded every sou of her frequently unpaid wages, and regularly threatened her with abandonment. And when Marie scorned her threats, insisted she had been paid everything she was owed and a good deal more than she deserved, and told her to pack up and go, then – 'Where do you think you'll go? Who'd take you in? Who'd put up with you like I do? Go, good riddance' – Jamyn hissed like a snake, and made her mistress wait a good long while for the tisane she'd demanded. Jamyn knew Marie could no more do without her than she could leave her mistress. A certain understanding was reached. Something was lost for ever, but habit was gained. They became a regular pair of old maids, just as the world viewed them, though the world could only continue to guess at their night-time activity. La Demoiselle de Gournay and her faithful spinster servant, Nicole Jamyn. The two bad-tempered old virgins and their cat achieved at last, after forty years together, the domesticity of the mutually disappointed.

In the silent, waiting hours of the previous night, Jamyn had drifted off on her stool beside her unconscious mistress. There was a noise and she woke to see the bed lit up in cold silver by the almost-full moon shining in at the window. She'd been watching the moon's progress earlier, before falling asleep, when it crept into view at the window's edge, so she hadn't closed the shutters. Piaillon was looking at Jamyn in the shadows from her bright place on the bed cover in the beam of moonlight. Being a cat, she must have seen Jamyn as clearly as Jamyn saw her. Her head was lifted up off the coverlet. When she saw Jamyn open her eyes and try to move her painfully stiff legs out in front of her, she made a small noise. Possibly the same as the one that had woken Jamyn. A sigh, a longish breath with a light note in it, almost a wheeze, but in fact a deliberate sound, a mew that skated on the sigh. There was nothing of pain in it. It was her greeting cry, but laboured, as often these days, with her heavy breath. Sometimes they played a duet, Marie and Piaillon, the sleeping cat on the bed at the feet of Jamyn's unconscious mistress, breathing high and low in counterpoint. Jamyn never heard her own breathing, of course, while she slept. Perhaps, she thought, they made a trio which no living being ever heard.

Jamyn leaned forward and lifted the cat on to her lap. She supposed Piaillon needed to be taken out, but her aching back and old knees required a moment to prepare for rising from the stool and making the long, dark, cold journey down the stairs. Jamyn forgave the cat her inconvenient needs, as she forgave her lady her inconvenient lack of consciousness. She did what she could for each of them. She sat for a moment with Piaillon on her wide lap and bent over her, partly to exercise her back and also to surround the cat's curled form in her arms to make the animal feel snug enough to wait for a few moments while she unstiffened. Piaillon raised her head and rested her chin on the enclosing forearm, and with the fingertips of her free hand Jamyn stroked the top of the cat's bony old head. Piaillon sighed again, just as heavily, but this time without the accompanying mew. Jamyn found her welcome warmth in the icy night and stroked on for a little while, feeling the weight of Piaillon's head on her forearm grow heavier. Still, she thought, I'd better take her downstairs, though it seemed a pity to wake her, and Jamyn's own temptation to doze off again was powerful.

'Come on, little one,' she whispered – so as not to disturb her mistress, though she knew that no sound of hers would wake her; even, absurdly, so as not to disturb Piaillon, in spite of the fact that Jamyn was making to rise and carry her down to the front door to put her outside. Or it might have been an attempt not to disturb herself or the degree of mutual comfort Piaillon and she had achieved. But as Jamyn worked her poor stiff thighs and began to stand up, there was no matching tension in Piaillon's relaxed body on her lap. There was no response from her to being disturbed, no adjustment of her muscles readying herself to land on her feet, rather than simply falling to the ground as the incline of the lap beneath her grew steeper. Jamyn was only inches off the stool, still with her arm around the cat, and felt her begin to slip. She sat down again. Piaillon remained still, a limp weight on her thighs, her head still lolling on Jamyn's forearm, but now she knew that it was a dead weight.

'Piaillon?' Jamyn whispered. And then, 'Piaillon. Piaillon. Piaillon,' but it was no longer a question.

Jamyn was reluctant to take her arm away. She didn't want to experience that absolute lack of response or to feel the full weight of Piaillon's head drop to her lap. So she sat on and continued to stroke the cat, playing with the soft, still-warm fur at the back of her neck. She had gone, though. No longer present. Probably not since just after she took her from the bed. In a little while, Jamyn's fingers began to feel as if they moved automatically, to be toying with a pleasing texture, rather than giving and receiving comfort. She stopped. Piaillon, the first of them to go. She hadn't expected that. She was to be the last sooner than she'd imagined.

First thing in the morning Monsieur Costar came round to see La Demoiselle. He knocked and woke Jamyn, but she still had the cat on her, and she found she couldn't rise to get to the door. He called out, and then let himself in. The door was always on the latch now. Only politeness made visitors knock and wait to be let in by the servant who led them to see the dying Demoiselle de Gournay.

He was kindness itself.

'Jamyn, have you been sitting here all night like this?' he asked in a soft voice.

She didn't answer. She didn't want to say yes.

Monsieur Costar lifted the cat off the elderly woman. Scooped it rather, expecting, in spite of the obvious, to feel a responsive creature in his arms, and having to adjust to the dead, stiffened weight.

'Poor Piaillon,' he said, looking at Jamyn's mistress, still breathing heavily but obliviously in the bed.

'There's no change, Monsieur. Did you know tomorrow is her eightieth birthday?'

'Would you like me to deal with . . . this?' He looked down at the dead animal he was holding.

'I couldn't ask.'

He was a fine gentleman, elegantly dressed. His kid gloves were already covered in cat hair.

'It's no trouble. I'll take him away and have him . . . don't you worry. You must get to bed and have some sleep.'

She said she thought she'd better stay by her mistress's bed. She doubted that it would be much longer. Monsieur Costar made her promise to send the boy downstairs out to get him if there was any change in Mademoiselle de Gournay's condition. At midday, he sent his servant with a pot of stew and a roll. Jamyn heated it up and had some of it down in the scullery. It was very welcome.

After the disaster of the Jesuit pamphlet, there was only work and keeping going. Marie did her best to avoid hearing the laughter that followed her in her chosen world, and she sometimes succeeded. It never died away, at least partly because she denied its existence, often noisily, which made her all the more comic to those intent on laughing. She laboured at her vocation in the cluttered attic, her eyes down on the page in front of her, seeing nothing but the next edition of the *Essays*, a new pamphlet to set politics, morality or literature straight, or a poem dedicated to someone with influence and money. She was for ever in search of her royal pension; always working to enhance her literary reputation; too busy to look up and observe the expression in the eyes of the world. Occasionally it was unavoidable, but it was like tripping in the street. She was the sort who got up immediately and walked on, head held high, looking steadfastly ahead, as if ignoring it could make such a humiliation never have happened. And only a step or two later it *was* as if it had never happened. Jamyn was the other sort. She watched their years go by and knew that it was too late for anything to change. For her; for Marie.

Except that each of them grew older. Jamyn began to understand how early a life narrowed into what it could decreasingly avoid being. There had been enough time now in their lives to look back and see how much had seemed, to each of them, waiting, yet all the while was life actually being lived and becoming what it was to be.

Jamyn had never had the large ambition of her mistress. Life had never seemed an opportunity to do something with. Her youthful reading had been for the pleasure it gave her father and herself. The secret reading she did in Marie's service had been to try to understand her mistress and what she wanted, and why she could never have it, no matter how it seemed to be so tantalisingly possible. Jamyn was a servant because that is what happened to her after her father died, and she remained one because it did not occur to her that she could do anything else. Life became waiting, and then that stopped; it became simply the smaller or larger cruelties the two women inflicted on one another for the intractable pain and disappointment each had in their life.

Watching, now, in the attic where Marie struggles with the last shreds of her life, Jamyn knows that she inflicted the greater cruelty. Her mistress hadn't known it. That was part of the cruelty. When the scorn from the world was at its noisiest, when Marie couldn't help but hear it, she received nothing from the woman, the one person in the world, who loved her.

By 1612 so many had died. Her father, Montaigne, her mother; recently Madame de Montaigne and her daughter, Justus Lipsius, Uncle Louis, the two sisters Madeleine and Marthe, and the youngest brother Augustine. All gone. Her older brother was soldiering abroad and her last sister Léonore was in her other life in the convent. Though love was not what had held the family together, though the family hardly had been together, Marie was nonetheless more alone in the world; she had no one apart from the few who from kindness or lack of a place in the world themselves, kept up their visits to what had become known to all of Paris as the Hotel Impecuniosity.

In all that time Jamyn did not speak. She might, she knew, have spoken either truth or untruth. 'Mademoiselle, you are a remarkable writer, your style, your editing skills, your gravitas are second to none.' But La Demoiselle would have laughed her to scorn, and condemned her to live in a petulant, punishing silence for weeks. 'Who are you to speak?' Jamyn could hear her saying in a voice like a rusty key turning in its lock.

Rightly. What use was praise from an illiterate servant? Jamyn was her servant, whatever else she was on those nights when her mistress's breathing was too smooth and regular for sleep, and Marie never wanted her servant to be more in daylight than her fetcher and carrier, no matter how alone she was. La Demoiselle's place in the world was, in her view, a lonely one by necessity. She had filled herself, and then emptied herself, with her beloved Montaigne. There could be no husband, no lover, no friend; only the written word and the dead mentor.

This was why, Jamyn told herself, any effort of hers would have been rejected and useless, and very likely she was right. But just as true was the thick black knot that rose in Jamyn's gorge whenever she'd thought of telling her mistress that she could read, and that she knew well enough the work of both her and her mentor. That, without Marie ever noticing, Jamyn was familiar with every book in her small library apart, of course, from those in Latin and Greek, and with every letter Marie wrote or received and left lying on her desk. This bitter, choking bile that blocked Jamyn's throat came at the thought, however unlikely she knew it to be, of giving her mistress pleasure. Marie was not the only one who punished. When Jamyn thinks now of the nights she lay close to her mistress, her forehead buried in the back of her neck, cupping her cunt in her palm, and receiving only a sad sort of comfort for and from herself, nothing all those years from the unresponsive body in her arms, that same black anger still swells in her.

The initial rejection was Jamyn's – *her* rejection of her mistress, right from the beginning. At fifteen years old, though lonely and longing for a mentor, a friend, a person who showed some recognition of her inner life, as Marie in her clumsy way tried to, Jamyn refused even to think about showing any interest in learning to read, or the books her mistress suggested she look at, or telling her how she and her father had read and talked about many books together. Jamyn was adamant, in her silent, sullen way. *I will not read the books you offer me. I will not be available to be tutored by you. I will not become your protégée, no matter how much my love for you grows and pains me*. There was always, right from the start, a bleak space in Nicole Jamyn where this hatred, it is hardly too strong a word, of her mistress resided, the place where the black knot lurked, swelling and subsiding, but always present, which Jamyn retained within the unbreachable shell of her pretence at irredeemable dull-mindedness. That place was where Jamyn was not the servant of Marie de Gournay, an empty orphan who might be brought on, filled up like a crock bought in the market, a shadow puppet of that strange and marvellous girl who had spent her lonely childhood in her father's library learning to read. She was Nicole Jamyn, whose own father had taught her to read and think and wonder, but who could only survive if she kept that her secret. Her secret was all she had of herself when she arrived, destitute, at Marie de Gournay's door. And though to have revealed it and given it as a gift would not, she knows, have brought her happiness with her mistress, it would have given them both a better kind of unhappiness.

Once his heirs had died, Montaigne's *Essays* were entirely Marie de Gournay's – by right and by effort. She worked her way further and further into them, producing new editions at regular intervals, in order, she wrote in her much shortened Prefaces, to keep Montaigne alive. Yet she made each edition a little more her own. She laboured, with some help from the likes of Messieurs Machard and Bignon, but prodigiously herself, to index and identify every Italian, Latin and Greek quotation in the *Essays*. Montaigne used quotations everywhere, and, perhaps deliberately, often failed to indicate where these had come from, or even to differentiate them from his own words. They were justifications of his arguments, but also a means to jump off into his own thoughts. Marie tracked down every one, and in her 1611 edition, included an index of subjects and authors Montaigne quoted. It took six more years to complete the translation of every quotation, but in the 1617 edition they were, every one, presented in French. She became Montaigne's caretaker, his executor now that his heirs were dead, and just as well, because his daughter having inherited the marvellous library had sold it to a monastery into which it had disappeared. The loss of those books, that study, the place of so many dreams in her youth, was the subject of much bitter muttering at all times of the day and night. If she could have nothing of the fabric of his life, she was entitled at least to Montaigne's soul, to be in charge of the words he'd left behind and of his reputation. Gradually, it came to have less to do with keeping his memory alive than with asserting her right to be regarded with respect. Montaigne, whose approval she had so dearly wanted, was long dead. What had occurred between them, other than his conferring the title of *fille d'alliance* on her, what he had or had not thought of her work, what letters he might have written to her, was now for her alone to say. She had taken control. It was as it should be. The child grows, the father fades. This is the way of things. And so in the 1617 edition of the *Essays*, she not only put the quotations into French, she also reinstated in full the original Preface that had caused Madame de Montaigne such distress, and Lipsius quite to alter his opinion of her. They were both dead. The *Essays* were hers. The Preface in which she claimed to be the rekindling of her adopted father's ashes, the only one who truly knew him, his other self, was reprinted just as it had been in her first posthumous edition. She had to please no one but herself, the *Essays* were hers alone.

There was, of course, still the matter of pleasing a wealthy patron so that she might continue to live and work. It seemed increasingly hopeless. With her in mind, Guez de Balzac wrote, to the fashionable young men's delight, 'I've always been opposed to learning in the other sex. I would much prefer a woman to have a beard than to be learned. Truly, if I were a policeman, I would drive away all women who want to write books.' Though there were a few women who held literary salons (Balzac and Marie both attended those of Madame de Rambouillet and Madame des Loges) it was clear to everyone to whom he was referring. Marie responded with her usual contempt. 'The chatterers' special target these days is anyone who loves learning who is neither a churchman nor a lawyer. Today nothing is more stupid or ridiculous, next to poverty, than being enlightened or learned.'

But in 1617, after the publication of the *Essays* with her reinstated original Preface, Marie got news that was beyond her wildest dreams. A letter arrived from an English canon called Hinhenctum, who was a representative of King James I of England. He wrote that His Royal Majesty, hearing of La Demoiselle de Gournay's fame, had ordered that her complete works be sent to him. He was so impressed with his reading that he had commanded his envoy to request a portrait of Mademoiselle de Gournay, and, as France's foremost writer and thinker, to beg her to write an autobiography for inclusion in a collection His Majesty planned to produce of the most notable men and women of the century.

It took Marie six months to complete her *Life of La Demoiselle de Gournay*, during which time she also sat for a portrait she had commissioned for His Majesty. After all these years of seeking out a sponsor, one had simply come to her, and such a one. The King of England. Marie worked, refining and shaping her autobiography, telling His Majesty about her childhood in the library, her refusal to marry and her commitment, at such an early age, to a life of learning and writing, her reading of the *Essays* and her subsequent collaboration and profound friendship with their author, and her literary achievements since his death. She sent it off and waited to hear from King James, convinced that a pension would surely result, and once it was known that he was supporting her, who else wouldn't clamour to help her, too?

It was a hoax. Three young courtiers, Moret, de Bueil and Yvrande, had invented the whole story. They sat patiently for those six months until they received the portrait and the autobiography, then they told the world of their grand joke. The crazy woman, blind to her own creaking lack of wit and talent, had actually believed that the King of England read her work, that he had even heard of her, and she was not at all surprised to be considered among the greatest minds of the century. Soon the manuscript of Marie's life was circulating all round Paris, but not before the jokers had added their own amendments to her text, describing, as if in Marie's own overworked prose, her sexual antics with Montaigne, an absurdly inflated account of how much she had spent in her alchemical pursuit of gold, and lewd hints about her private life with her so-called servant, Nicole Jamyn.

When she realised what had happened, later than everyone else including Jamyn who said nothing to her mistress, and heard what had been done in the name of vicious fun to her manuscript, not on its way to London, but doing the rounds of the Paris salons, Marie demanded its return, and loudly threatened the perpetrators of the hoax with the law, as well as everlasting disgrace among the society of the learned. But she had no money to take them to court, and the society of the learned were fighting for their turn to see the defaced manuscript. She never got it back, and the laughter which had not gone away but merely levelled off since her defence of the Jesuits, rose again to a deafening howl of malign delight.

Perhaps, already in her fifties, she knew it was too late. Perhaps she was gratified by her fame whatever form it took and told herself that public ridicule was a sign of her standing, and their envy. The world was full of fools, let them laugh, but let them know that she was a senior figure in the literary world. And she was right. There were those who had mocked Montaigne. But there was none of the gravity or the respect that she had believed went with a literary reputation, and which she had imagined if not named in those hopeful days of her youth in the library.

She stamped around Paris, muttering to herself, shouting at those who disagreed with her at the salons she visited, and received those guests who chose to visit her in her miserable rooms as though they were literary demiurges come to pay homage to their true mistress. Indeed, by now, she was an acknowledged figure in Paris, and even those who laughed had, for form's sake, to include her in their world. Even Guez de Balzac: though he explained to his friends that he called on her at times when he guessed she wouldn't be at home, so that he could leave a card and be considered to have done his well-mannered duty. She was still known as the 'thousand-year-old virgin' and now also 'Mademoiselle Quarrelsome'.

Marie was undaunted, at least in her behaviour. She had her own way to keep derision at bay. Over the years she worked and reworked her existing writings, adding to them copiously, expanding the philosophical asides, the examples and the analogies. She had learned early on, from her great teacher, that work could be revisited and republished. She produced new editions of *The Promenade of Monsieur de Montaigne* with ever lengthier digressions into the moral nature of love and loyalty both in the past and present, citing the ancients and taking all the time in the world before returning to her story of passion and despair. She also republished new editions of her poems, pamphlets, commentaries and translations of Latin verse.

She wrote some new work, too. Two irate complaints that fell on deaf ears, inevitably, but which were, of all her writings, Jamyn suspected when she read them, the ones which might one day be her posterity. Her posterity rather than his.

The Women's Grievances and *The Equality of Men and Women* were not exactly original in their protests about the silencing of women's minds. The Woman Question was an ancient and rather rhetorical debate that men (and a few women) had been having for a century. Taillement – the originator of her romantic novel – had called for women to have a right to proper education. Even Montaigne had said he thought that wasn't such a bad idea, though elsewhere he contradicted himself. There were even those, like Taillement, who had written that women were more than the equal of men. Marie would have none of that. Not lesser, not greater: she demanded flat equality. Her sharp tongue was at its best. 'Nothing so resembles a male cat on the windowsill as a female cat.' Women were only hindered by men, not inferior to them. It was an outburst of personal rage and frustration: 'Even though the Ladies had those powerful arguments of Carnéades, there is not even the puniest of men who does not rebuke them, with the assent of most of those present, when, with just a smile and a nod of the head, his silent eloquence proclaims: It is a woman speaking.' But, of course, they smiled and nodded, if they bothered to read her essays at all. It was a woman speaking. And not a beautiful one, or a rich one, or a soft-voiced one. Marguerite de Valois, dead these past ten years and finished causing scandal, could be remembered as exceptional. Marie de Gournay, alive and angry with none of the graces, just made a noise.

Jamyn was moved by her essays on women as by nothing else her mistress had written. They were just as strident, just as pompous in parts ('Was not Christ himself the son of a woman?'), but she was demanding her own voice, not speaking in the words of others who had spoken already, and she was speaking for others who were silenced. In any event, the fashionable courtiers and men of letters took no more notice of her original voice than of her ventriloquised one.

Finally, at the age of sixty-one, she collected those two essays and most of her other writings together and published them as *The Shadow of the Demoiselle de Gournay*, a 1,200-page compilation of her life's work. As well as her old material it contained sixteen newly written chapters on the subject of the great cause she had taken up – the preservation of the French language.

Even before the laughter began to die down about the foolish old spinster's vanity in believing the King of England was a fervent admirer, she launched herself into the great debate on what was to become of the French language. She stood toe to toe (theirs finely tooled and elegantly shaped, hers lumpish abominations) with the young crowd of radical poets, led by the passionate moderniser Malherbe, who stripped their work of the flowery archaisms of Ronsard and his fellow Pléiades, and brought their language (and in doing so they hoped French itself) into the seventeenth century by abolishing the ancient poetic forms, the ornate, twisted syntax and paring away the accretions of metaphor and allegory. The cry was for a poetry of new simplicity and directness. What Malherbe did for verse, Marie's old enemy Guez de Balzac attempted for prose. They were passing heroes in the eternal battle to renew the world and cleanse it of the ways of the generations that had gone before them. If the young men ever had a moment's doubt about their crusade, Marie de Gournay reinforced their beliefs both about poetry and herself by coming down at very great length on the other side. If anyone was of an older generation, epitomising what needed to be swept away, it was La Demoiselle of the Creaking Prose. There were others, of course, the last remains of the old poets themselves, and antique newcomers determined to follow Ronsard's lead, like Du Perron and Racan, but she was the most vocal in the salons and in her writing.

'I have just come from a gathering where I saw the ashes of Ronsard and of his fellow poets thrown to the wind as completely as the effrontery of ignorant people could do so.'

But with her increasing passion for the cause of conserving the old came another self-inflicted catastrophe. Not only did she want to protect the language of Ronsard as noble, rich, royal and celestial, and therefore to be encouraged, she also decided to show the poetic hooligans that the Prince of Poets was just as capable of modernity as they were when he felt it necessary. She produced an edition of Ronsard's *Harangue du Duc de Guise aux Soldats de Metz* in a dual text: his original poem of 1553 and a second version 'corrected by his own hand', as she said, that showed considerable modernisation of language and form. She dedicated the book to King Louis XIII in thanks for a small pension which at last she had been given. The problem was, however, that the corrections to the poem were actually in the hand of La Demoiselle de Gournay, not Ronsard. She rewrote 159 of the 291 lines, and passed it off as Ronsard's own work. Malherbe was not impressed with the revisions, and those who knew the corrections were hers and not Ronsard's were horrified by what she'd done – the woman who had once defended his writing by declaring, 'What person of judgement would be willing to strike out a single word or phrase of Ronsard's work?'

Jamyn wasn't so sure. She was quite pleasantly surprised when she discovered in secret from the manuscript on the desk that her mistress had, after all, a capacity to change her mind and to tinker with the sacred. It almost gave her hope. But nothing essential changed in their lives or the way the world treated Marie. La Demoiselle argued and wrote and stood her ground even while it shook under her. By now, the derision was so great that even more of it hardly made her reputation or her existence worse.

Indeed, there was even a little more money from the King, so that Jamyn found life a little easier. Marie noticed nothing and continued to write and fret and complain. She was now 'the old Sybil', the pedantic recreator of the past stuck in the folds of time. In her sixties she had more or less caught up in actual time with her reputation. One other essay, collected into *The Shadow*, caused a further wave of hilarity. It was entitled *Apology for the Woman Writing*. It was an apology as Plato's was an apology for Socrates. She took all the criticisms that the gossips had set scurrying around society and explained herself in enormous detail. It veered from the very practical ('And here to conclude the story of my management of resources, I confess, that my generosity, too confident in others, has cost me five hundred ecus, and the vanity of youth five hundred more, although it nevertheless always contained itself within the bounds of my condition, which I have acknowledged to be decidedly of a middling sort') to the classically obtuse ('The fact remains that anyone who would wish to

subject honourable people to every vulgar convention and formality would resemble those who, to render a king thoroughly
accomplished, would wish him to know how to make his own
shoes. Did Alexander shrink from taking the very royal diadem
from his head in order to bind the wound of an injured man?')

She defended herself not just as a woman rejected by society
because she attempted to be a thinker and writer, but complained
at her betrayal by false friends who slandered her once she could
no longer afford to entertain them royally. She was a paragon. She
was ill used. 'No man or woman of sound judgement and
demeanour among my acquaintance could allege, even if they
wished me ill, that I am false at heart or capricious in my good
feelings or lukewarm in discharging my obligations or unduly
secretive or importunate or rash either in manners or company, or
less than honourable in my associations (if innocence counts for
anything), or, moreover, aggressive. Neither can I be portrayed as
disorderly, disputatious, or quarrelsome, as opposed to sensitive,
firm and earnest – qualities which, just as they would amount to
thorns, or produce them, in a soul unilluminated by Reason,
become seedbeds and nurturers of many laudable effects and
necessary to society in those souls unenlightened by that torch.'

In the *Apology* with its accounting of her alchemical costs
('The first year, then, that I worked on that art cost me, I admit,
a not inconsiderable sum (although not greatly excessive), which,
of course, came from the productions of my wits and my labours,
not from my inheritance'), and what had become of the family
legacy, she justified her behaviour with all the detailed ammuni-
tion and self-pity that her opponents needed.

There was one final burst of laughter to come for France from

La Demoiselle, before the young began to grow middle-aged and started to worry about what those coming up behind them were doing, rather than continue to bait the irascible old scarecrow. She sent a copy of *The Shadow of the Demoiselle de Gournay*, when it came out, to the poet, Racan, a writer who still clung to archaic language, though he was quite young. His work, along with his physical clumsiness and excruciating social awkwardness, caused nearly as much laughter among the radical poets as Marie did herself. When he decided to call on Marie at home the following day to thank her for the gift, a young courtier, Boisrobert, heard him say so, and passed the information on to his friends de Bueil and Yvrande, who had perpetrated the King of England hoax.

La Demoiselle was writing a poem when the doorbell rang. Jamyn nodded brusquely at the visitor and pointed him to the stairs to the attic room while she made the slow climb up behind him. He opened the attic door and introduced himself as Racan the poet. He stood smiling at her, a tall young man in fine clothes. Marie noticed that he was remarkably handsome.

'I came to thank you for your marvellous volume. I've longed to meet you. But Mademoiselle, I'm mortified. I'm afraid I've interrupted you at your work.'

Piaillon complained ferociously when Marie got up from her desk and tipped her to the ground.

'No, Monsieur, don't distress yourself,' Marie said, pleased with the young man's words. 'It was a very fine poem, but the muse will return. As always. She is my devoted servant. Please sit. Jamyn, take Piaillon out so that I can hear Monsieur Racan. And tea for the gentleman.'

He thanked her and covertly brushing the only chair with his silk handkerchief sat for a while, sipping his tea from a worrying cup, put into his hands less than graciously by Jamyn. In between sips he praised La Demoiselle's work mightily before he left her to return to her poem, promising to come again soon.

Five minutes later, the bell rang again, and Jamyn grunted in yet another young gentleman, snapping at him that her mistress was at the top of the house as she herself no longer was, again.

'I've come to thank you for sending me your recent masterpiece, Mademoiselle,' he said in the attic doorway.

'I've sent you nothing,' Marie replied, a little testily at being interrupted once more, and feeling confused. Surely she should know if she had sent this person a copy of her book? But she liked the word 'masterpiece'. 'I will give you a copy, nevertheless. What is your name, young man, so I can inscribe it?'

This one was somewhat shorter, stockier, but his smile was as wide, and his manner even more congenial than the last visitor.

'I am the poet, Racan.'

'Don't be ridiculous, Racan has just left. Are you making fun of me?'

The poet looked quite crushed.

'No, Mademoiselle, who would dare to do such a thing? I am Racan. Always have been.'

Marie was more confused, but he began to praise her work, which he seemed quite familiar with. She decided that the previous young man must have been an impostor, and offered this one tea. He couldn't stay, alas, having a previous appointment, but yes, he would be delighted and honoured to attend her weekly literary evenings.

When the third visitor rang the doorbell, Jamyn threw down the key into the street and told him to let himself in, she had better things to do than run up and down the stairs every minute of the day. When he finally reached the attic, this visitor, very short indeed, round-shouldered and scrawny, was wheezing asthmatically from the climb up the steep stairs. He staggered into the room, whooping for breath, and without waiting to be asked, collapsed into the chair.

Marie jumped up from her desk.

'What do you want? Who are you?' she shouted at the dishevelled person who was splayed out with his eyes closed.

It took another moment before her visitor caught his breath enough to pant his name, speaking with a pronounced stammer.

'M . . . m . . . m . . . Mademoiselle, I am Ra . . . ra . . . Racan the p . . . poet. I have come to thank you for the b . . . b . . . book you sent me. Such remarkable p . . . p . . . prose, such fine p . . . p . . . poetry. I have the p . . . poems by heart. If I could only get my breath, I could rep . . . p . . . peat every one of them . . .'

Marie did not wait for him to begin.

'You dare to mock me? You worthless bag of bones! Scoundrel! Impersonator! Do you think you can fool me?' she screamed at him, catching hold of his sleeve and dragging him off the chair. She pulled him by one arm to the open door and with uncanny strength heaved him down the stairs, then took off her heavy black shoes one after the other, and threw them after him.

Only the next day did she discover which of her visitors was the real Racan and, mortified, hired a carriage to take her, far too early the following morning, to his house to apologise to him and present him with a fine, signed copy of her latest edition of Montaigne's *Essays*. And once again, Paris roared.

Perhaps Boisrobert regretted his part in setting up this game because when, several years later, he was charged with the job of finding needy writers by the arts-loving Cardinal Richelieu, he suggested that the chief minister of France meet La Demoiselle. It was said Richelieu greeted her in a French so antique that even Ronsard might have disapproved. But La Demoiselle was not impressed.

'Very good, Your Grace. Very amusing. Mock an old lady. Why not, shouldn't everything in the world be at the ready to entertain you?'

The Cardinal, gracious after all, accepted her rebuke and apologised for his levity. He turned to Boisrobert beside him.

'We must do something for Mademoiselle de Gournay to show our appreciation of her untiring efforts to sustain the French language and to thank her for her services to literature, Boisrobert. I'll give her a pension of 200 ecus.'

'But she has servants,' Boisrobert is said to have replied.

'Who are they?'

'Mademoiselle Jamyn, Your Excellency.'

'I shall give Jamyn 50 ecus a year.'

'But there is also Madame Piaillon, her cat,' Boisrobert continued.

'Madame Piaillon shall have 20 ecus, so long as they feed her tripe.'

'Your Excellency, Piaillon has just had kittens.'

'A *pistole*, then, for the kittens.'

*

So at last, and as always to the sound of laughter, Marie de Gournay was granted a pension that she could live by. It was so easy, and so late. The constant worry had gone, more for Jamyn than her mistress who concerned herself with receiving her due rather than the difficulty of running the household. But it made very little difference to the two women apart from that. The food hardly improved, though now there was enough of it, and they had grown used to the cold, so the fire in the stove was still kept low.

The laughter died down, the world had had enough of amusing itself with La Demoiselle de Gournay. It ignored her, apart from the few old regulars who still attended her soirées, and she ignored it. She had almost ten years more to live. She sat at her writing table and continued her endless task of reworking her poetry, her essays and her novel.

In the new edition of the *Essays*, this one dedicated to the Cardinal, Marie de Gournay cut out the passage at the end of 'On Presumption' that praised her as beloved more than a daughter, with wisdom beyond her years and sex. She explained in an addition to her Preface, 'On one point only have I been bold enough to take out something of a passage which concerns me: following the example of the man who tore down his lovely house, in order to rid himself of the annoyances people caused him on account of it. This is because I want to belie now and for the future, in so doing, those who believe that if this book praised me less, I would also cherish it less.'

She was done with Montaigne.

Jamyn always knew there could only be two possible endings. One or other of them would die. And she was faithful Jamyn, so there was really only the one ending: that Jamyn would be sitting here, as she is, on a stool beside her mistress's bed, listening to the death rattle in her throat, waiting out her time. She had often rehearsed this scene once it became clear to her that she would never leave. And here it is. There is nothing surprising about it. Nothing different from the way she expected it to be. She thought there might be. There isn't. This sitting and waiting for her mistress's end is as familiar to Jamyn as the weight of Piaillon in her lap. She can feel equally the impress of the future and of the past. Piaillon is curled, lightly snoring, a pressure on her thighs, for all that she is gone; and the final breath of her lady which has yet to come and go, has already been exhaled many times over. The silence of the breath that will not be taken after the final one has been in Jamyn's ear these forty and more years. Even as her wheezing inhalations and rackety out-breaths disturb the air, Jamyn can catch the silence that will shriek through this oddly peaceful, repetitive noise very soon now. She can hear it like the cry of an owl invading the implacable night.

Among those who have come to see her mistress in these last hours are some of the very same gentlemen who tormented and mocked her while she was alive and vigorous. They are solemn as they stand at the foot of the bed, a little remorseful in the face of death, but no more or less than would be required for them to remain fine gentlemen. When they leave, they fingertip Jamyn's shoulder and deposit a few sous in her lap, as you would the keeper of a grotesque exhibit at the fair. She rises up with difficulty to show them to the door, and when she hears that they have left the house, she throws their money rattling down the stairs, spitting after it. She can dispense with their coins and their elegance.

Astonishing how the old hag hangs on. She's trying to outlast her own death, in all likelihood, in order to read the tributes to her life and work. It's a bitter irony that she of all people cannot see the honeyed words they will fashion, even those who sneered, for the sake of form, and to signal their familiarity with the worth of the great Montaigne. Those are precisely the words she has been waiting for all her life. But even she can't survive her own death, not even La Demoiselle, with her determination and self-blinding confidence, with her stubborn refusal to know what there is to know. Unless, of course, that is exactly the condition of ghosts: stubborn fools who can't accept the truth of the end of themselves and think that they have cheated death. Jamyn wouldn't put it past her. If anyone could . . .

Would she want her mistress to haunt her? She wouldn't deign to, of course, Marie de Gournay's ghost would have much more important fish to fry. She would ignore and exclude her faithful Jamyn in death as in life. Let her die a final death. Jamyn will have no coming back for her mistress to cause her further pain.

Tomorrow will be Marie de Gournay's eightieth birthday. She will not reach it. And now there might be twenty more years of life to come for La Demoiselle's faithful servant. Free at last.

Boisrobert has assured her, after his farewell visit, that her pension of 50 ecus a year from the late Cardinal will continue for the rest of her life. She will have a life of her own. Jamyn looks at her mistress, her dying gathering pace and sees the years to come.

sent. A tant dire, il faut qu'ils dient, & la verité & le menson-
ge ne les estime de rien mieux, pour les voir tôber en quelque rencontre: Ce seroit plus de certitude, s'il y auoit regle &
verité à mentir tousiours. I'ay veu par fois à leur dômage, au-
cunes de noz ames principalesques s'arrester à ces vanitez. Le
demon de Socrates estoit à mon adys certaine impulsion de
volôté, qui se presentoit à luy, sans le conseil de son discours.
En vne ame bien espuree, côme la sienne, & preparee par cô-
tinuel exercice de sagesse & de vertu, il est vray semblable
que ces inclinations, quoy que fortuites, estoyent tousiours
bonnes & dignes d'estre suyuies. Chacun e en soy, quelque
image de telles agitations ausquelles ie me laissay
emporter si vtilement & heureusement, qu'elles pourroyent
estre iugees, auec quelque chose d'inspiration diuine.

De la Constance. CHAP. XII.

LA Loy de la resolution & de la côstance, ne porte pas
que nous ne nous deuions couurir, autant qu'il est en
nostre puissance, des maux & inconueniens qui nous
menassent, ny par consequêt d'auoir peur qu'ils nous surprei-
gnent. Au rebours, tous moyens honnestes de se garentir des
maux, sont non seulement permis, mais loüables. Et le ieu de
la constance se iouë principalement à porter patiemment, &
de pié ferme, les inconueniens, où il n'y à point de remede. De
maniere qu'il n'y à souplesse de corps, ny mouuemêt aux ar-
mes de main, que nous trouuions mauuais, s'il sert à nous ga-
rantir du coup qu'on nous ruë. Toutes-fois aux canonades,
depuis qu'on leur est planté en bute, comme les occasions de
la guerre portent souuent, il est messeant de s'esbraler pour la
menasse du coup. D'autant que pour sa violêce & vitesse nous
le tenons ineuitable, & en y à meint vn, qui pour auoir ou
baussé la main, ou baissé la teste, en à pour le moins appresté à

The annotated copy of the *Essays*, which Montaigne left on his desk in the tower while he went about his dying, survived by luck. Since the beginning of the twenty-first century (oh, let him smile a little) it has rested in an unlit vault in the Library of Bordeaux, and will remain there unobserved, like a famous twentieth-century cat in a closed box, for at least fifty years because his inked additions, last made in 1592, days before his death, are deteriorating and would if exposed to light slowly but surely disappear. In 2002 (his grin is now as broad as the cat in the box) a fine scholar of remarkable taste and discrimination, Professor Philippe Desan, was permitted after much official resistance to photograph it in the vault. Oh, the wonderful care and fuss. He writes: 'We had tremendous trouble finding a photographer who was designated by the French government, and we had to work in almost total darkness, without using a flash, within what we call in French a *chambre forte* – a safe. We had to design a special camera, actually a special chamber, with a lens that was specially built. Three times the French government sent someone to Bordeaux to verify that we were not using more lumen than we were allowed to. They would not allow light to be on the copy itself.'

Even then only designated people were permitted to turn the pages, and so that there was no excessive disturbance, all the rectos were photographed first, then the book was turned over and all the versos shot.

Montaigne's phantom heart pumps with pride and his ghostly lips manage a wry smile, as both his vanity and his sense of the absurd shimmer on from beyond the grave. His daughter inherited the Bordeaux copy, of course, along with the tower library, but she was not a reader, his only child. She sold it and the entire library. For a while it was in a convent in Bordeaux. In 1789 the convents were seized during the Revolution (which he cannot, as a moderate man, condone) and the Bordeaux copy was taken to Paris. Then it disappeared and resurfaced in the nineteenth century, since when it has been owned by the French Ministry of Culture and held as a national treasure in the Library of Bordeaux. He cannot complain that he has not been appreciated.

But how extraordinary that the Demoiselle de Gournay should have been the one responsible for keeping his work alive. That moment of enticing youthful promise whose plainness he was so disappointed by. That deranged child who pricked herself with her hairpin. That devoted young woman whose hospitality and care he took and to whom he gave only the most minimal, most miserable show of gratitude. That writer of over-worked poetry and overwrought prose whose devotion and self-regarding blindness caused such a fury in his friends and family after his death. Who was the laughing stock of France. She was and is the one responsible for his posterity and for colour reproduction in paper or on DVD of the *Exemplaire de Bordeaux* that anyone can purchase from http://hum.uchicago.edu/montaigne/order.php?lang=en.

AUTHOR'S NOTE

What shall we call this one? I suppose 'historical novel'. It doesn't much matter to me, except that I understand that the designation brings questions to the mind of the reader. About what is true and what is made up. Well, it's all made up, of course, but some of it is true – at any rate verifiable by means of other texts.

The main source for the life of Marie de Gournay – actually the only published one – is *A Daughter of the Renaissance* by Marjorie Ilsley, an American academic from Wellesley who died before the book came out in 1963. It is a lushly written biography, designed to retrieve La Demoiselle from the bad-mouthing she had received from history. It defends her against all accusations, although even Isley can't deny that she is not the most original or elegant of writers. Writing in the ladylike late 1950s and early 1960s, Ms Isley is quite sure that Marie remained 'pure' throughout her meetings with Montaigne in Paris and the months in Gournay with him, and I couldn't bring myself to imagine otherwise when making her up myself, so fervent are her admirable biographer's declarations of her heroine's innocence.

Marie has been picked up in the last twenty years by more

recent feminists for her remarkable life and dedication to her improbable ambition. She is admired for her determination and her fury, also for her demands that women be regarded as the equal of men, but no one pretends that her own work is of the highest quality or very original (even the *querelle des femmes* had been batted about by women and men for centuries). She is also written about by literary academics with an interest in psychoanalytic theory: both from the point of view of Montaigne's underlying motivations and her own. The father/daughter, mentor/acolyte possibilities are psychoanalytically delicious. There are excellent and intriguing essays to be found in the journal of *Montaigne Studies* from the University of Chicago, and other books on Montaigne, as well as – particularly fun – in *Montaigne's Unruly Brood* by Richard Regosin.

Montaigne's American biographer, Donald Frame, mentions Marie, as he must, as part of Montaigne's life and legacy, but he doesn't give her very much consideration, though he does analyse the changes in the elegy in 'On Presumption', and concludes that Marie made the changes as described in this book. This is generally agreed by most writers, except Marjorie Ilsley, who rather fudges the issue and uses occasional phrases like 'Who can blame her if . . .' Not me, for one. Though she is a little more judgemental about her Ronsard deceit.

There are no letters extant from Montaigne to Marie or from Marie to Montaigne. It might not be surprising if Montaigne did not keep her letters, but it would be extraordinary if she had not kept his. Even the devoted Ilsley says that Marie de Gournay told lies (though she doesn't elaborate). But all we have are her own brief explanations of their meetings, mostly their mutual admiration, in the Preface, and her autobiographical works. Montaigne does not mention Marie de Gournay beyond her appearance in the elegy, and the 'young girl' whom he did not say was from Picardy.

All the interaction between the two is muddy, and I have taken what she said and then invented one version out of a large number of possible interactions. On the whole I have kept to historical events and timings. That would be the historical bit. The rest is the novel. As is Nicole Jamyn. She certainly existed and is mentioned here and there as Marie's long-time devoted servant who outlived her. She gets several lines, including the story about her will, from Marjorie Ilsley, who applauds her for her loyalty and the companionship (along with the cat) she provided. Aside from the contemporary gossip, there is only the barest suggestion (that special use of the word *companion* for the most part), and certainly not from Marjorie, that Jamyn and Marie were lovers. There were rumours (dismissed by Marjorie but probably encouraged by Marie) that Jamyn might have been the illegitimate daughter of the poet Amadis Jamyn (1538–92). There is no evidence for this. Beyond that Jamyn is silent. So I made her up.

I'm very grateful to Clarissa Campbell Orr for reading the manuscript for historical solecisms. Any remaining combustion engines or polyester clothing are entirely my fault or my choice.

If you want to sieve the history from the make-believe, or just dive into a season of excellent reading, the following list of books and publications in English or translated into English will be of interest. None of these books, writers, editors or translators, of course, bear any responsibility for what I found in their pages.

A Daughter of the Renaissance: Marie le Jars de Gournay: Her Life and Works by Marjorie Henry Ilsley, Mouton & Co., The Hague, The Netherlands, 1963

Montaigne: A Biography by Donald M. Frame, North Point Press, San Francisco, 1984

Apology for the Woman Writing and Other Works, edited and translated by Richard Hillman and Colette Quesnel, University of Chicago Press, 2002

Preface to the Essays of Michel de Montaigne by his Adoptive Daughter, Marie le Jars de Gournay, translated by Richard Hillman and Colette Quesnel, Medieval & Renaissance Texts & Studies, Arizona State University, Tempe, Arizona, 1998

Montaigne Studies, vol. VIII, nos. 1–2, Woman's Place: Within and Without the Essais, edited by Dora E. Polachek and Marcel Tetel, University of Chicago Press, 1996

Montaigne Studies, vol. IX, nos. 1–2, Psychoanalytical Approaches to Montaigne, edited by Lawrence Kritzman, University of Chicago Press, 1997

French Women Writers and the Book: Myths of Access and Desire by Tilde A. Sankovitch, Syracuse University Press, NY, 1988

Montaigne's Unruly Brood. Textual Engendering and the Challenge to Paternal Authority by Richard L. Regosin, University of California Press, 1996

Montaigne by Hugo Friedrich, 1949, edited and introduced by Philippe Desan, University of California Press, 1991

Montaigne and Melancholy by M. A. Screech, Penguin Books, London, 1983

The Discipline of Subjectivity by Ermanno Bencivenga, Princeton University Press, NJ, 1990

Michel de Montaigne: The Complete Works, edited by Donald Frame, 1943, Everyman Library, 2003

Michel de Montaigne: The Essays, edited by M. A. Screech, Penguin Classics, London, 1993

The Essays of Montaigne, translated by John Florio, first published 1603, World's Classics, 1906–29

The Je-Ne-Sais-Quoi in Early Modern Europe by Richard Scholar, Oxford University Press, 2005

Plutarch Essays, translated by Robin Waterfield, Penguin Books, London, 1992

And, as mentioned on the final page of the novel, the *Montaigne Studies* website of the University of Chicago, organised by Professor Philippe Desan.

Jenny Diski

2008